Capturing
Their Destiny

The Eyes of Destiny Series: Book 2

By: S. Roach-Seymour

Dedication

I want to thank those who set the stage for my craft long before I knew it was a possibility. I find inspiration from so many places, including but not limited to renown authors, artist, musicians, and digital creators, but must importantly my mother – Brenda Renfrow-Roach. She has always pushed me to follow my dreams. Her love and persistence has motivated me to become the best version of myself as her daughter, a sister, a mother, a wife, an author, and a friend. Thanks Ma.

A Note from The Author

This sequel, Their Destiny, is the second installment to The Eyes of Destiny Series; however, it is a standalone book. You can enjoy it without reading The Eyes of Destiny: The Chasm; but for a better understanding of characters going forward in the series you have to start at the beginning.

Trigger Warning:

This novel contains graphic depictions of violence and sexual assault. Reader discretion is advised.

Chapter 1 – Fear

The instant message from an unfamiliar phone number came through Destiny's Blackberry while she hovered over her economic textbook at Harry Elkins Widener Memorial Library.

You can't hide from me.

The text immediately threw off her concentration, forcing her to slowly observe her surroundings. The study hall was littered with people cramming before a midterm, just like her. The idea of someone waiting... lurking.. stalking turned her stomach. With so many students walking to and from, she couldn't decipher if someone was watching her.

Destiny became uneasy as her hazel eyes searched for someone, but no one in particular. It wasn't the first text message she'd received since publishing a series of articles in the *Harvard Crimson Newspaper* about police brutality and law enforcement's microaggressions on campus toward the Black students. This was just the first one she received since she had changed her number. Destiny exhaled loudly as she bounced her pencil's eraser against a ruled notepad. This meant the messages were from someone she knew personally. Someone with access to her personal information, possibly someone she trusted.

Searching the hall for prying eyes, she questioned if the constant threats were even about the articles. *Was something more sinister at play? Was someone retaliating*

1

for the things she'd been an accomplice to over the past few years?

Breathing slowly, trying to focus on her studies, Destiny couldn't resist the anxiety rushing over her.

Another text: *Bitch, you think it's a game.*

Instantly Destiny gathered her things, throwing her backpack over her shoulder, she headed out of the door. Upon hitting the cool, damp March air she dialed the unknown number.

"Don't play on my fucking phone!" she shouted into her Blackberry as she descended the library steps.

No one responded. *Call ended* flashed across the screen.

As she galloped down the last step, Destiny realized nearly everything she had thrown inside of her backpack was spilling onto the concrete. She turned around to hold her bag in front of her, recognizing that she hadn't zipped it completely. As she picked up her pens and notepad, a familiar hand, adorned with a year 2000 high school football state championship ring, reached out to assist.

"Everything okay?" her ex-boyfriend, Myer, asked. "I saw how you left study hall... I just wanted to check on you, make sure everything was cool," he insisted, dropping her lip gloss into her backpack.

Destiny looked up at him. Despite his attractive physique, and promising future as a Fortune 500 CEO or NFL draft pick, all she could think was – *he was such a waste of my time.*

2

Standing erect, she responded, "Still getting these crazy-ass instant messages."

"Unless someone actually approaches you, I wouldn't trip," he urged. "But if you're afraid, I could come over and keep you safe."

Destiny laughed. "You can't bust a grape in a fruit fight."

"Shittt," he disagreed. "You're just talking to hear yourself talk."

Destiny looked Myer over with mixed emotions. She would love to have someone comfort her at night. She could cuddle against his muscular chestnut-brown arms, wrap her legs around his long, toned legs. But in reality, she couldn't. She felt like Myer compromised her persona on campus. Therefore, dismissing her temporary need, Destiny simply rolled her eyes.

"I'm just saying. I wouldn't let one of these punk-ass computer geeks hiding behind some burner scare you," he continued, wrapping his arm around her shoulder. "Ain't nobody messing with your crazy ass, anyway."

Destiny looked at him from the corner of her eye as she removed his arm from around her and teased him, "You want to."

"Well, I know another side of you," he reminded her while licking his full lips.

Destiny looked him over, wishing she felt secure with him. But she didn't. As she confirmed to herself that

3

she was in the situation alone, a droplet of rain hit her nose. They both looked up at the dreary sky.

"I gotta go," Destiny replied, zipping her bag. "If I need you, I'll call you."

"I'm here for you, Destiny," he assured her.

"You're here for me and every young bitch from Cambridge to Central Boston," she recounted, as she headed for her dormitory.

Destiny threw her hood over her head and scurried toward Adams House — the coveted dormitory she'd done unmentionable things to live in. As she walked, an uncomfortable, yet familiar feeling came over her. Scouring her surroundings for the predator, she was reminded of visiting home for Columbus Day in 2002, during the D.C. sniper attacks. A time when it was terrifying to just get gas or even walk around D.C.

The tightening in her chest almost caused her to hyperventilate as she trekked the brick walkway to her dorm. Even with the rain picking up, she was forced to stop at the gate of the dormitory. Gripping the wrought iron gate, she took deep breaths to gain her composure before entering the building with a fearless face.

Since Destiny found her footing at Harvard, she only patronized the most exclusive social clubs, wrote controversial articles for the newspaper, hosted parties that paid her to attend, and stayed to herself. She prided herself on being a champion for equality while actively participating in various advocacy groups and being on staff at the Undergraduate Council. She also held mutual secrets with several students who had as much to lose as she did if Pandora's box was opened. She kept with her family motto, 'The less they know, the better'. Which made it hard for her to determine which of her trusted associates was torturing her.

Once in her room, Destiny immediately turned on the CD player, grabbed a pillow from her futon, and screamed into it, her chest heaving with frustration. Every strained breath made the weight in her stomach feel heavier. She gripped the fuzzy decorative pillow so tightly that the stitching began to unravel, threads pulling loose like her own fraying thoughts. The sound of her own voice, muffled by the fabric, seemed to twist inside her, amplifying the tight knot of anguish she couldn't seem to escape. Just as she finished her muffled cry, there was a knock at her door.

Taking a deep breath, she shouted, "Who is it?!"

"Myles!" her neighbor yelled.

Casting the pillow aside, Destiny swung open the door without concern that her 5'1" neighbor could be the stalker considering his pill habit financially contributed to her residency in Adams House.

"I'm really trying to focus on this Lit paper. Would you mind turning it down?" Myles requested.

"Sure," the assurance barely escaping her mouth before she slammed the door back shut.

Behind the closed door all of her insecurities bubbled to the top. She started to pace the floor, trying to convince herself that it was a random cyber geek messing with her. She tried to rationalize that no one was crazy enough to approach her because she had an opinion on social injustices and police brutality.

But she couldn't shake the feeling of being betrayed. This afternoon's text message felt like proof it wasn't a stranger. In that moment, with confusion swarming in her head, Destiny wanted to be as small as she felt during her first month at Harvard. However, she wasn't. As a member of the graduating Class of 2004, she knew there was no turning back.

After laying there for a moment, wracking her brain — no closer to identifying a possible suspect, Destiny opted for her computer. Logging onto Thefacebook.com, she sifted through her classmates' profiles, intensely studying their comments and interactions with each other. Deeply focused on her research, the sharp shrill of her ringing phone startled her. Pulling in a deep breath, Destiny was already answering the line, acknowledging her mother.

"Ma, I'm still getting the messages," she exclaimed into the phone.

"What did the police say?" Mrs. Peay asked.

"They can only do something if someone vandalizes my property or tries to break into my room."

"What?" her mother exclaimed. "They gonna wait until someone harms you before they act? They can't trace the number?"

"It was a burner the last time, and I'm sure this is the same thing."

"Someone is giving them your number," her mother quickly concluded.

"Ma, I can't live like this!" Destiny screamed.

"Destiny, calm down."

"I've tried bypassing Harvard campus police and going to the Sheriff's office, but all of them take it lightly. Saying I just have an admirer," Destiny said as she pushed away from her desktop.

"Just get through midterms and come home for spring break. I'll send you a plane ticket to come home."

"Ma, I have to work," Destiny responded. "We're in the middle of this case, I can't just bail now."

"I'll come there," her mother pushed. "Your father and I will drive up and we can bring some of your things back, so it will be less of a hassle at graduation."

"I can barely concentrate," Destiny admitted, instead of admitting that she didn't know if she would be returning to D.C. after graduation.

She was still filling applications for legal assistant and clerk jobs across the country, trying to avoid returning to her childhood bedroom. She knew she needed to do something to avoid falling back into the family business.

"I just want to be left alone," Destiny admitted somberly.

"Destiny, you have no idea who it is?" Mrs. Peay questioned.

"At first I thought Myer was the psycho," Destiny confessed. "But what would he gain from it?"

"Y'all didn't break up on bad terms, did you?"

"Ma, I found out he had a baby on the way... of course we ended on bad terms," Destiny sighed.

"Well, that will do it," Mrs. Peay said in a matter-of-factly tone.

"It sure did," Destiny mumbled, lost in the thought of how foolish she felt for allowing him to meet her family.

Out of all the men she'd dated while in college, she thought Myer could be the one – not knowing he was the one for anybody. She quickly shook off the tainted memory, knowing she was a hypocrite when it came to Myer. She had an ex lurking for most of their relationship.

As if on cue, her mother asked, "Where is Jasiah? I'm sure he could get somebody to start snitching."

Destiny sucked her teeth. Though she knew the mention of her first love was inevitable, she didn't want to hear it.

"Ma, I don't think he even talks to his old high school classmates that go here." Destiny sighed, leaning against the mantle of the inoperable fireplace in her bedroom. "No one recognizes the person Jasiah's become."

"Well, you certainly haven't introduced us to anyone else worth mentioning."

"Stop asking me about him," Destiny demanded. "We are worlds apart."

"Destiny, that boy loves you," her mother assured her. "And I just want you to be happy."

"I just want to feel safe," Destiny retorted as tears dropped from her eyes.

"God hasn't brought you this far to leave you now... this too shall pass," her mother sighed. "Anyway, here's your father."

Destiny could hear shuffling within the phone before her father's familiar voice was heard. "Hey, Pumpkin. What's going on?"

"Someone got this number too."

"Hmmm," her father grumbled. "You got that taser gun and pepper spray?"

"Yes," Destiny answered.

"Don't hesitate to use it," he urged. "Never hesitate."

"I don't want to feel like I'm always looking over my shoulder," Destiny expressed as she tried to dry her face, but the tears continued to fall.

"Aren't you Black?" her father posed. "You're supposed to be doing that anyway."

Destiny rolled her eyes as she shook her head. Being from the city, she'd always had to keep her head on a swivel–constantly cognizant of her surroundings. She'd never had the luxury of being oblivious to danger unlike most of her counterparts at Harvard.

Destiny was reluctant to get off the phone with her parents. Though she didn't miss D.C., she missed her family. She was left to cherish the memories of family gatherings and certain securities that came along with being a well-known family.

In D.C., the last name Peay held weight; the streets talked to them, confided in them, and shielded them. But in Cambridge, her lineage held no credit. She slowly hung up the phone and tried to regain her composure. She needed to keep a level head to get through midterms and maintain her GPA.

Once Destiny dried her face, she went over to the small table by the window and wrote down the latest incident in the log she'd created. After noting the date, time, and verbiage, she flipped through the pages of the journal. *103* entries in *28* days.

Destiny grabbed her last pint of Ben & Jerry's strawberry cheesecake ice cream from her small fridge and sat in a corner with her Econ book, prepared to study. Every time she heard steps near her suite's door, she paused. What used to be white noise — the comings and goings of students entering and exiting dorm rooms — now filled her with alarm. Every footstep, door swing, every jingle of a set of keys – she paused to listen, ensuring her door was bypassed.

Unable to concentrate, she closed her textbook and leaned her head against the wall. She thought about sending Jasiah a message. She started to ponder if he could have one of his old high school classmates, since there were a number of them attending Harvard, snoop around their friend groups to find out who secretly hated Destiny. She quickly dismissed the notion, trying to focus on her studies again.

But as the formulas blurred before her eyes, thoughts of contacting Jasiah plagued her mind. Considering he was an economics major, she knew Jasiah could be more of a help than a hindrance for the Econ course. As Destiny dialed his number, a sudden surge of anger came over her as she reminisced on how simple life once was. In frustration, she stopped dialing and tossed her Blackberry onto her futon. In the midst of indecisiveness, she quickly retrieved the device and began twirling it between her fingers. One conversation with him about economics would bring some normalcy to her evening, but she feared unloading her drama on him.

She was convinced she needed to move on from Jasiah. Not because of anything he'd done in particular, but because she no longer wanted to hide the person she'd become without him. In the moment, she stood firm on the notion that they needed to live two separate lives and move on. But she needed some type of release before her anxieties consumed her.

Destiny went to her dresser drawer and pulled out the details to an invite only 'stress relief party' happening every night during midterms – deemed *The Pill*. Without a second thought, she found herself dressed for entry into the members-only club she belonged to.

"So, you're working tonight?" the policeman moonlighting as security asked. "I asked Emmanuel where you were."

"I'm just a spectator tonight," she responded, stepping inside.

Chapter 2 - Parents

When the doors opened, the blazing morning sun greeted Jasiah before anything else. He slid on his Prada sunglasses and casually walked off Baton Rouge's *Hollywood Casino* steamboat with a small leather saddle bag over his shoulder. The Louisiana heat caused sweat to develop on his brow before he reached his emerald-green 2000 Mercedes Benz C-Class, a high school graduation gift from his stepfather. Wiping the sweat from his brow, he started up his car with auto start as soon as it was in sight and lit a cigarette. Taking a drag, he enjoyed the slow pace of his morning, even though he knew he needed to put some pep in his step.

Jasiah moved his bag to the other shoulder and laughed to himself as he popped the trunk of his car. He'd done it again. He was $17,320 richer from a night of poker. Moving his tennis racket and gym bag to the side, he secured his riches in a secret compartment and started his voyage back to The Big Easy.

Lil Jon blaring through the Alphine speakers was Jasiah's shotgun driver for the nearly one-hundred-mile voyage. He still needed to make it to his 11 a.m. class. As he hit traffic on I-10, Jasiah quickly realized he wouldn't be able to stop at his condo to change clothes before his lecture hall. Yawning, he contemplated stopping for a cup of coffee but opted for another cigarette instead.

However, when he awoke from the sound of glass shattering, as he struggled to lift his head from an inflated airbag, and he wished he'd followed his instincts.

"We're gonna get you out sir," a firefighter called out to him.

Jasiah groaned, attempting to lift himself up again. A mechanical whirring close by caused the throbbing in his head to intensify. He started to choke on the smell of toxic fumes filling his nostrils. *Get yourself together* he coached, opening his eyes to only make out flashing lights.

"Stay with us," someone urged.

He struggled to make out anything familiar around him. His heart pounded rapidly against his chest as everything became even more hazy and sounds became muffled. He failed to make out what was happening to him before he lost consciousness yet again.

The next time Jasiah opened his eyes, the throbbing in his head was still persistent but his vision was no longer blurry. Surveying his surroundings, he became anxious at the sight of the cold, bleak hospital room. He tried to lift his body, but the pain in his abdomen wouldn't allow him to move much. He took deep breaths, trying not to panic as he realized he was in bad shape.

Jasiah took inventory of himself. His left leg was immobilized, and his wrist was wrapped in gauze. His throat was dry. Every muscle in his body seemed to ache except his feet. He took a deep breath, pressing his thumb against his glabella, as if it would eliminate some of the throbbing in his head.

"Shit," he cursed, assuming he had fallen asleep at the wheel and ended up hitting a guard rail along I-10 East.

Turning his body slowly, he searched for a phone. But suddenly, a nurse entered the room.

"You're awake," she smiled at him.

Jasiah, though out of sorts, couldn't help but notice the nurse's wide hips and cinched waist. Before attending school in the Deep South, Jasiah usually preferred his women petite but as time went on, he'd started to appreciate the softness and comfort in women's curves. In that moment, he couldn't deny the nurse's natural beauty. He was momentarily speechless, trying to focus on himself and fight against his naturally flirtatious ways.

"I know you feel like crap, but you're lucky," she informed him. "I saw your accident on the news. That truck nearly demolished you."

"What happened?" Jasiah's raspy voice questioned. He hoped she could provide a clearer picture because he had no recollection.

"A semi-truck driver had a heart attack at the wheel and as he tried to pull over, he hit some cars, including yours and wedging two of you against the guard rail... terrible scene. You're lucky you escaped with just a broken leg."

"My ribs?" Jasiah added, realizing his tennis season was over. It was his last semester in college, and they were so close to making it to the National Championship.

"Your ribs are bruised. Nothing's broken but the fibula," she replied nonchalantly. "You have some chemical burn from the airbag. Your hand and a little on your face," she continued as she checked his vitals. "Don't worry, you're still handsome though," she winked at him.

Jasiah started to blush, but it hurt him as his cheeks raised.

"We called your emergency contact in Maryland — Faye Netaspend. But do you have someone you would like me to contact in the Nawlins area?"

Jasiah sighed, "My dad," he responded. "Do I have any of my personal things?"

"They only brought you in. I'm sure everything else is still in your vehicle."

Jasiah thought about the money.

"Here's the phone," the nurse smiled at him again. Jasiah enjoyed the warmth of her smile which seemed to light up her walnut-brown face. "The doctor will be in at some point," she informed as she shook her head. "You've downed this IV bag though," she continued, as she looked up at it. "Most guys your age don't drink enough fluids," she shook her head again. "I'll be right back."

Jasiah didn't bother to look at the empty bag of fluids looming close to his head. He knew his diet of long island ice teas and cola wasn't the best. As the nurse exited, he tried to dial his father; however, his hand shook uncontrollably. "Ugh!!" Jasiah groaned in frustration, dropping the phone.

The nurse came back with a fresh IV bag before Jasiah could operate the phone. He recognized the light scent of tobacco mixed with a floral perfume looming over her as he admired her voluminous pear shape. He surveyed the nurse's body as she changed out the fluids in an attempt to distract himself.

"I went ahead and added a little something for you to get some rest," she winked at him. "I doubt they'll keep you for the night. You just have to take it easy, Mr. Sheffield."

"They gonna send me home like this?" Jasiah questioned, not knowing how he would manage with bruised ribs and a broken leg.

"You're lucky, the orthopedic surgeon was in this morning to set your leg. Only time can heal your wounds, boo," she continued to smile, showing a beautiful set of teeth.

"Can I get something for this headache?" Jasiah requested.

"Sure, that shouldn't be a problem. But why don't you call your dad? We prefer it if someone takes you home later."

Jasiah thought about his support system at home, in Maryland, versus what he had in New Orleans. At home, he had his mother, stepfather, an aunt, cousin, and a host of friends. In New Orleans, he was limited to his father, a few loyal frat brothers, and his girlfriends. However, glancing at the nurse, with her slanted eyes, thin lips, and flawless skin, he could imagine her giving him a sponge bath during his recovery.

"Can I have your number in case I need some medical advice?" Jasiah flirted.

"That's a possibility," the nurse's cheeks turned pink as she blushed. "If no woman comes here to claim you first."

"No woman is coming here for me," Jasiah sighed heavily in attempt to seem sad. He knew his girlfriends would come if he called. But even in his condition, he wouldn't dare let the nurse know he was a third wheel to a lesbian couple. "Unless my mother hops on a plane," he added in a low tone rid of the confidence that Jasiah normally displayed. He hoped his act would spark empathy from the nurse.

"Well, I'll get that pill for you. You should call someone," she reiterated before leaving the room.

After Jasiah watched the sway of the nurse's hips, he picked up the phone again. And despite his hands still trembling, he was able to dial his father.

"Who dis?" his dad, Big Siah, asked, in a groggy tone.

"It's Siah," Jasiah cleared his throat.

"What number is this?"

18

"Tulane Hospital. I need you to come pick me up."

"What?!?" Big Siah exclaimed into the receiver. "Fuck happened to you?"

"Pops, my shit totaled. I was in a wreck this morning. I need you to pick me up."

"Okay, okay, shit. I'll figure out how to get there."

"And I need clothes."

"What?" Big Siah yelled again, as if he was hard of hearing.

"Clothes, Pops... like some basketball shorts and a shirt."

"I think you're on the news now," Big Siah cleared his throat. Jasiah could hear the television getting louder in the background on the phone. "You caused all that traffic this morning?" Big Siah suddenly questioned.

"Honestly, I don't know what happened," Jasiah admitted with an exaggerated sigh. "I kind of remember them cutting me out of the Benz," he yawned as his eye lids started to feel heavy while he talked.

"From the likes of what the news anchor said, you're the only survivor," Big Siah informed him.

"Pops, my shorts are in the second drawer of my dresser... don't go through my shit," Jasiah ignored the news from his father. He didn't want to think of the devastation he was victim of.

"Shit! I'm on my way, gottdamn it," his father cursed before hanging up.

Jasiah hung up, wishing he had his cell phone with him. He would call Destiny, his ex, to tell her about his situation. He hoped she would be sympathetic and maybe, she'd come visit him. He secretly longed to hear her voice daily but continued to fight the urge to contact her.

As Jasiah started drifting off to sleep, the nurse came back into the room pushing a cart. He welcomed her with a small smile as he tried to fight closing his heavy eye lids. The nurse mistook his fatigue for sadness. "There are better days ahead," she said gently, handing Jasiah two pills and a small cup of water. "Don't worry."

Jasiah liked her optimism. "I didn't catch your name," he responded, taking the medication, and trying to focus his eyes on the name on her employee badge.

"Amelia," she flashed a genuine smile. "I'll be back to check on you before my shift is over," she retrieved a blanket from the cabinet of her cart and laid it over Jasiah. "I thought you could use another one of these. I see you're shivering."

"So kind," Jasiah recognized with a yawn. He tried to wink at her and continue his flirtatious ways, but he couldn't open his eyes. Sleep came upon him fast. A dreamless rest that he awoke from at the sound of his father's voice.

"Yeah, I don't know what happened to this gottdamn boy," Big Siah rambled.

Jasiah turned in the direction of his father's voice and immediately asked, "Who you talking to?"

"Your uncle," Big Siah responded, referencing a man that Jasiah had only found out existed four years ago.

"In D.C.?"

"Yeah."

"Did you call collect?"

"Don't worry, your muvha gonna pay the bill."

"Pops, you're reckless man," Jasiah's head instantly started to hurt at the thought of his mother complaining about the medical bill. "Hang the damn phone up," Jasiah yanked the cord from his father. "My mother shouldn't even know you're here."

"Yeah, too late for that. I answered when she called."

Jasiah's eyes widened with shock.

Big Siah laughed and sat back in the chair, placing his hands behind his head as if he didn't have a care in the world.

"How long have I been asleep?" Jasiah inquired, searching for any indication of the time. His eyes landed on a partially open curtain. Looking out of the window, he could see that the sun had just set. The sky wasn't completely dark yet, but it was definitely late into the evening.

21

"Oh, it's been a minute, this nice young nurse came in to check on you a few times. She a little thick for your usual taste but more cushion for the pushing, right son?" Big Siah laughed.

"Pops, did you say you talked to my mother? *Faye Netaspend*?" Jasiah recalled.

"Yeah," he shrugged. "She should be in flight by now."

Jasiah closed his eyes as he fought the anxiety quickly building within him. He had not seen his mother since Christmas. At that time, he didn't reveal he was in contact with his biological father, let alone that they were sharing the condo she paid half the rent on.

"You gotta find somewhere else to stay before she gets here," Jasiah declared, attempting to move out of the bed.

"Hold, hold, hold," his father jumped up and came to his aid. "Take your time."

"Pops, I don't need this right now."

"Look, you're a grown ass man. What's the worst she could do?"

Jasiah thought about it. She could take his car, but it was totaled. She couldn't stop paying his tuition at Xavier University because he was on a full athletic scholarship for tennis. However, she could stop paying his half of the rent. But he had more than enough money from gambling to handle that. Maybe she would get so pissed that she would disown him.

"I don't want to deal with it," Jasiah admitted.

"You're lucky to be alive, son," Big Siah suddenly got serious. "Don't worry about your mother. Worry about your recovery."

Jasiah didn't know how to explain to his mother that he'd kept his relationship with his father a secret for four years. Rubbing his temples, he searched for the right words as he tried to prepare his confession.

How could he admit that Big Siah had gotten permission to visit a year ago from his parole officer and never left? Would he reveal that Big Siah had convinced him to change his major from political science to economics? Would he be able to explain to her that for the past year, they'd been raking in cash at poker and roulette tables on steamboats across Louisiana and Mississippi? Would the truth that the summer internship that prevented him from coming home last summer was really him and Big Siah traveling the country for poker tournaments?

Jasiah shook his head, mumbling, "Shit is about to hit the fan."

"I can handle Lady Faye," Big Siah affirmed. "Just let me do the talking."

Peering at his father, Jasiah was met with a slightly older reflection of himself. Twenty-four years his senior, Big Siah could pass for Jasiah's older brother. He hadn't aged much in his fifteen years behind bars. He hoped his father's youthful appearance would be a distraction to his mother in some way. But he knew that wouldn't be enough to subdue her wrath.

By the time Jasiah and his father made it back to their apartment, his mother, Faye, stood in the middle of the floor, with her arms crossed. The scowl on her face all too familiar.

"Hey, Ma," Jasiah greeted, trying to manage on his crutches.

"What will come of your tennis scholarship at this point?" she uttered, devoid of concern for her son's current condition.

"I have two more months of school, what could they do for an accident?" Jasiah countered, irritated with her usual lack of concern for *his* wellbeing. "Hello to you too." He slowly lowered himself onto the sofa, the pressure on his rib cage causing him to release a pained moan as the pain medication started to wear off.

His mother didn't say anything, her eyes fixated on the father of her eldest son. Big Siah took a seat at the breakfast bar and stared back at her. Jasiah stared at them and hoped he wasn't watching a train wreck.

"Faye," Big Siah shook his head. "You still got it, girl."

"What are you doing here with *my* son?" she spat, her neck rotating.

"*Our* son," he casually corrected, using his palms to smooth out his Hugo Boss collar shirt.

24

"*My son*," she emphasized again, pointing to her chest. "Explain yourself, Siah?"

"You gonna have to differentiate," Jasiah told is mother. "Big Siah, Lil' Siah, so we know how to answer."

Big Siah chuckled. "I know you just got off a plane, Faye. Do you still like Lemon Drops?"

Faye rolled her eyes. "Why are you down here with *my* son? Don't you have another son that needs you?"

The room fell silent.

"One panty dropper, I mean, Lemon Drop martini coming right up," Big Siah responded, ignoring Faye's statement. He hopped off his stool and headed for the liquor cabinet. "You still looking good, Lady Faye," he complimented her again.

Faye gave a long eye roll. "What happened to Daquon?" she probed.

"Ma, can you fill my prescriptions?" Jasiah asked, butting into an awkward conversation between his parents.

"Tell your roommate to do it," she flopped down on the loveseat and flung her 24" weave. "Jasiah Sheffield Senior, I can't believe you don't have a relationship with your older son," she shook her head. "You focusing all your energy on the cash cow?"

"He was killed back in '95," Big Siah finally responded, without making eye contact with anyone as he moved around the kitchen gathering ingredients for cocktails.

Jasiah and his mother locked eyes for a moment. Her eyes saying, *'I kept you away from those Sheffield's for reasons like this'*. But she managed to choke out "I'm sorry to hear that. My condolences."

"I'm sorry to say it," Big Siah looked at his namesake. "That one right there is all I have left."

"I ain't going nowhere, Pops," Jasiah smiled.

Big Siah smiled back.

Jasiah watched his mother's eyes move from him to his father, gazing over them while comparing their resemblance. Jasiah had to admit that their resemblance shocked him at first. The height. The chestnut-brown complexion. The dimples. Even their eyebrows were shaped the same.

"You know people mistake Jasiah and I for brothers," Big Siah mentioned, running his hand over a head full of waves.

Faye rolled her eyes and sucked her teeth as she fell back against the loveseat cushions. The fellas laughed.

"Pops, can you fill my prescriptions?" Jasiah asked, as he thought about the pain creeping through his body.

"You've known this muthafuckah five minutes and he's Pops? Roy has been taking care of you for almost twenty years and he's still Roy," Faye referred to her husband. "Unbelievable!" She smacked her hands against her thighs.

"You should be happy me and my son have a bond," Big Siah declared as he shook up the martini. "It's certainly a relationship I only dreamt about while on the inside."

"How long has this been going on?"

"Since I came home," Big Siah answered, pouring the drink into a martini glass. "Right before he graduated high school."

Faye's mouth flew open. She glared back at Jasiah, in disbelief that her son had kept a secret for so long.

"Spring 2000," Jasiah mumbled as he leaned his head back and closed his eyes.

***

It was a warm April day when Jasiah sat in front of a halfway house off Montana Avenue Northwest, trying to figure out if he wanted to go inside to connect his father for the first time in fifteen years. He had no memory of his childhood with his father, considering he'd been arrested when Jasiah was two years old, and had been serving time since Jasiah was three.

Seated inside of his tinted bubble Chevy Caprice, Jasiah pondered if he had made the right decision by coming to the halfway house without his mother knowing. She had lied to him for as long as he could remember about his father's whereabouts. Until a few months prior, Jasiah thought his father was dead because of the lies his mother told him.

But now, he just hoped that he and his father would recognize one another. Jasiah wondered would they instinctively embrace or greet one another with a handshake?

"Come on, young. Let's get this over with," Lafayette, Jasiah's cousin, urged as he got out of the car.

Jasiah shook his head as he exited the driver's side. Questioning why he hadn't come alone. But really, he knew why. If he'd pulled up to the location on his own, he probably would have turned around. He was content knowing his father was alive. He would have left it as that if his girlfriend didn't get involved in helping him reconnect with his father.

"Why you moving so slow?" Lafayette asked.

"This shit is crazy," Jasiah uttered, as he leaned against his car, hesitant to go inside. "I'm trippin'."

"What?" Lafayette glanced at Jasiah. "We ain't come over here for nothing."

"You put in on this gas or something?" Jasiah retorted, reminding Lafayette that he had nothing to lose.

"Look, Siah, I could be spending time with my shawty... What you scared of?" Lafayette pried.

"I kept thinking I want to know about my father, but now, I'm thinking what is knowing him going to do for me?" Jasiah pondered. "He's been in prison for the past fifteen years, what the hell is he going to tell me?"

"I know my father and it does nothing for me," Lafayette shrugged. "At least you both want to build something. My father intentionally destroyed our relationship."

Jasiah didn't comment. He looked at his nails, plucking the little dirt that had accumulated under one.

"Nigga, come on... Since our dads came up together, I'm curious if your father knows what turned mine into a monster," Lafayette admitted.

"Don't count on it," Jasiah mumbled, as he stood up and took a deep breath, suppressing his anxiety. He decided to move forward. "A'rite, let's do this."

"It's about time," Lafayette let out a sigh of relief. "I didn't know how much more pep talk I had in me," Lafayette acknowledged, following Jasiah.

When they entered the halfway house, Jasiah was surprised at the homely feel in the place. The boys gave their identification at the desk and were directed into a den area to wait. Jasiah tried to figure out whether he wanted to stand or sit on the worn sofa covered with various quilts. He opted for a small wooden chair by the window littered with a variety of house plants. Lafayette stood. The ten minutes they waited in silence felt like an eternity.

"Yo, where this nigga at?" Lafayette whispered, as he finally sat on the sofa.

"I was thinking the same thing," Jasiah uttered, glancing at his watch.

"I mean, he only meeting his son he ain't seen in like fifteen years. Not a pen pal," Lafayette whispered.

Jasiah chuckled just as the glass French doors opened. Holding his breath, he turned his attention toward the door to see a white man walk in.

"I know that ain't your father," Lafayette gritted through clenched teeth.

Jasiah didn't respond as he watched the guy pick up a book without speaking to either of them and walk out of the room.

"I think he was sent to scope things out," Lafayette recognized as he stood up and stretched.

"You think so?" Jasiah exhaled. "That was weird."

"Man, I'm about to go sit in the car," Lafayette informed Jasiah.

Jasiah continued to sit there.

When Lafayette noticed his cousin not budging, he tried another tactic to mask his nervous energy, "Let me go see where that nigga at."

"Man, sit down," Jasiah responded. "Chill."

Just as Lafayette started to pace the floor like it was his father that he was going to become reacquainted with, Big Siah walked through the door. Jasiah knew instinctively that was his father. Big Siah smiled at his son. "Jasiah?" he questioned.

Jasiah nodded and stood up to greet his father. He nervously extended his hand for a handshake. They shook hands and looked one another in the eye. The handshake *spanned what felt like a lifetime as the men surveyed one another.*

"Y'all can hug," Lafayette whispered.

Both men chuckled and broke their hold.

"I'm glad you came," Big Siah confirmed.

"I ain't gonna lie, I'm freaking out on the inside," Jasiah recognized, taking his seat by the window again.

"Hi... over here... I'm Lafayette," Lafayette waved, feeling invisible. "Jasiah's cousin."

"Boy, I know who you are. I remember when you were born," Big Siah extended his hand to the teen. "Your mother didn't even know she was pregnant until she went into labor."

"So, I've been told."

"That was wild," Big Siah exhaled as if he could remember it vividly. Jasiah and Lafayette waited with bated breath for him to go into detail about the ordeal but instead, Big Siah changed the subject. "I'm assuming you both are keeping out of trouble?"

They nodded.

"Jasiah, I'm really glad you're open to a relationship with me," his father acknowledged quickly.

"Why didn't you want one with me?" Jasiah blurted out the question that had been swarming his mind since he'd discovered his father was alive. "As soon as my mother had a man, you decided to let him be the father."

"Jasiah, I didn't just decide to let him your father. I felt betrayed by Faye and Mr. Netaspend. And a lot of things transpired that aren't worth rehashing."

"How did they betray you?" Jasiah asked.

"I'm not going to talk about that," Big Siah shook his head as he refused to elaborate for his son. "Mr. Netaspend gave you more opportunities than I ever knew existed. I don't have no ill will toward that man anymore."

"That's crazy," Lafayette cut in. "Your father calls him Mr. Netaspend, and we call him Roy," he shook his head. "Y'all see how crazy that sounds?"

"Shut up, La," Jasiah spat, irritated that Lafayette had cut off his father.

Lafayette held his palms up, indicating he didn't want any trouble.

"Tell me how it was going to school with George Bush daughter," Big Siah tried to lighten the mood.

"It was Chelsea Clinton," Lafayette interjected again.

Jasiah cut his eyes at his cousin before answering, "She was a little older than me and not in my crowd. There was just a lot more security at the school when she was there."

"Yeah, I thought I saw you on television one time in the background. Folks ain't want to believe that you were my son. I imagined you living a life like those kids on American Pie."

"How did you recognize me?"

"You're my son. Seeing you is like seeing a younger version of myself."

A short pause fell between everyone as Big Siah's words floated around the room.

Finally, Jasiah cleared his throat and broke the silence, "My life was like American Pie until last summer."

"Who you got beef with?" Big Siah quickly assumed the only thing that could change his son's life had to be an altercation.

Jasiah didn't feel like getting into the sexual assault accusation at the end of his junior year of high school that changed his social circle. Lafayette watched on, waiting to see what he would say.

"Not worth talking about," Jasiah refused to go into detail.

Big Siah nodded. "Look, you have a heads up in life with just the high school education Mr. Netaspend provided for you. You stay on the right path and your network will get you far in life," Big Siah ran his hands over his waves. "Don't let anyone fuck up those connections."

"Yeah, Siah been to bat mitzvahs and quinceañeras," Lafayette interjected with a smirk.

"So, what kind of student are you? You play any sports?" Big Siah asked his son as he finally sat down.

Lafayette did the motion of playing tennis and Big Siah excitedly said, "You play baseball?"

The teenagers chuckled. "I play tennis," Jasiah responded.

"So, you going to Wimbledon one day?" his father asked.

Jasiah sighed. "I don't play competitively anymore."

"Jasiah is going to join Roy's law firm in the future," Lafayette added. "It's gonna be Netaspend, McMillian, Sheffield and Associates."

"Doubt it," Jasiah shook his head. "I want to set my own path."

Big Siah was quiet as he listened to the cousins.

"What did you want to be when you were our age?" Lafayette asked Big Siah.

"At your age? Eighteen?" He sat back and rubbed both of his thighs with his palms as he thought. "I was already a father. But I wanted to be that nigga."

"Already a father?" Jasiah questioned.

"My oldest son, your brother, was named Daquon," he responded.

"Was?" Jasiah looked at his father.

"He was killed five years ago, over on 9th Street NW."

"Damn," Jasiah and Lafayette uttered together.

34

"He was seventeen," Big Siah voice cracked with a mixture sadness and guilt. "Before his murder, I hadn't seen him in three years."

"That's tough," Jasiah sympathized, the weight of his father's words burdening him. He rubbed his temple, processing the news that he had an older brother. "I wish I could have met him."

"I wish you two could have met too," Big Siah exhaled.

"You have my condolences," Lafayette spoke. "But can you explain what that nigga is?"

"Damn, La, can I process that I had a brother?" Jasiah eyed his cousin. "I'ma need you to go wait in the car."

Big Siah chuckled. "He's cool. I'm happy to switch subjects," he explained. "Yeah, I wanted to be that nigga," Big Siah confirmed proudly. "As a kid, I thought it was the Number Man."

"Number Man?" Lafayette questioned.

"Yeah, the Number Man — the neighborhood lottery," he smiled as he explained to the boys. "Mr. Charles was our Number Man. Everybody knew Mr. Charles. He was the best dressed man I ever saw, with a gold tooth right here," he pointed to his canine tooth. "And he drove a clean white LTD. He was smooth, clean, and had a pocket full of money. He was the opposite of my grandfather who got up, went to work at the Old Soldiers Home, and came home to drink himself to sleep every night."

Jasiah and Lafayette listened intently.

"Later on, I learned that Mr. Charles was running numbers for Elkridge. And Elkridge was that nigga. He owned a pool hall on 7th and S Street, rented out rooms above it. He had a liquor store across the street and the barber shop behind it. He was a loan shark and supplied reefer."

"Elkridge sounds like an entrepreneur to me," Lafayette shrugged.

"And what happened to Elkridge?" Jasiah asked.

"Me," Big Siah answered.

***

When Jasiah regained focus, he noticed his parents engulfed in a conversation in hushed tones. His mother had moved to the breakfast bar, and his father stood behind it, making her another cocktail. They were smiling at one another. The scene made Jasiah question his mother's motives his entire life. She didn't speak ill of his father until Jasiah discovered he was in prison and not a cemetery. Then, Faye acted as if Big Siah and his family were the devil's spawn.

Jasiah watched them intently. He secretly hoped time had healed some of his mother's wounds and she would grow to appreciate Jasiah's relationship with his biological father. He didn't want to lie to her any longer. But when he heard his mother giggle, there was a pain that shot through his being.

"Hold up!" Jasiah yelled. "Ma, you acted like he was the devil and now you're sitting here reminiscing over what my father calls his *panty dropper* martini?"

"I never said he was the devil. I said he was gone," Faye corrected her son.

"Siah, I would think us getting along is a good thing," Big Siah looked at his son. "It's what most kids want for co-parenting right?"

"Who starts co-parenting when the kid is twenty-two?" Jasiah's brow twisted. "Make that make sense, Pops."

"I taught you the game," Big Siah retorted.

"What game?" Faye snapped. "What the fuck do you have my son into?" her demeanor instantly shifted.

"Nothing," Jasiah quickly tried to dismiss his father's statement and his mother's concern.

"The boy is amazing with numbers. I just taught him how to use them in the real world," Big Siah answered, refilling Faye's glass.

Jasiah threw his hands in the air as he braced himself for his mother's negativity. He was prepared for her shock on his graduation day about his changed major, but not in this moment.

"My son could be amazing at many things if he wasn't trying to be captain save a hoe," she jabbed. "I mean, he loves a project bitch," Faye sneered.

Jasiah looked at his mother like she was crazy, but he was unfazed at the opportunity she took to criticize him in various ways with only one shot. When Big Siah started laughing, Jasiah's eyes deviated between his parents in anger.

"What project bitch?" Jasiah questioned.

Faye just rolled her eyes.

"You know your son," Big Siah uttered, as he poured himself a glass of Johnny Walker Blue.

"What project bitch?" Jasiah repeated.

"Those girls you got coming through here from the Graveyards," Big Siah mentioned in a low tone.

"*Graveyards?!*" Faye shouted. "Now that definitely sounds like an unsavory place."

"Tiffany got a good job in the French Quarter," Jasiah defended his choice of companionship.

"Yeah okay," his father mumbled, as he sipped his scotch. "What about the that other one?"

"That Destiny was straight from the hood too," Faye assumed who 'that other one' before taking a sip of her cocktail.

Jasiah and Big Siah locked eyes, knowing the truth about 'the other one' went right over his mother's head.

"You know you cannot say anything bad about Destiny, she ain't talk to that boy since Thanksgiving and he still sensitive about her," Big Siah covered for his son and kept the conversation moving. "You know that's what brought me down here. Lil Siah sounded so depressed when I talked to him. I said let me go check on my son."

"Pops, you know that's a lie," Jasiah shook his head but didn't bother to correct his exaggeration.

Big Siah shot him a glare, silently questioning if Jasiah wanted him to expose the truth.

With flared nostrils, Jasiah grabbed his crutches. His anger slowly bubbling to the surface as he struggled to his feet. Pain seared through his body as he moved toward his bedroom. He refused to continue watching his parents interact like this— after everything. He felt like he was in the twilight zone.

"See how he's gonna run off at just the mention of her name," Faye shook her head. "I swear she put some roots on that boy."

"She's a nice girl," Big Siah shrugged. "If it wasn't for her, we wouldn't be here at all."

Jasiah ears burned as he listened to his mother degrade Destiny as he struggled to his room.

"Exactly! If it wasn't for her, my son would be at Harvard. She stole his dream."

The havoc the accident wreaked on his body coupled with the sting of his mother's words stopped him in his tracks with a wince. "Harvard was your dream, Ma. I made the decision to come here," he repeated for what felt like for the hundredth time.

"If you were so in love with her, why wouldn't you go to Harvard to be with her?" Faye questioned with a raised eyebrow and tilt of the head.

"Because I'm smart enough to know that my college experience can't be based on anyone but me!" he yelled and immediately regretted it for the sharp pain that ran through his abdomen. He slowly turned to continue his struggle to his room. "I'm getting my degree for *my* future. Remember?" he concluded.

"Faye, let it go," Big Siah whispered.

"I ain't letting shit go!" Faye yelled from behind Jasiah. "I told him to leave that girl alone before he even graduated high school and he couldn't get enough of her bullshit."

Jasiah finally managed to maneuver to his bedroom — slamming the door behind him. He couldn't understand why his mother held a vendetta against Destiny. Destiny was always the one person that wanted him to be himself above all else. She was the one who encouraged him to explore his dreams of playing tennis competitively again and ultimately, to attend Xavier once he had the offer. Destiny had always been the one to push him out of his comfort zone, urging him to make impactful changes to his life. She'd sacrificed their relationship so that he could pursue his own dreams without worrying about her.

It was Big Siah who'd helped Jasiah realize his hidden talents and take them to heights that made them both plenty of money. During his visits to the halfway house, Big Siah taught Jasiah how to play Poker, Tunk, and Spades.

And when he was released from there, Big Siah taught his namesake how to gamble.

The summer before Jasiah left for college, he'd spent less and less time with Destiny as he attempted to get to know his father. Initially, she was understanding, then she'd found out from her brothers that Jasiah was gambling in afterhours spots with his father. That swayed Destiny to end things with Jasiah, citing it was best for both of them to split and concentrate on their futures.

As Jasiah focused on writing emails to inform his professors, coaches, and the school's administration of his accident and condition, there was a tap at his bedroom door.

"Yeah?" he answered, without looking away from his laptop.

Big Siah cracked the door open, only peeping his head into the room. "We'll fill your prescriptions," he assured.

"Okay, thanks," Jasiah uttered, still not looking away from his laptop.

"I'ma drop the top on the E450 for your mother," Big Siah whispered in a witty tone.

Until that very moment, Jasiah couldn't have ever imagined his parents cruising down Common Street, Bourbon Street, or any street together. He nodded but wanted to warn his father. He'd seen how his mother could be kind to a person, coaxing them to let their guard down, before she went for the jugular.

"You want something particular to eat?" Big Siah asked. "I was thinking of getting some wings off Claiborne, what you got a taste for?"

"A pain pill," Jasiah answered honestly.

"You gotta eat," Big Siah voiced his concern.

"A Shrimp Po Boy and some gator bites," Jasiah rambled off a quick order as he finally looked up at his father. "Watch out for her," he warned.

"I heard that!" Faye yelled.

"She better watch out for me," Big Siah retorted with a wink, and closed the door behind him.

After Jasiah heard the front door close, he picked up his house phone and dialed the number he knew by heart – Destiny. He needed her to tell him he would be okay. That despite his burned face and broken leg, he was still handsome. He knew that she could reassure him that he would play tennis again.

Before Jasiah could hit the last digit, he hung up. The memory of the last time they saw one another flashed in his mind and he became less confident that she would answer the phone. He rotated his neck, trying to alleviate some of the tension in his body, but it only grew as he admitted to himself his approach with Destiny over the holidays was faulty. Showing up to her parents' house with Lafayette, inebriated; but still, he hadn't thought Destiny's rejection was warranted.

Everyone in the rowhouse was happy to see him toting bottles of Moet and a pocket full of money to bet on a Spades game, but Destiny wasn't impressed. She wasn't impressed with the New Orleans slang he spoke to make her brothers and father laugh. Even more, she was disturbed by the lingering cigarette smoke on his Versace sweatshirt that choked her every time he tried to hug her.

After Jasiah was full of the Peay's traditional Thanksgiving dinner, he sweet-talked Destiny outside into the cool autumn night and tried to convince her to come to Morton's Steakhouse with his family, as they had always done. But this time, she refused. "This is it, Jasiah," she'd told him. "This is where we part ways."

"Destiny, just come with me. I'm not asking for anything in return," he lied. He'd wanted her the way he'd always had. Even though they hadn't been an item for nearly three years, and he'd had many women to satisfy his every whim, no one had compared to her. She was his kryptonite.

"Jasiah, you're drunk, your mother's gonna be super critical. She'll assume I'm the reason. I just don't want to deal with it," Destiny admitted. "Plus, my man's coming in on the last flight."

"Fuck him," Jasiah retorted, jealous at the idea of any man being as familiar with her softness as he was. "You didn't tell that nigga I get the holidays?"

"Jasiah, you invited yourself to my parents' house!"

"I have an open invitation," he corrected. "And I know that muthafuckah ain't about to come eat my mac and cheese," Jasiah tried to lighten up the mood. "You know I worked on that with your dad last night while you and Bria were at the club."

"Where is La?" she asked, ignoring Jasiah's commentary. "Is he still in the house, because he needs to take you to your next destination."

"Destiny, stop playing with me," Jasiah grabbed her around the waist and landed a wet kiss on her before she could push him away. She accepted the kiss for a moment, but then regained her wits and bit his tongue.

"Get yourself together, Jasiah," she pushed him away. "The smoking, drinking, the gambling — you have to cut the shit out."

"There you go judging me," he threw his hands in the air. "I'm living, Destiny! Are you?" he questioned. "You up there in Massachusetts with a stick up your ass."

"Fuck you," she uttered, turning her back to go into the house. Jasiah had no idea of the life she'd created in Cambridge. No idea of how she'd managed to make ends meet.

"I didn't mean that, Destiny," he grabbed her by the shoulder. Swiftly, Destiny removed his hand and twisted his wrist, as she'd learned in self-defense class years ago.

"Leave, Jasiah," she demanded, applying pressure.

"You know I need my wrist for a match," Jasiah mentioned, *pain shooting through his arm.*

She released him and continued into the house.

Jasiah stood on Destiny's parents' stoop and lit a cigarette, waiting for his cousin to drive him to an uncomfortable dinner with the Netaspends. As he rubbed his wrist to soothe the discomfort she'd caused, he worried a little less about her being alone in Cambridge.

But now, three months later, Jasiah still preferred Destiny's company to anyone else's. She'd understand, more than anyone, how weird he felt having his parents in the same room together. With her family's connections, she'd found out his father was serving time and how to get in contact with him.

Jasiah threw away his caution and dialed her number again, this time letting it ring. He was surprised when he got a disconnection notice from the operator. He dialed again, making sure he hit the right numbers, and received the same error message before his hands covered his face in frustration.

After letting the disappointment settle in, Jasiah shifted his energy, deciding, finally, to call his girlfriends and tell them about the accident.

Chapter 3 – Admissions

Destiny sat at her desk and combed through the case file to prepare the final judgement. As she found the information needed, she surveyed people walking the halls outside of her dimly lit office, wondering if her stalker was a coworker. She quickly dismissed the lawyers on staff and focused her attention on the people who attended school with her. The head litigator at Rossi and Associates was a Harvard alumnus and also a professor who gave Harvard students preferential treatment for employment at his office.

Destiny started with the receptionist, Emmanuel, that also went to Harvard. She couldn't see him from her office, but she heard him in the hall rambling on about something. Emmanuel, with a charismatic personality with flamboyant style, he was always in-the-know on campus. He'd taken the simplest job at the firm to appease his parents. He was a senior, like Destiny, studying Sociology with plans of going to law school, but it was only under the tutelage of his father.

Emmanuel and Destiny worked well together in whatever situation they were in. He was known for his coveted lavish parties off campus, that Destiny had an exclusive membership to, and often hosted. She dismissed him, considering he not only hooked Destiny up with this job, but he also spilled the beans about Myer impregnating his ex-girlfriend.

Then there was Megan, a third-year criminal justice major. She was a legal assistant for the litigation attorneys and had started at the firm soon after Destiny. She and Destiny never had a problem at work, but there was always something about her that didn't sit right with Destiny. She often looked at Megan as a threat. Not to her job, but to equality. She was envious that Megan could call wolf at any time and the world would shift. But Destiny was dealing with a cyber stalker, who'd recently left a dead rose on her doormat and she'd been told by campus police to be flattered.

Destiny stopped observing the office and looked at her Blackberry. She had only come up with Megan as a suspect, but again, she tried to convince herself that she had to be wrong. She had never heard Megan use any profanity other than *damn* and the way the mysterious texter used the word *bitch*, would seem to disturb Megan's debutant disposition.

"Destiny, I have a courier coming for that file at two p.m. Mr. Rossi would like to get it to the courts today," Harold, the office manager, informed as he peeked his head into her office.

Destiny nodded as she looked at her watch. She knew she would finish her tasks by noon. She planned on taking a walk during her lunch hour and didn't want any looming deadlines on her mind while she tried to get some fresh air. Since midterms were over, she had some weight lifted off her shoulders academically, but she still felt the weight of being someone's prey. Yet, with determination, she continued in her normal routine- refusing to succumb to fear.

When Destiny felt the cool, vernal air on her face during her lunchbreak, a billboard from a travel agency caught her attention. It made her question herself. She felt like she had made a mistake staying in Cambridge for spring break to work full time hours. Destiny inhaled the damp air and regretted not visiting somewhere tropical during her final spring break like her best friend, Bria. She had more than enough money stashed to do whatever she wanted, but Destiny continued to work and hustle in preparation for law school.

As Destiny strolled past businesses on Massachusetts Avenue, she thought about how she was exactly where she wanted to be in life, but the circumstances didn't make her feel as ecstatic as they should. To her parents, she was the family's first-generation college graduate. Despite their checkered past, they had raised a Harvard graduate who was well on her way to becoming a lawyer. Notwithstanding that accomplishment, Destiny's personal life felt like a failure.

She thought of herself as smart and charismatic. Her vibrant hazel eyes attracted attention, but she had a hard time picking the right man. Destiny thought she would have found her husband at Harvard after she let go of the notion of marrying her high school sweetheart. Inside, she was a hopeless romantic. She gave men a hard time initially, but once she let them in, she always thought they'd be the guy to share life's journey with. There had been a few *"the one"* guys at Harvard. James Blake from Brooklyn. And David

McKinsey from Baltimore before Myer Williams from Boston.

As Destiny pondered her choices in men, she realized she'd aligned herself with men with familiar upbringings; top of their class in under-served major cities, trying to adapt to the ivy league culture just as Destiny was. And though they could relate in their commonalities, there was always an idiosyncrasy that turned her off – their lack of resources. Jasiah had spoiled her from the moment they met. He had the resources, even as a teen, to do so. But as she aligned herself with men that could relate to her struggles on campus to fit in and excel, she found they were never good enough.

Destiny entered Andy's Diner to escape the gloom of the day. Seated at the counter, she searched through her oversized tote for a magazine to entertain her. Her hand grazed the taser gun she carried with her everywhere. Destiny cringed at the idea of someone invading her space in a way that she felt threatened enough to use it. She hoped she didn't have resort to such measures. She hoped the police were right – that the text messages were idle threats that no one would dare cash in on.

But sitting at the lunch counter, tears threatened to pour out of the corner of her eyes. Destiny thought she'd escaped threats of violence when she left DC. A tinge of disappointment swept over her at the realization that if something didn't materialize soon, she would be returning there. She dabbed the corners of her eyes with a paper napkin from the dispenser in front of her and pulled the latest edition of *Harvard Law Review* from her bag.

Just as she flipped through the first page, she felt a firm hand on her shoulder. She instinctively knocked it away, jerking her body around to see who was touching her without warning. Her eyes landed on Mr. Antonio Rossi, the owner of the firm. She let out a sigh of relief and said, "Mr. Rossi, you shouldn't sneak up on people like that."

He nodded with a smile. "I didn't mean to startle you."

Destiny tried to fix her disposition and appear pleasant as she stared up at him. She could only manage a pressed lip smile.

"I saw you walk in and thought I would join you. I can't get enough of that raisin bread French toast."

Destiny nodded at the older, distinguished gentleman. She lowered her gaze after staring into his steel gray eyes for what she felt was far too long. She'd always thought Mr. Rossi, a man in his early 40s, was attractive. To her, he resembled Andy Garcia in The Godfather III. His olive complexion and dark hair made his sparkling eyes stand out even more. He dressed well, always smelled expensive, and was cunning whether it was the conference room or courtroom. Destiny loved to see him at work. He was crafty in his thought process and often asked her poignant questions during her research to help her think outside of the box as well.

"I'm here for the chicken parm sandwich today," Destiny informed him. His gold scale of justice cufflinks catching her attention. She knew instinctively that he'd been in court this morning, or he would be that afternoon.

"Let's get a table," Mr. Rossi suggested as he turned quickly, not allowing Destiny to decline the invitation.

She gathered her things and followed him to an open booth. He helped her out of her trench coat. She tried to hide her surprise and pleasure in his chivalrous act. As she smoothed the lines in her pencil skirt and slipped into the booth opposite of Mr. Rossi, she started to wonder about the motive behind his kindness. For the first time, she felt like his eyes devoured her petite frame.

"Soooo, I'm sure you received your acceptance letter by now?" Mr. Rossi referred to Destiny's admission to Harvard Law as he took off his suit jacket, neatly folded it in four, and laid it beside him on the booth's seat.

"Yes. Thank you again for the reference," Destiny replied, noticing how his fitted pinstripe shirt hugged his broad, muscular shoulders.

Mr. Rossi shrugged. "It's the least I could do with the commitment you've shown to the firm and your academics." He smiled at her. "I hope you turn out to be a lifer like me."

Destiny's eyebrows raised. His words made her feel seen, like someone thought she actually belonged there. Through the years, she'd dealt with so much self-doubt when being compared to her peers. The competition for everything, including her seat on the Undergraduate Council and getting a single room at Adams House, made her feel like she was constantly in a rat race on campus. She was often questioned if being a lawyer was what she really wanted to do.

The people that believed in her dream were few and far between. Several times, she was told she would be a great teacher or executive. But now, with one of the most prestigious lawyers in Boston and one of the most notable faculty members at Harvard Law School sitting in front of her, telling her he supported her dream, she felt relieved.

Destiny couldn't hide her joy. Her small, pressed lip smile turned into a full grin as she told him her plans, "I've deferred my admission for a year," she admitted.

"Who approved that?" he asked with raised eyebrows.

Destiny shrugged. "Someone who understood I needed a mental break from this place."

"So, you'll fill in full-time for a year at the firm," he assumed nonchalantly. "Awesome."

"I've been applying for fellowships and positions on the Hill that would be able to diversify my resume."

"You show a lot of promise," he acknowledged, staring Destiny directly in the eyes. "I would love to keep you on staff in hopes of grooming you to be my partner one day."

Destiny felt a rush come over her. She didn't know whether it was the seductive eye contact or his sly innuendo. She wasn't naive to the implications of his words. She pondered the kind of partner he wanted to groom her to be. He had ten associates in the office, some had been with the firm for over ten years and their names still didn't grace his letterhead. Instead of questioning him, she reiterated, "I'm heading back to DC after graduation."

Mr. Rossi's grayish-blue eyes widened, "You're not even taking my offer into consideration," he looked up at the waitress that had come over. "Two of my usual," he told the slender woman.

"I hope your usual is chicken parm," Destiny interjected.

"I have the best place to take you for chicken parm this evening," he replied casually.

Destiny's eyes narrowed. Over the past year, she had worked at his office without incident. She had no inkling that Mr. Rossi was the least bit attracted to her. She questioned where the shift came from. However, surprisingly, she liked it.

"I mean, I have to do something to convince you to stay," he added.

"You can't convince me," Destiny shook her head. "I need a break from Cambridge."

"If you were homesick, why didn't you get your fix during spring break?"

"I've been waiting my whole life to get out of DC," Destiny admitted. "But I've been second guessing myself for the past four years here. Honestly, I wish I could take a break from both but in this situation..." she looked directly as Mr. Rossi as she spoke because she knew he was still a part of the Harvard culture. She hoped her direct eye contact would give her words credence, not allowing him to ask any questions about her personal life. "I've picked my poison."

"Where else did you apply to law school, Ms. Peay?" Mr. Rossi asked quickly, as if he was convinced there was something more to the story.

Destiny was relieved that he didn't try to pry into her personal life. She happily responded, "Howard and Columbia," before thanking the waitress for sitting a cup of black coffee in front of her.

"Howard?" he looked stunned that she named a historically Black college.

"Yes, Howard," she confirmed confidently. "I always thought I would be at an HBCU. Harvard was somebody else's dream."

"But you're still here," Mr. Rossi recognized as he sat back, looking at Destiny to explain her statement.

"I had something to prove," Destiny sighed. "You know my story."

"Tell me the unadulterated version," he requested, stirring cream into his coffee.

Destiny took a deep breath and tried to figure out how much she wanted to share. After Destiny's silence stretched on, Mr. Rossi finally began to fill the void with his own words.

"Okay, I'll tell you the truth about me going to Harvard," he shrugged. "My older brother's name is

Anthony and as you know, my name is Antonio. There was always mix ups with our records at school. In the '70s, there was a huge mix up and I ended up in the same grade as Anthony. My mom suffered from Schizophrenia and couldn't keep up with shit," he brushed that part of the story off with a hand sweep, like it wasn't worth going in to.

"Now, I was smart, but not book smart like Anthony. He'll read the whole book to learn. I use cliff notes and a lot of common sense to figure things out," he stirred his coffee slowly as he talked. "I ended up so smart, I could fake it all! I had someone take the SATs for me, intercepted, and forged my transcript, discovered the rugby coach had a thing for underaged girls and bribed him to put me on a scholarship," Mr. Rossi cleared his throat and chuckled lightly as he continued his story.

"We didn't even have a rugby team at my high school in Camden, New Jersey. Then I had to teach myself to play rugby just to sit on the sidelines for four years."

His storytelling ability, with hand gestures and facial expressions that amused her. It was reminiscent of Joe Pesci or Robert DeNiro moderating how things worked in Las Vegas throughout the movie *Casino*. Destiny was blown away by his candor.

"Now, with computers and such, I could never get away with the things I did," he sipped his coffee. "I worked my ass off to not just fit in here, and also to take advantage of every opportunity those entitled kids had," he tapped his index finger on the veneer wooden table, emphasizing his point. "Now, I know your story is nothing compared to mine."

"You're right about that," Destiny agreed.

For some reason she wanted to recite lyrics to Jay Z's "Renegade" and tell the man that signed her checks *I drove by the fork in the road and went straight*. But instead, she opted for a less poetic explanation.

"I was a kid that decided I was going to do something different. Something better than what I'd seen anybody in my family do," Destiny sipped her coffee before continuing. "I started out with dreams of attending any college that would give me a scholarship, then I met my high school sweetheart, a boy from a well-off family, whose mother was determined for him to attend Harvard like his stepfather.

"I never even thought of applying to Harvard or any ivy league school before meeting him. Long story short, I ended up at the ivy league school and he ended up at an HBCU."

"You came here following a boy?" Mr. Rossi asked.

"Sorta," Destiny admitted. "I really applied to prove to myself I was worthy of the experience; that I was as good as the kids who had access to everything. Things just worked out in my favor to be here. And he's exactly where he wants to be."

"Well, you've done well here," Antonio acknowledged before taking a big gulp of his coffee. "Despite the competition."

"And you did well here, despite faking it until you made it," Destiny pointed out.

Mr. Rossi nodded and smiled in agreement. "I've been looking at all the angles since I was a kid."

"What made you be so honest with me?" Destiny asked as the food was delivered to their table.

"Well, I know if I want to get to know you, I have to open up about me," he shrugged, lifting his knife and fork.

"Mr. Rossi, you know me," Destiny stated, grabbing her coffee mug again.

"Not like I want to," he looked up from his plate and winked at Destiny. "So tonight, I'll send a car for you at 8 — if you really have a taste for the best chicken parmigiani in town."

Mr. Rossi stared at Destiny, not moving. He awaited her response with bated breath. Destiny let the silence linger as she sipped her coffee slowly. Her eyes held Mr. Rossi's glare from over the aged porcelain mug's rim. He bit his bottom lip as he stared back at her. Destiny sat her cup down slowly, deliberately licking her lips before agreeing.

"Well, now that's settled, tell me, did you find anything new on the J. Morgan case?" In a heartbeat, Mr. Rossi's familiar air of authority returned, and he was once more the firm's name partner and managing attorney as he cut up the French toast on his plate.

"There is some dicey language in the contracts from August 13th. I have it flagged on the file for Monica's review."

Mr. Rossi nodded as he poured a heavy amount of syrup on his food. "I'm going to put Megan on contracts. I'd like you to look over the financial data I subpoenaed."

Destiny's bottom teeth sank into her top lip to stop herself from cursing aloud. She hated looking at numbers.

"What's that face about?" he inquired.

"Nothing," she refused to admit her weakness.

"Destiny, you have the ability to be great at this, but you have to push yourself."

Destiny nodded. "I understand that, but often I like to stick with my strong suits," she reasoned.

"I have faith in you," Mr. Rossi didn't waiver in his decision as he relished in the first bite of his food.

Destiny blushed.

For the first time since she'd left The Pill, the harassing texts weren't at the forefront of her mind. She was in a daze as Mr. Rossi helped her back into her trench coat after they finished their meal. Their eyes locked again when Destiny looked over her shoulder at him.

"I'd like to see you in a vibrant color," he whispered. "It would really accentuate your eyes."

"I wear a size 4," Destiny replied. "If you want to see me in something particular."

Mr. Rossi let out a light chuckle as he backed away, "Noted."

She grabbed her tote bag and followed him out of the diner.

"I'm headed to the court building," he informed her, speaking over his shoulder. "The car will be on Plympton and Bow at 8."

Her eyebrows twisted with curiosity - *how does he know what dorm I'm in*. She stared at the back of his head as they weaved through the tables to exit the diner. For a moment, wondering if he was her stalker then laughed at herself. There was no way a man of his stature had time to play little mind games. They parted ways on the street. Mr. Rossi only winking at her as his chauffeur opened his car door.

On her solo walk back to the office, she remembered a quick conversation about her housing assignment with Mr. Rossi. She recalled how he'd been amazed at her ability to score a single room in the coveted Adams House. The recollection gave her a brief moment of relief.

Once back at the office, Destiny fixed herself a hot mocha latte to warm up from the brisk walk. Sipping the piping hot drink, she eased into the conference room that held stacks of boxes marked J Morgan.

"That was an extended lunch," Harold acknowledged from the conference room doorway.

Destiny quickly turned to see her immediate supervisor staring at her with a disapproving eye. She returned her attention back to the files, not wavering from her task. "I ran into Mr. Rossi," she admitted, "We discussed the J Morgan case."

"Any particulars you would like to share?" Harold pried.

Destiny looked up at him again. *Is he the stalker-* she wondered, as his disapproving gaze made her uncomfortable.

"Not at the moment," she replied, turning her attention away from Harold again. Picking up her Blackberry, she scrolled through the assorted stream of hostile messages before she came across an email from Mr. Rossi that simply read - *Call me Antonio.*

A smirk formed on her lips. The arrival of that singular email faded the barrage of messages calling her a black bitch from her thoughts and Harold's attempt to micromanage her.

Chapter 4 – First Date

Mary J. Blige crooned in the background as Destiny restlessly raked through the makeshift clothing rack in the study area of her dorm room. She was determined to find something just right for her first date with the distinguished gentleman from Camden, New Jersey – Antonio Rossi. Combing through her array of corsets and pencil dresses, she imagined sitting across from Antonio in a dimly lit Italian restaurant. She knew she needed something elegant for the occasion.

After pacing the floor, cracking open an individual bottle of Moscato and nibbling on pretzels, Destiny settled on the little black satin halter dress she wore to Winter Feast the previous December. However, once she was fully dressed and applying eyeliner in the mirror, Destiny paused, as if she finally had a conscience.

"What are you doing?" she asked herself aloud. Antonio Rossi was a triple threat. He was her boss; he was married; and he would one day be her litigation professor. But as she applied mascara, Destiny focused on the positive attributes of Antonio Rossi that she didn't want to resist. He was powerful. His charisma was magnetic. But most of all, he was an influential resource. Destiny wanted him in her corner if she ever had to protect herself from her stalker or if the secret of how she afforded more than what student aid covered was revealed.

As Destiny slipped into the 4" black patent leather stilettos, there was scuffling on her door. Her gaze flicked to the pocket knife her father had given her freshman year, and she quickly shoved it under her futon mattress. Instead, she grabbed the taser gun, praying she wouldn't have to use it —and praying she didn't ruin her night or someone else's future.

'Don't hesitate' her father's voice lingered in her mind as she opened the door and aimed.

She was relieved yet frustrated to see some of the boys playing in the hall. They were tossing a Nerf football back and forth and faking plays as they moved down the hall. Destiny rationalized that someone or something hit her door accidently. "Look at you, Destiny," Connor said, his eyes widening with admiration. "Where you off to tonight?"

Destiny rolled her eyes and slammed her door without a reply. As she threw the taser in her clutch, her conscience resurfaced. She remembered meeting Mrs. Rossi briefly at the Harvard-Yale game, and when their paths had crossed again at the office Christmas party. Her appearance was underwhelming compared to her husband's. She had a head full of long dark hair, stout in figure, and she was always adorned with pieces of the most beautiful jewelry. Destiny sipped her wine and flushed out the guilt starting to arise within her. "This is only dinner," she said to no one.

Lastly, Destiny unleashed her hair from her scarf, letting her auburn tresses fall past her shoulders. Humming Mary J Blige's "Not Today" in the bathroom mirror, she ensured her straight hair laid perfectly. "It's only dinner," she repeated into the mirror before checking her watch. It was 7:50 p.m. "Gametime, Destiny," she told herself, as she draped her trench coat over her shoulders, and headed out to the black Suburban parked exactly where Antonio said it would be.

"Good evening, Miss Peay," the driver greeted her as he opened her door. "Buckle in and we will head over to Mr. Rossi."

Destiny nodded, slipping into the plush vehicle. She sat back and watched the landscape as they headed toward Boston. She nervously gripped the edge of her seat when they pulled up in front of a high rise on Newbury Street instead of a restaurant.

"Do you have the right address?" Destiny questioned, searching the building entrance for a door to a storefront restaurant.

The driver smiled in the rearview window. "Mr. Rossi is expecting you," he responded, exiting the car and opening the door for Destiny.

Destiny rubbed her nasion with her index finger before she stepped out into the cool night air. She was slightly irritated at how presumptuous Antonio was by bringing her to an apartment building. She hoped he didn't think she was an easy lay. But as the bellman opened the door, and revealed the exotic wood floors of the lobby, she became intrigued. Sucking in a deep breath, she walked through the opulent lobby confidently. But while alone in the elevator she slumped against the rail and exhaled.

"What are you doing girl?" she asked herself as she stared at her reflection in the pristine brass elevator doors. Gaining her composure, she stood tall again and exited the elevator. Before knocking on the door, Destiny mumbled, "Fix your face," to herself. But she felt like she might have said it loudly because before she could place her fist to the door, it opened. Destiny was surprised to be greeted by the scent of Italian spices mixed in with the array of candles lit throughout the space. A young lady at the door in something close to a nurse's uniform ushered Destiny into the apartment and took her coat.

"Do you have a cocktail of choice?" the woman Destiny perceived as the housekeeper, inquired.

"I have it, Mary," Antonio interrupted, as he revealed himself further into the apartment.

Destiny pursed her lips, as she moved toward Antonio, taking in the entire scene before her. Dressed in casual black slacks and a black casual silk button down shirt with gold medusa head loafers, Antonio's attire fit the contemporary space perfectly. Destiny quietly marveled at the design of the apartment as she moved closer to him.

"You're right on time," he smiled at Destiny.

"I was under the impression we were going out," Destiny admitted as she clutched her purse tightly in front of her.

"I only told you I was gonna get you the best parm in town," he continued to smile. "How about we start with some champagne?" he insisted.

Destiny moved further into the apartment. Her heels clicked against the marble tile before they sunk into a plush rug in the living room. "I thought you lived in West Cambridge," Destiny confessed – taking in the view of the city from the floor to ceiling windows.

"My family lives there," he responded.

She admired the lights and movement of those under the cloak of the evening sky from her advantage point until she heard a cork pop. She turned to see Antonio popping a bottle of Veuve Clicquot champagne. Destiny took a deep breath and told herself – *smile*.

When he offered her a flute of champagne, his fingertips grazed hers. "You look amazing," he complimented her.

"Thank you," Destiny blushed as she finally looked beyond Antonio and saw another person moving around the kitchen. "Are you sure you are the chef?"

"I am," he smiled. "But that's all I can do. If I were left to my own vices, you would have walked into a mess."

"We could have gone to a restaurant," Destiny pointed out, as she gave him another once over. She had to admit, seeing him in a more relaxed state faded some of her worries about the evening's direction.

"I figured this way we could really get to know one another with no inhibitions," Antonio motioned for them to take a seat on the sofa. Destiny obliged.

"I like inhibitions on a first date, if that's even what we're calling this," Destiny retorted, as she crossed her legs at the knee.

Antonio chuckled. "I'll be a gentleman," he assured her.

"Pinky promise?" Destiny asked as she held up her pinky finger.

"Scout's honor," he replied quickly, holding up two fingers as if he were still a Boys' Scout.

Destiny couldn't resist smiling as she let her guard down a little. "Antonio," she took the opportunity to call him by his first name for the first time. "What is this about? Truly?" she inquired, wanting an answer to the lingering question in her mind.

He chuckled a bit and cleared his throat before responding, "I've noticed the way you look at me."

Destiny rolled her eyes. "Now that's a lie," Destiny disagreed.

"Maybe once I caught you checking me out," he insisted. "But truly, I overheard Emmanuel mentioning that you were single and then Harold might have hinted that you would be resigning before our summer retreat. So, I thought I would take a chance."

"Very risky," Destiny pointed out, as she sipped from her glass.

"No risk, no reward," he acknowledged, as he reached over and touched Destiny's hair with the back of his hand.

"Now you know you're not supposed to touch a black woman's hair," she moved to the side after she allowed him to stroke her mane twice.

"I can't walk up on a black woman; I can't touch her hair..." he laughed. "What other lessons am I going to learn before the night is over?"

Destiny shrugged. "The night is still young."

Antonio tilted his glass toward Destiny's to toast, "That it is, that it is," he agreed.

As their glasses clinked, Destiny caught a glimpse of a record player. She sipped her champagne and insisted that Antonio show her his collection.

"After dinner," he stood and extended his hand to help Destiny from the lavish sofa.

The way he clasped her fingertips sent a tingle through Destiny's being. She blushed, enjoying the way Antonio escorted her to the dining room. *Calm down,* she told herself watching him pull out her chair to the single slab of redwood table just off the kitchen, adjacent to another wall of windows. Destiny turned to the city view as she sat in the dimly lit space while answering Antonio's mundane questions about weather in Cambridge.

"So how did you get into Adams House?" Antonio inquired, shifting the conversation. "Even I couldn't pull that off," he added.

"I'm resourceful," she responded, as the chef placed a Caesar salad in front of her.

"Come on, spill it," he insisted.

"I know how to leverage people's secrets as well," Destiny hinted. Knowing she would never tell what she had to leverage for the funds unless she was the co-defendant in a criminal case.

"Well enough," Antonio held his hands up. "But I would like to know more about you and your family. Your persona has always been intriguing to me," he added.

"I feel like I should pay you $1 before we do a deep dive into my life," Destiny acknowledged.

"One dollar?" Antonio looked puzzled.

"For attorney client privilege," she responded.

Antonio laughed.

"To be honest, talking about my upbringing is a broken record," Destiny insisted quickly. "The lower middle-class kid from public school, who was the top of her class but came to Harvard and struggled to adapt."

"Aren't you tired of giving the trailer? I want the pilot episode of your series," Antonio insisted.

Destiny raked her fingers through her hair and inhaled deeply. She contemplated what she wanted to disclose about herself. She always followed her family's motto – *the less they know- the better*. But she knew she needed to give Antonio just a nugget of herself.

"I'm an opportunist," she admitted before finishing off her glass of champagne. "I align myself in friendships and relationships that I perceive will benefit me in one way or another."

Antonio's eyes widened as he moved to refill her glass.

"Don't look at me like you've just seen your predator," Destiny narrowed her eyes at him. "We are probably one in the same... It's just that the statute of limitations on the things I've done isn't up yet."

"I would love to take that dollar now," Antonio mentioned, trying to urge her to keep talking.

"I'll probably pay you before the night is out," Destiny lied as she started to eat her salad. "This chicken parmigiana better be good," she mentioned with a smirk.

"I promise you, anything I serve you will be amazing," Antonio winked.

Destiny blushed and reached for her glass of champagne.

"Your eyes are memorizing," Antonio commented just before his phone rang in another room. "The way they catch the candlelight..." he stopped mid-sentence as he rose from his seat.

"Thank you," Destiny tilted her head slightly as she looked at Antonio from across the large table.

"I have to get that," Antonio excused himself from the table. "I'll be right back."

Destiny nodded as she picked up her fork to continue eating. Before Antonio returned to their meal, Destiny finished with her salad. She asked the housekeeper who cleared the table to refresh her glass as she stood to take a look at the view of Boston streets for a moment. She grew agitated as the third glass of champagne was nearly empty. Turning around, surveying the grand apartment again, her eyes landed back on the record player. She started to fumble through his album collection, shuffling through the stacks until she came across a Bob Marley record. Just the sound of the record player being turned on and watching the turntable spin was nostalgic for Destiny. She could recall her father playing albums on a Friday night when she was young adolescent.

"Let me help you with that," Antonio's hand hovered over hers.

Destiny didn't notice the trance she'd fallen into until Antonio touched her. Her mind had been stuck in 1987 for a moment. Incense burning from a hanging pothos plant. Her brothers playing with a Rock 'Em Sock 'Em Robot toy. Her mother standing in the kitchen archway with the corded telephone stuck between her ear and shoulder, while Destiny spelled out words on the album covers as her father played the role of a DJ.

"Have you been to Jamaica?" Antonio asked, pulling Destiny completely away from her pleasant childhood memory.

"No," Destiny responded, as she released the album and moved away from the player, allowing Antonio to take over. "Not yet."

"Allow me to find something to play more fitting for the evening," Antonio suggested, sliding her choice back into its place on the shelf.

Destiny nodded as she picked up her champagne glass, that had been replenished while her back was turned. She sipped slowly, her eyes shifting from the view of the city to Antonio amongst his records. She waited anxiously for a glimpse into his taste in music.

Soon, a familiar angelic male voice crooned over a base guitar as the record turned.

"Nat King Cole?" Destiny questioned, as she turned toward Antonio.

He nodded. "So, you're familiar?" Antonio questioned.

Destiny didn't want to tell Antonio that she'd mainly heard Nat King Cole singing Christmas songs. So, she simply nodded.

Destiny wished that he would ask her to dance. She would have loved to sway in his arms to the ballad. But he didn't. They stood there, staring into one another's eyes as if their feet were glued to the marble floor. In that moment,

Destiny searched his eyes for his true interest in her. She wondered if he wanted her as his hidden secret, a fetish, or if he wanted to love her out loud despite adversities. Destiny was about to ask her boss what he wanted from her so that she could stop wondering. But as her lips parted, someone approached Antonio and asked if he was ready for the second course.

Chapter 5 – A Mother's Love

Jasiah took inventory of his demolished vehicle and thanked God he survived the accident. He leaned on a totaled car adjacent to his and lit a cigarette as he watched his parents work together to retrieve his personal effects from the vehicle. Seeing them working together, laughing at age-old inside jokes was still an unimaginable sight to Jasiah.

He could vividly remember when Destiny left printouts from *The Washington Post* detailing his father's arrest and trial. Since then, he had worked diligently to keep the world his father introduced him to and the world he lived with his mother separate. He feared the day his two worlds would crash into one another. But in a distorted reality, they seemed to meld together in a matter of moments. Jasiah felt like he was watching old friends gathering his loose change, disheveled tennis equipment and schoolbooks from his totaled vehicle.

"Where are the keys?" Big Siah asked as he uncovered the aftermarket safe in the trunk.

"What the fuck do you have my son into?" Faye questioned for what seemed like the hundredth time.

"Getting this muthafuckin' money," Big Siah answered, retrieving the small key from his son's fingertips. "You know what it is."

Faye rolled her eyes and started to fan herself. She turned her steely gaze toward her son, her lips curling in disdain. "And when did you start smoking cigarettes? That can't be helpful for tennis."

"It's neither here nor there at this point." Jasiah hunched his shoulders and blew smoke away from his mother.

"He developed that habit after somebody tried to carjack him at a gas station," Big Siah revealed, while he wiggled the key in the makeshift safe.

"Why didn't you tell me that happened to you?" Faye asked her son.

"I couldn't call to say, Ma, I was in the lower 9th with Pops running a game of Texas Hold 'em when these CTC niggas rolled up on me," Jasiah explained.

"You have no business over there," Faye shook her head.

It was the same sentiment Faye expressed years prior when he was held at gunpoint in an attempted carjacking in Northeast D.C. But from that situation and many more, Jasiah had learned to keep his head on a swivel. This time, he saw the would-be carjackers coming. It was the first time he pulled the 9mm his father insisted he purchase at a gun show. It was the first time he unloaded it outside of a shooting range.

"You would have said more than that," Jasiah insinuated.

"It's okay. Siah let them know what's up," Big Siah smacked palms with his son as a smirk formed on his lips.

"I'm going to call the parole board when I get home, see if they know you're down here," Faye uttered.

"Damn, you cooperating with the 5-0?" Big Siah looked at Faye. "You would do that to me?"

"You should know by now... I'd do anything to protect *my son*," Faye snapped, her glare sharp enough to cut through steel.

"So, you say," Jasiah mumbled sarcastically, as he took another drag of his cigarette.

Big Siah didn't interject as he concentrated on freeing the small knapsack from the safe. "Gottdamn!" Big Siah exclaimed in frustration.

"Let me see," Faye pushed him back and reached her slender fingers inside to free the bag hooked within the aluminum box. "There," she yanked the bag free and handed it to her son.

Jasiah opened the bag and revealed his winnings from days prior.

"I'm not paying your rent another month!" Faye threatened as she ran her manicured fingers across the cash. "That is over ten thousand dollars."

Jasiah smirked, and announced, "Lunch on me," while the cigarette dangled from his lip.

"I'm not bailing you out of jail, Jasiah Sheffield," his mother announced.

"Ma, you would not be my first phone call," he retorted, shaking his head.

"How long you in town for, Lady Faye?" Big Siah asked in an attempt to diffuse the situation before the mother and son duo fully erupted into an argument.

"You got it... I'm leaving in the morning," Faye crossed her arms over her chest and looked over the sea of vehicles in the impound lot.

"Why don't we hit a spot? You can see our son in action," Big Siah suggested. "The boy is amazing on any table."

"I'm not in the mood," Jasiah threw his cigarette down and left it smoking as he headed towards his father's car. "This is weird enough as is."

He could hear his parents giggling like teenagers behind him as he struggled to fit his 6'3" frame into the backseat so he could stretch out his leg. Once Jasiah was situated, he exhaled. Still feeling the slight discomfort in his healing ribs, he reached in his pocket to pop a Percocet to dull the aching pain. Closing his eyes, he rubbed his temple, trying to figure out how he'd ruined his senior year of college for $17,000. He punched the back of the seat as an attempt to alleviate the tension growing within him.

Reality hit him: he wouldn't be able to finish his senior year on the 2004 ITA All-American team; his tennis career was probably over; and he would have to hobble across the stage on crutches to receive his degree in May. Anxiety started to build up as he thought about how he might have to start his job at a hedge fund in New York in a boot.

Jasiah gritted his teeth as he tried to keep his composure. He recounted his last night in the casino on the poker table. He had told himself to leave by one a.m. if he wasn't up by two thousand. By one a.m., he was up by four grand. At the time, he felt like he was on a lucky streak; but as he sat in the cramped backseat, he felt like his luck had run out on I-10.

Adjusting the vent to blow cool air directly on him, Jasiah took a deep breath, trying to convince himself that he'd be fine, though his chest felt like it might collapse under the weight of his thoughts. He continued breathing slowly while glancing at his totaled vehicle. His plans to take it to New York after graduation were ruined. Without another thought, Jasiah punched the back seat again and again. He felt like it was the only way he could release his anger, disappoint, and pain coursing through his veins. His internal rage only escalated as he heard his mother's cackle.

His eyes burned when he caught a glimpse of his mother and father having a conversation in the scorching heat as if they were at a pool bar and not an impound lot. But then something flicked inside of him. They were his parents. Being civil. Working together to take care of him. He exhaled and sat back, trying to control his feelings. Throwing his head back, Jasiah covered his face with his palms and told himself, "Get yourself together."

Looking at his destroyed vehicle again, Jasiah told himself "You're lucky." The driver's side door was laying on top of the crumpled hood. His custom rims were bent and contorted inside of all flat tires. He thought about the people that died that day and finally felt fortunate. He had escaped death.

Closing his eyes again, Jasiah recounted the times he had been spared. The crack of the butt of the police officer's gun against his temple, the attempted car jackings, the shootouts where he'd been an innocent bystander. Jasiah was so deep in his memory; he didn't notice he'd fallen asleep until he heard his father ordering Jungle Juice from New Orleans Original Daquiris.

"You sweating bullets back there, you could use one of these," his father handed him a frozen daiquiri.

Jasiah took one sip of the drink and nodded back off. When he woke up again, only his mother was in the front seat. "Where are we?" he asked, stretching his arms.

"Some spot your father swears has the best pork chop in town," she sucked her teeth.

Surveying his surroundings again, Jasiah noticed they were parked on Dante Street. Jasiah knew his father was inside of Brigsten's. "I know you do not care about a pork chop," Jasiah sipped his watered-down daiquiri.

"You don't know me, boy," his mother concluded.

"I definitely don't know Lady Faye," he expressed, as he shifted in his seat for comfort.

"Why have you been keeping this from me?" Faye turned and looked at her son. "I thought you let the shit go with your father, but come to find out, you have him living with you."

Jasiah drummed his fingers on the roof, wishing it were open so he could escape.

"What does it look like for me to pay your rent for you and your father?"

"There you go worrying about how you look; that's always your only concern," Jasiah uttered.

"My number one concern is keeping you safe. I bet if you had just gone to Harvard, like we originally planned, he wouldn't have followed you there."

Jasiah sighed. "Harvard didn't give me a full ride like Xavier. Remember?"

"That didn't matter," Faye replied.

"Roy helped me get this scholarship when he saw my acceptance letter. You do know that. Don't you?" Jasiah divulged a secret he had been holding on to, no longer fearful of his mother's reaction. "His frat brother from Harvard is our athletic director."

"Roy did not," Faye gasped in disbelief.

"Roy helped Destiny get more on her financial need scholarship at Harvard too," Jasiah kept talking, knowing that the information would infuriate his mother and deflect her attention from his secrets. "I grew up thinking Roy was the bad guy, but now I give him credit for providing guidance when I really needed it."

Faye sat silently for a moment, fuming in her seat. "Roy did everything on the strength of me," she spat. "You have always been unappreciative for the life that Roy and I have provided for you."

"Whatever," Jasiah sipped his daiquiri, disregarding the watered down taste. "I've told that man thank you many times," Jasiah dismissed his mother's sentiment. "Roy and I speak more than you and I," he continued to dig at her. "And do you know who I attribute that to?" He paused for a split second before adding "Destiny."

"Ain't that some shit," Faye uttered.

Jasiah continued adding fuel to the fire. "You know what I can give you props for, Ma?"

Faye sat mute, facing forward.

Jasiah knew his mother was gathering her thoughts. He envisioned her mind tinkering, figuring out a venomous rebuttal. "My fashion sense," he answered. "Thanks, Ma."

"You—"

"You what?" his voice immediately filled the car, daring his mother to be combative.

Faye flinched but didn't say a word. She allowed silence to fill the car as they awaited Big Siah's return.

Faye turned to her side and looked at her son. Jasiah refused to make eye contact with his mother. "I don't know what gotten into you, but I'm telling you that you better part ways with your father as soon as possible. He will do nothing but bring you down," Faye declared calmly as if it were her last resolve.

Jasiah thought about the experiences he'd had with his father over the years. Big Siah parlaying Jasiah's math skills into bank rolls. Coming to New Orleans and watching over him as he detoxed. Showing up to every tennis match and every poker tournament. Those times together were irreplaceable.

"Do you understand me, Jasiah?" Faye asserted.

"Ma, did you know I'm a poker champion? As in, featured on ESPN-level champion? I'm on my way to being on Poker Players All-Time Money well before thirty, if I even pursue it," he questioned. "And I would have never found passions in this way if it wasn't for my father."

"What are you talking about, Jasiah?"

"I'm talking about the fact that you don't know me. You've never taken the time to know me!"

"You're my son. I know you better than you know yourself," she sucked her teeth, dismissing what Jasiah was saying.

"If you knew me you would have never thought I raped that fucking girl!" Jasiah retorted - his words imbued with years' worth of resentment.

"I never thought that my son—"

"You thought I did it. You wouldn't even come to the school with me. Roy stood by me."

"I had RJ to care for," she tried to defend her actions.

"Let me out," Jasiah began to feel even more cramped as her excuse fueled a rebellion within him.

"Jasiah, you need to—"

"Let me out!" he hit the back of his mother's seat as he began to get enraged.

"You better calm down!" she turned all the way around in her seat.

Seeing the anger in her eyes calmed Jasiah's tantrum. But his cheeks still puffed as he started to breath hard.

"What has gotten into you?" Faye inquired, surprised at how much anger her son had toward her.

"Ma, you haven't been to one family day since I've been here... not one of my tennis tournaments. My father has been to every one of them since he got here. Even with his parole situation, he has been here. You have no limitations and couldn't even try to make it to the championship game last year."

"Boy, I've provided for you your entire life. I fixed all your fuck ups while you were in school. Do you know how much stress you put me through while you were in high school?"

Jasiah laughed at his mother's statement. "What did I put you through, Ma? Did I put you through anything or did I have to go through shit? Were you just my parent while I experienced it?"

"There was the rape charge—"

"False accusation," Jasiah quickly corrected his mother.

"The... the police brutality."

"That Roy sued the Montgomery County Police department over and we will eventually get a check. You're talking about an incident that happened to me!" Jasiah exclaimed.

"Destiny's pregnancy."

"Thank you for giving me money for an abortion because you were too young to be a grandmother," Jasiah looked out of the window for his father.

"When stuff happens to you, it happens to me!"

"Bullshit!" Jasiah shook his head in disagreement. "The only thing you helped me with is finding an abortion clinic. Other than that, you left it for Roy to figure out," Jasiah referred to his stepfather.

"I should slap you in your face! Anything Roy did was on the strength of me!" she insinuated again.

"Hey, hey, hey, hey... lets calm down here," Big Siah stated as he entered the car. "I can hear you screaming from the street, Lady Faye."

"Get me to the airport! Get me away from this ungrateful—"

"Ungrateful?" Jasiah cut his mother off with another condescending laugh. "I'm grateful for everything you have given me, Mother. Including your cynicism."

"Siah, chill out," his father demanded. "Don't talk to your mother like that."

"She wouldn't be here if you didn't answer the phone at the hospital! She would have sent Lafayette or maybe even Roy to check on me. She doesn't give a damn about me as long as I'm out of her hair."

"You know that's not true," Big Siah looked at Jasiah through the rear-view mirror as he pulled off.

"Pops, do you ever hear me on the phone with her? You ever see me eager to visit her at any point?" Jasiah pulled out his bottle of pain medication and popped another pill before continuing, "She didn't even know I was on TV three times!" Jasiah yelled. "Once for the tennis championship and then twice last summer for poker tournaments... she had no idea I was in Vegas or Florida. Nor does she care."

His father pulled the car over quickly. "You are a grown man," he turned in his seat, glaring at Siah. "That's what you've been telling me since I met you... this is how mothers treat grown men."

"Where you're from," Jasiah corrected his father. "That's how mothers treat grown men where you're from... them bitches on Wisconsin Avenue barely got their titty out their son's mouth when they graduate from high school."

"That's what you want, son? Some of your momma's titty?" Big Siah asked, cracking a smile.

"I just want her to stop worrying about how I make her look and more about my well-being." Jasiah admitted. "That's it."

Big Siah turned around in his seat. Faye was silent even though she knew all eyes were on her. She opened her mouth to say something but instead she turned up the radio. Her unwillingness to continue the conversation spoke volumes to Jasiah. It only reinforced his sentiment that she didn't care.

"I'm so glad I got away from you," Jasiah mumbled, but his words hung in the air, penetrating the heart of his parents.

"That's not cool, son," Big Siah recognized in a solemn tone.

In an instant, Faye took off her seatbelt and turned around to attack Jasiah. He blocked her wild swings until his father pushed Faye against the passenger side door.

"What the fuck?" Big Siah yelled. "Faye, chill!"

"This little ungrateful, entitled muthafuckah!" she screamed, as she flung her hair over her shoulder. "You know what I went through to keep a roof over our head because of this son of bitch?" she pointed to Big Siah. "I sacrificed my whole youth for you, Jasiah, and you want to be the fuck away from me?"

"What twisted dimension are we in?" Jasiah questioned, as he looked at the scratches on his arms. "Ma, cut it out. The jig is up."

She lunged at her oldest son again, attempting to use her manicured nails as a weapon.

Big Siah slammed her against the door. "Cut the shit out, Faye," he demanded, pointing at her. "You're no victim! Let's not forget how our story really goes." His usual jovial voice had dissolved.

Faye heaved as her eyes narrowed onto Big Siah.

"You don't need to look at me like that, shawty, I should be the one with the axe to grind in the car. I got the short end of the stick," Big Siah continued.

Faye rolled her eyes.

"Now, ya'll chill the fuck out!" Big Siah demanded. "I'm trying to get us home so we can enjoy these pork chops."

Jasiah leaned his head back and wished he had an escape route. Big Siah pulled off again and turned the radio off, leaving everyone to their own thoughts. Jasiah welcomed the silence as looked at his parents from the back seat. He watched their body language and tried to figure out who was the villain between the two of them. His father never spoke ill of his mother. His mother never really spoke of his father until Jasiah showed interest in meeting him. Jasiah started to question if his mother was innocent all of those years ago. He wondered if she should have been behind bars alongside his father.

Back at the apartment, Jasiah ate his food in his bedroom at his desk, just has he had eaten his dinner many years as a teenager. He tried to drown out his parents' conversation with the television but every so often, he could hear their laughter an octave above the commentator on Sportscenter. He slipped on a set of headphones, tuning into Ginuwine's "In Those Jeans" as he took in his view of Common Street. He bobbed his head to the music, trying to release the anguish that was rooted within him.

He reminisced on when he first arrived in New Orleans. Everything about Xavier's campus and the surrounding city was new and exciting. The town hardly slept. It felt like everyone was on a never-ending party cycle. The hospitality seemed amazing. The culture was intriguing. And fun never stopped on campus. He tried to stay focused. He attempted to stay grounded. Juggling his academics, the tennis team, and a social life was getting the best of him during his sophomore year. When he admitted to his father that he started popping Adderall to stay focused, Big Siah started visiting. Jasiah attributed his father's presence to him staying on track to graduate on time.

"Hey!" his father's voice cut through the music, turning Jasiah's attention toward his bedroom door. "You done?" Big Siah asked from the doorway.

"Yeah, thanks," Jasiah stated as he removed his headphones. "Can you help me bag my leg up when you get a chance. I want to take a shower?"

"I ain't gonna keep doing this for you," his father admitted. "I felt sorry for your last night, you better call Ava and Tiffany over here."

"Not while my mother is here," Jasiah protested. "She's too judgmental." He knew his mother wouldn't understand that he was in a menage a trois.

Big Siah shrugged. "I'ma take your mother to listen to a second line band, get her liquored up, and see if she let me see those titties you still want stuck in your mouth."

Jasiah looked at his father plainly, showing he was not amused by his father antics.

"It was a joke," Big Siah collected Jasiah's plate and trash. "Well, kind of."

"Pops, that is still my mother," Jasiah frowned.

"I just gotta see for old times' sake," Big Siah admitted.

Jasiah pretended like he was going to throw up.

Big Siah chuckled and started to close the door.

"Ah, Pops," Jasiah called his father before the door closed. "After she's gone, can you tell me how the story really goes between you two?"

"Naw," his father declined, shaking his head. "You're not ready."

Chapter 6 – News

Destiny's eyes flicked nervously from one figure to the next in the corner of the conference room. The low murmurs of the opposing counsel felt like a quiet storm brewing around her, and she couldn't shake the feeling that they were talking about the evidence she'd uncovered in the J Morgan finances. The hidden profits she had discovered were a key component that would push them to start negotiations.

"Do you need the room?" Antonio mockingly asked the opposition while his pen tapped against his folder of evidence. "We can give you a minute."

The opposing counsel held up his finger, inaudibly requesting more time.

Destiny shifted her weight in her seat as her discomfort continued. She couldn't imagine the amount of anxiety their client felt.

"Okay, I think we can settle at three million," the attorney finally spoke.

"We're still at five," Antonio stated firmly without blinking an eye.

In her head, Destiny danced the cabbage patch, her victory dance. The due diligence had paid off—she could feel it in her bones. After the lawyers agreed on terms, Antonio turned to Destiny and gave her a nod. His actions seemed simple to most but to her, it was a stamp of approval. She had conquered one of her most difficult tasks at work to date and Antonio's nod was recognizing it.

Destiny relished in the gratifying moment. I only made her want to dive deeper into her pursuits of being a lawyer.

"Team, what a way to pull it together!" Antonio raised his celebratory glass of champagne in the conference room after the clients left. "If we can pull this off next quarter, imagine what the end of the year bonuses will be."

Everyone cheered but Destiny. She would be long gone before bonus checks would be cut. For a moment, she pondered Antonio's proposal for her start working full-time at the firm while she took a break from Harvard. Not only could she get an end of year bonus, but there was an opportunity to negotiate a better salary and really stack her money. She roused from her thoughts at the sound of Antonio's voice near her. She didn't want to risk a lingering gaze between the two of them, so she made a swift exit of the conference room and made her way the reception area to chat with Emmanuel.

"I know you didn't come out here with only one glass in your hand," Emmanuel teased, as Destiny leaned against the counter of his desk.

She rolled her eyes. "Your headset is mobile. If you want something you can get it."

"I'm not fooling with you, Destiny Peay," Emmanuel hissed before he answered the ringing phone. "Rossi and Associates. How may I help you?"

"What would you like?" Destiny whispered, sipping her glass of bubbly.

Emmanuel placed the caller on hold, "A shot of tequila and a handsomely hung doctor, but I'll settle for whatever you're drinking and a few slices of that good brie cheese with the brioche crackers. Thanks, Hun," he quickly rambled.

Destiny headed back to the conference room to get Emmanuel what he requested. As she reached for the bottle of Chandon Champagne, Antonio reached for it as well.

"Let me get that for you," he insisted.

Destiny quietly tilted an empty flute toward him.

"Great work, Miss Peay," he complimented her. "Very impressive."

"I try my best," Destiny smiled.

"I hate to see you go after graduation," he shared the sentiment that he'd already stated several times.

"I just received an interview request for a law clerk position in D.C. Superior Courts," she notified him proudly, knowing it would agitate him just a little.

Antonio turned his head slightly to hide his disdain. "I think you're overlooking better opportunities."

Destiny gave a simple shrug and walked away. She could feel his eyes on her, watching her hips sway in the fitted maroon sheath dress. She imagined he was longing to brush his lips along her jawline, the way he normally greeted her when they were in private.

"What has you smiling so hard?" Emmanuel asked once she approached his desk.

"Just thinking about my future endeavors," Destiny handed him his glass. "We're graduating!" she exclaimed as she raised her glass.

"Cheers to that!" Emmanuel toasted with Destiny. "Now, we have to get this money," he produced a small envelope before her. "Are you game?"

Destiny took a deep breath and sipped her champagne.

"Come on, your brother is already on his way. I need you to host."

The mention of her brother, Jax, made her release an exaggerated sigh. There was a part of her that no longer wanted to be complacent in their shenanigans – but she loved the payout. She knew that if her brother was coming up to Massachusetts from D.C., there would be some real money at Emmanuel's secret society event. She was confident that if she played her cards right with the thirsty clientele, she could collect enough tips that she wouldn't give missing out on the end of year bonus another thought. Destiny reached for the envelope.

Emmanuel snatched it back, "This means you're in. Right?"

"In what? What are you two up to?" Megan interrupted in her deep southern accent.

"Just our normal shits and giggles," Emmanuel answered smiling at Destiny.

Destiny snatched the envelope from him and looked at Megan. "What's up Megan? Did you get tasked with putting us back to work?"

"Mr. Rossi just received an urgent call. The Robinson family is on their way, and he told me to greet them at the door."

"Robinson family?" Emmanuel and Destiny questioned together.

"Yeah, they're from Potomac, Maryland. Their son just got charged with assault and battery."

"Jason Robinson?" Destiny questioned in shock.

"I'm not sure of his name," Megan looked at Destiny. "Is D.C. close to Potomac, Maryland?"

"They must have plenty of money and connections to get Mr. Rossi directly on a criminal case," Emmanuel interjected.

Destiny gulped down the remainder of her champagne – ignoring Megan's question. She had not seen the Robinsons since Jasiah and Jason's prom send off in the spring of 2000. She couldn't recall ever seeing them assist their son move on or off campus in any of the years they'd been at Harvard together.

"Finish yours so I can take the glass," Destiny instructed Emmanuel.

"So, do you know them?" Megan pried.

"I may," she responded casually.

Before Destiny could take Emmanuel's glass, the suite door opened. They quickly pushed their glasses out of sight under the reception counter.

"Mr. and Mrs. Robinson," Megan greeted the couple with a pageantry smile as though she'd met them before.

Mrs. Robinson, a tall, slender Black woman, whose style resembled Jasiah's mother to Destiny, smiled at Megan. Mr. Robinson, a short, bald White man, turned to the familiar face in the room. "Destiny, right?"

Destiny smiled. "Hello, Mr. and Mrs. Robinson."

"Oh," Mrs. Robinson's head tilted toward Destiny. "Faye did say you were at Harvard — are you graduating this year?"

"I am," Destiny assured her.

"We haven't seen Jasiah come home much," Mr. Robinson recalled.

"You remember he was in that terrible accident before spring break," Mrs. Robinson turned to her husband.

"But even before that," Mr. Robinson looked to Destiny like she could spare some details.

"An accident?" Destiny's head shot back in shock at the statement. "Did you say Jasiah was in an accident?"

"Oh, you two *have* lost touch," Mrs. Robinson shook her head. "That's a shame... but yes, Faye mentioned that he nearly lost his life."

Destiny gasped. But from her peripheral view she could see her coworkers' eyes on her. She swallowed hard and managed to say, "That's unfortunate to hear."

The joy Destiny had been feeling all day quickly left her body. She held her midsection, finding it hard to believe that something devastating had happened to Jasiah and she wasn't there for him.

"Mr. and Mrs. Robinson, Mr. Rossi is waiting for you in his office. We were having a small celebration, please excuse the chatter in the halls," Meagan spoke when she noticed the disbelief plastered on Destiny's face.

Destiny excused herself. With the envelope crumpling between her fingers, she quickly walked toward her office. After closing the door, she leaned against it in the corner and tried to regain her composure. She could hear her own heart thumping in her chest with nervousness about the unknown. Even though she had intentionally pushed Jasiah away, she could never imagine not seeing him again. In that moment, she pushed aside all of her animosity towards Jasiah and reached for her Blackberry. Her fingers trembled as she dialed the number from memory. With each ring, she felt like a rope was tightening around her heart. She feared he wouldn't answer. Or maybe he changed his number. She nearly hyperventilated at the thought that he didn't want to speak to her.

After three rings, a groggy, familiar voice answered. She didn't realize she had been holding her breath until he asked, "Who is this?" in agitated tone.

Destiny cleared her throat and took a seat at her desk before saying, "Hey, handsome."

***

Jasiah sat up in the bed in his dimly lit bedroom, allowing his girlfriend Tiffany's head to fall on to the pillow to the right and almost crushing Ava as he tried to get out of the bed at just the sound of *her* voice on the other end of the phone. A chill went through his body at her signature greeting.

"Hey," he managed to return as he used the slither of sunlight coming through his blackout curtains to maneuver in the room.

"Is this a not a good time?" Destiny inquired – recognizing he didn't greet her as he normally did.

"It's fine," Jasiah replied, hopping to his dresser to retrieve a pair of shorts.

"You can just call me when you get up. I just—"

"It's fine... It's fine. Just give me a second. Hold on for a minute."

Jasiah placed the phone on mute and threw it on his dresser before sitting in his desk chair to dress.

"Are you okay?" Ava questioned as she sat up, exposing her full C-cup breasts.

"Go back to sleep. You have to work in a few hours," Jasiah told her. "I'ma take this call in the living room."

He grabbed his phone from the dresser and unmuted it. "Hold on, one more second. Don't hang up."

He placed the phone on mute again and slipped it into his pocket before grabbing his crutches and making his way to the living room. He plopped on the sofa and hoped Destiny hadn't hung up.

"Hey, Beautiful," Jasiah finally answered out of breath.

"Are you okay?"

"No," he responded, as he sat back and tried to catch his breath. "No, I'm not okay after the way you carried me."

"Jasiah," Destiny sang his name sweetly.

The way she said his name relaxed every muscle in his body. "I just need to catch my breath," he acknowledged. "Crutches are not made for big boys like me."

"What happened to you?" she questioned.

"Why you change your number?" he asked in return.

"Answer my question, boy," she demanded.

97

"I nearly died, and you were nowhere to be found. THAT is what happened," he answered.

"Jasiah, what happened?" Destiny asked again.

"An eighteen-wheeler tried to take me out," Jasiah sighed. "I woke up with a broken fibula, some bruised ribs, and chemical burns from the air bags."

"Ouch," Destiny finally took a full breath since Mrs. Robinson gave her the news of Jasiah's accident.

"This is more than ouch," Jasiah shook his head as he looked at his cast. "But I still have space on this cast for your signature."

"I'm sorry," Destiny whispered into the phone. "I'm sorry that happened to you."

"But not sorry enough to come see me right?" Jasiah looked up at the ceiling.

"Jasiah, you don't need me."

Jasiah held the line, intentionally not giving Destiny the assurances, she wanted. There was a part of him that enjoyed hearing the sound of her voice. There was another part of him that hated the grip she still had on his heart.

"Why are you calling me?" he asked. "You changed your number to be rid of me. Right?"

"I have a stalker!" Destiny blurted out. "I have someone playing on my phone every day, calling me black bitches. Threatening to rape me. Telling me I will not get away with things I've done. Changing my number had nothing to do with you. It was an attempt for me to protect myself when no one else can."

Jasiah sat silently in shock.

"I just didn't want to burden you with my problems," she added.

"Destiny, you know that's not how we roll," he whispered. "You can always count on me."

"I'm sure whoever you were in the bed with at four in the afternoon wouldn't want to hear that."

Jasiah chuckled at the obvious. "How I feel about you hasn't changed," he mumbled. "So, what made you call me?"

"Jason is in trouble," Destiny informed him. "His parents are in my law office now seeking counsel."

"What kind of trouble?"

"I don't have the specifics," she sat back in her office chair. "But for his parents to be here — its serious."

"Ummm," he looked out of the window of his apartment. "I'll check on him later."

Destiny wanted to tell him to wait a few days, but she kept quiet.

"But back to you; this stalker—"

"It started as just a cyber stalker," Destiny divulged. "But then I started to get dead roses in front of my dorm room every so often."

"What? What are the police doing? The administration? Mr. Peay hasn't been up there to raise holy hell?" Jasiah was alarmed.

"I've been told to be flattered; that there's nothing they can do if no physical harm is done."

"That's bullshit!"

"Calm down, Jasiah."

"Destiny, if something happens to you... man... I could never forgive myself."

She could feel the sincerity in his voice. "Jasiah, put your energy into healing... next time I see you, I need you at the top of your game."

"Shawty, even with these crutches, I'm still the best that did it and got away with it."

"Boyyyyy," Destiny hissed, as they shared a laugh. "There you go with that cockiness."

"Destiny... I'm serious though. I'm concerned about you," he interrupted their playful banter.

"My head is on a swivel," she tried to play down her worries. "I just can't wait to be out of here in a few weeks."

"Then what, Destiny?" he asked.

Destiny took a breath and started tapping her finger against her desk. She didn't know how to answer him.

"What's the plan, Shawty?" Jasiah continued to pry. "You always have a plan." When she didn't respond it disturbed him. "Destiny, I'm here for you... you don't have to shut me out. I got you."

"Jasiah, I called to check on you and your near-death situation," Destiny tried to take the attention off of her. "I'm so relieved that you—"

"Time will heal my wounds," he cut her off as he stared at his cast. "I'm more concerned about this stalker situation."

"Me too," Destiny admitted.

"Is it that bum you let eat my mac and cheese on Thanksgiving?"

Destiny laughed. "Boy, you are crazy."

"Did you tell Jax and Junior?" he asked about her brothers as he watched Tiffany come out of the bedroom in one of his t-shirts.

"Jax on his way up here... he may figure it out while he's here," she sighed.

"Are you okay?" Tiffany quizzed, as she rubbed his shoulders.

"Jasiah, I didn't mean to intrude. I just wanted to check on you," Destiny stated when she heard the female voice.

"Don't hang up, Destiny," Jasiah replied. "Just give me a second."

To Destiny, the phone went mute. She was instantly irritated at the confirmation of her suspicions that he was in a woman's arms. She sat back and shook her head, asking herself why she cared so much. She wanted to hang up, but there was another part of her that didn't want to keep the distance between her and Jasiah.

On the other end of the phone, Jasiah turned to Tiffany. "Baby, everything is fine. I'm just talking to my homegirl. Go back to bed."

"No, I'ma cook us some dinner before I head to work," she insisted, continuing her way to the kitchen.

Jasiah gritted his teeth and took the phone off of mute.

"Destiny, your safety is a priority," Jasiah recognized, knowing how much trauma she had already been through growing up in the nation's capital.

"I wish the police or even the administration thought that way," Destiny replied. "But I'll figure it out."

"Boo, you want fried chicken or pork chops?" Tiffany asked from the kitchen.

"Jasiah, I'ma let you go," Destiny said, even more annoyed to hear someone giving him a pet name.

"Destiny, I'm worried about you," Jasiah admitted.

"I'm glad you have someone to take care of you," she retorted sarcastically.

Jasiah wanted to tell her how he wanted it to be her. That he would rather her comforting hugs and head rubs. He wanted to tell her that the thought of her running her nails up his back as she straddled him still sent a chill up his spine.

However, all he could say was, "Destiny."

She hung up. Jasiah cut his eyes at Tiffany, who was busy in kitchen. He wished she had stayed in the bedroom instead of making her presence known.

"Pork chops or chicken?" she asked again without looking at Jasiah.

"Chicken," he answered, as he turned to prop his leg up on the sofa.

He locked Destiny's new number into his phone as a myriad of feelings fell over him. He was concerned for both Destiny, and his childhood friend, Jason. He felt useless as there was nothing he could do for either of them.

Chapter 7 – Weight

Destiny grabbed her patent leather stilettos and stumbled out of Jax's rental car, her bare feet splashing against the wet pavement. Any other time, she would have been telling her brother to turn down Rare Essence's "Overnight Scenario" to avoid unwanted attention. But in the moment, the inebriated Destiny didn't have a care in the world. Jax laughed at his sister as she rapped along with "Whiteboy" and moved her body to the congas and drums embedded in the go-go music.

"Aye, Destiny, you sure you gonna get to your room okay?" he asked, rolling his window down.

"I'm good," she smiled back at her brother, as she bopped to the beat and snapped her fingers under the black iron gates on Plympton Street. A soft breeze flowed through her hair as she moved her hips rhythmically.

"Get your ass in that building," her cousin, Ron, yelled from the passenger seat, his voice laced with playful urgency as he and Jax laughed together.

"Go Destiny... go Destiny," Jax coaxed his sister's fun on.

At 3 a.m., their laughter echoed off the narrow street. At that moment, they were three kids from DC, lost in their hometown music amidst the historic Harvard campus. Destiny felt amazing, like so many things were going well for her that day.

She had spoken to Jasiah, and they had started instant messaging in a playful banter all evening. Antonio had pulled her into his office and snuck a kiss before she left for the day. And then there was the money she made hosting Emmanuel's exclusive clientele. She felt like all of the chips were falling into place. She smiled at her brother as he continued to hype her up and imitated the beat of the drum on the steering wheel.

All Destiny could think was, *this is what I needed*. A carefree night where she felt confident about herself. However, when lights flickered on from several of the dorm rooms at once, Destiny dashed into the building, giggling, as she could only imagine someone making a noise complaint. She was safely inside the building when she heard the tires screeching against the wet pavement as her brother sped away.

She was on cloud nine when she made it to her dorm room but cursed when her bare foot crushed a dried red rose at her doorstep. Destiny rolled the flower under her foot in a backwards kick, sending the stem flying across the wooden hallway floor and scattering dry petals along the way. Her mood soured instantly. Entering her room, she didn't bother to turn on a lamp, fearful that the bright light would irritate her eyes. The glow of the streetlight from her open window illuminated her room enough for her to see.

She closed the door behind her, dropping her bag and shoes, but stumbled over the whip that tumbled from her bag. She caught herself by gripping her mantle and then leaned against it to hold her balance as she started stripping out of her trench coat. She slowly disrobed from her black, shiny patent leather corset and matching boy shorts. She was too tired and intoxicated to get into the shower to wash off her body glitter and she figured the futon was the perfect place to sleep after the night she'd had. Closing her eyes and snuggling under a throw blanket, Destiny thought about the money she made hosting a stripper party with Emmanuel and her brother. Though she didn't undress for anyone, she found great pleasure and amusement in narrating the event on the microphone. She smiled, thinking of the props she used, like whips, to capture the audience's attention and how she was often tipped like she was a dirty dancer.

A chill swept through the room; Destiny's first instinct was that her blanket had slipped off her. Groggily, she blinked her eyes open, only to find that the darkness had lifted. Dawn cast into the room with an eerie blue haze. But there was unfamiliar scent in the room that made her think of a sour mop. Her gaze fell on the fluffy pink throw discarded on the floor. She reached for it, but then she felt it - the pressure on her back, too heavy, too unnatural.

She groaned and continued to reach for her blanket, her mind foggy, chalking it up to the weight of a sluggish hangover. But as her fingers stretched out, a firm, unyielding hand clasped down on her shoulder, forcing her arm to hang uselessly in the air, frozen in place. The realization hit her like ice in her veins: this wasn't a hangover. This wasn't her mental state weighing her down. It was a person. Someone was on her back.

Her breath caught in her throat, and her scream tore from her lips—but before it could escape, the hand on her shoulder whipped around, clamping over her mouth with brutal force.

Her eyes widened as her new greatest fear was unlocked. The fear of being violated in her own sanctuary. With the new fear, she became aware of everything violating her personal space. His pale, clammy hands. His tobacco tainted breath. His acne, sandpaper skin against her cheek. His smell —oddly familiar – yet still disgusting.

Destiny screamed even though she doubted anyone was awake to hear her muffled cry. But she wanted to awake the entire House. She wanted someone to bang on her door, wondering what was going on, as she tussled. Her arms flailing about as she felt like a fish fighting to get back to water. Her heart beating like she was losing air. Her skin shriveling under unwanted touches.

He released her mouth and turned her over. Destiny came eye to eye with a familiar, nameless face. The voiceless nemesis that once only lived in her mobile phone now shared the same air as her. His eyes were blue lasers burning her flesh. He licked his lips, admiring her exposed breasts glistening with body glitter under the rising sun.

Destiny screamed, releasing the fear within her. The same adrenaline filling her veins that had driven her to attack the assailant who put a gun to her head while she was in high school. Her nose flared as she tried to claw at him, but he caught her wrist midair and held it so firmly, she thought he would snap it. She screamed in agony and tried to kick her legs, but he sat on them. She tried to hit him again, but he grabbed the other wrist as well. He didn't attempt to quiet her screams; it was almost as if they were fuel to his flame.

He leaned in, as if he would kiss her, smell her, lick her. Destiny's eyes grew with fear. She whimpered under her loss of control. *Why me?* she thought. But in that same instant, she felt his body lift off of her legs. Giving her the opportunity to draw her legs up and she tried to lock her knees and ankles, as a last-ditch effort to maintain her dignity. He released one of her wrists to pry open her legs. She didn't miss the opportunity to pry at his hollow eyes. Her manicured nails sinking into his right eye, causing him to holler in agony. His pain fueled Destiny's determination. He attempted to pry her hands from his face as Destiny told herself, *don't let up!* She tried to dig in deeper, but he grabbed her by the throat. His sweaty palms squeezing the life of her. She gasped for air. In a split second she had to decide whether she would rather die than live as his victim.

Don't let up! – she told herself again.

Quickly, Destiny moved her grasp to his hair, while twisting and turning her other hand, a defying attempt to free her other wrist. She pulled hard as he squeezed her throat. She could feel the follicles giving way on his head. He yelled in pain again and released her throat but thrashed her to the floor. Destiny hit the ground with a thud and for a split second, she looked at the door. It was locked. No one was on the other side of it, trying to see what the ruckus was about. A tear dropped from her eye when the reality of no one caring fell upon her. She screamed again, feeling him pick her up by her hair before she could gather herself to get to the only way out.

"You fucking pompous Black bitch," he spewed – his voice coated in hatred.

He inadvertently put a voice to her entire log of instant message insults. It was him.

He threw her against the futon. And started unbuckling his pants as Destiny searched the room for a weapon within reach. Her taser was in the tote on the floor closer to the door. She managed to get her hand on her heels. She threw them at him and tried to scramble to her feet, but he only grabbed her by her hair and slammed her against the futon again. Pain shot through Destiny's back as she hit the metal frame. Her body crashing against it nearly made it topple over. When the feet landed back on the floor, the knife Destiny had stashed under the futon mattress weeks prior, fell. Destiny and the attacker's eyes fell upon it. Destiny could hear her father's voice, *'don't hesitate'*, as she grabbed the blade, instantly spearing his leg. She bit down on her bottom lip as she turned the blade, pulled it out, and stabbed again.

He hollered, tried grabbing her by her hair again, but Destiny withdrew the knife one more time and went for his inner thigh with the next stab.

He staggered away from her. With ragged breath, Destiny fumbled to her feet. Her entire life, she'd avoided being a casualty to the gun violence that plagued her hometown. She avoided going to go-gos in clubs during her teenage years, dark alleys, and house parties her entire adolescence – always erring on the side of caution at her father's advice. The reality that a rape could happen anywhere hit Destiny like a ton of bricks, as she stood in the middle of her dorm room, ready to continue the fight.

The intruder took an MMA fighter stance, hunched over, slowly moving as blood trickled from his eye and pants leg onto the floor. Destiny's eyes narrowed, rebuking the familiar feeling of being someone's prey. Only one thought crossed her mind –

This will end today.

Chapter 8 – Moonlight

Jasiah waved off the wheelchair his father offered, determined to make it on his own to his doctor's appointment. As he approached the hospital doors, his left crutch snagged on the rug, while the right skidded on the slick linoleum, wet from a spilled drink. His arms flailed, heart lurching as the ground rushed to meet him. He landed hard on his back, a sharp jolt shooting through his body.

"Damn it!" he hollered, frustration burning hotter than any pain.

A few bystanders helped him sit up, as his father picked up his crutches. A nurse came with a wheelchair for assistance. Jasiah and the nurse looked at one another. As their eyes met, it was as if they knew one another but Jasiah didn't know how. He admired her warm smile as she extended her hand to assist him.

"Where you headed?" the kind nurse asked in a thick Louisiana accent.

Jasiah was speechless as he used both her and his father's assistance to get into the wheelchair she'd brought over. Seated, Jasiah surveyed her entire physique. His eyes caressed her hourglass shape before snapping back up to her full face.

Before Jasiah could find a response, his father answered, "Back into surgery if he doesn't learn to sit down." He quickly turned to his son. "Was all of this to get her attention?"

"You saw me losing my balance, why didn't you catch me?" Jasiah asked his father, half joking and half serious.

Big Siah handed his son the crutches. "You would have taken us both down."

"I should sue this damn hospital for a trip hazard," Jasiah mumbled, as he looked back at the beautiful nurse. The beauty of her face only added to her luscious hourglass curves. He smiled, despite feeling an aching in his leg, admiring her head full of bouncy curly hair similar to his very first girlfriend, Tangey.

"Well, I see you have help... you take care of yourself," the soft-spoken nurse dismissed herself.

Jasiah instinctively reached out for her hand, "I feel like I know you," he admitted, staring into her familiar eyes.

She shook her head, "Maybe you've seen me in passing," she smiled and surprisingly didn't snatch away from Jasiah. Their fingertips parting slowly.

"Of course, you know her," his father insisted, as he took the brakes off of the wheelchair. "She is the nurse who helped you after the accident."

Jasiah eyes widened as he vaguely remembered a nurse talking to him after he became conscious. "Oh yeah... I was so out of it that day, you have to forgive me."

"*You are the one* from that pile up a few weeks back," the nurse recalled, nodding her head at the recollection. "Your face has healed nicely," she reached out and touched his cheek, where the airbag chemical rash once was.

Jasiah blushed and tried to mask the aching pain that was intensifying as he sat there. "I'm sorry, I forgot your name," he confessed.

"Are you okay?" she asked, noticing his change in facial expression.

"I'd be better if you let me put my number in your phone," Jasiah continued to try to mask his pain with his charm.

"It's Amelia," she replied, her cheeks rosy from blushing as well. She quickly obliged in taking his phone and storing her number in it.

"I'm Jasiah, by the way."

"Oh, I remember," she winked at him as she handed him his device back and walked away.

Both Jasiah and Big Siah's eyes followed her walk, admiring the view of her nursing uniform hugging her natural waistline.

Big Siah looked away first, beginning to push his son to their destination. As they made their way down the hospital hall, he uttered, "This boy can't even wash his ass good by himself and pulling bitches."

Jasiah laughed, still trying to mask the pain he was in. He quietly feared the fall had caused a setback. He quickly popped a Percocet into his mouth to subdue the discomfort.

"You're mighty quiet," his father recognized, once they were in the elevator.

"My leg is killing me," Jasiah admitted.

"Healing isn't painless," his father uttered.

Jasiah was aware that healing wasn't painless, but he didn't want the process to go on forever. As the doctor spoke to him about going to physical therapy, Jasiah felt lightheaded. He couldn't believe he was going to walk across the stage in a boot. That he would probably have to start his life in New York with a knee scooter.

"Temporary setback," Big Siah tried to convince him when he saw the devastation on Jasiah's face. "Things could be worst."

"I don't know how," Jasiah moped.

"You could be dead, paralyzed, in prison. I can think of plenty scenarios," Big Siah responded. "I'm going to get you to class then I'll update the lawyer on your progress, and we'll figure out what's for dinner."

"I'm going to hobble to class, try to stay awake, then I'm going to get home and continue to be uncomfortable in my own body, in my bed, on the sofa, trying to wash my ass," Jasiah retorted.

"You want a referral for a therapist while we're here?" Big Siah questioned.

Jasiah didn't respond.

"Boy, you've been up your whole life, you don't know what down looks like." Big Siah shook his head. "These eight to twelve weeks of your life will be a distant memory by Christmas," Big Siah encouraged.

Jasiah looked his father in the eyes. He wasn't there when a white girl accused him of rape. That was definitely down. His father was a figment of his imagination when a racist police officer knocked him unconscious with the butt of his service gun for driving while Black. He was literally pinned to the ground. That was down. His father's existence had just become a reality when he was confronted with being a teenage father. Watching Destiny's mental anguish was yet another down for him. Jasiah certainly didn't feel like he had been up his whole life. All he felt was – here we go again.

"Distant memories still hurt," Jasiah mumbled.

"Tell me about it," Big Siah agreed. "But look on the bright side," he nudged his son on the shoulder.

"What's the bright side?"

"You got me," Big Siah laughed with a huge grin plastered on his face. "I mean, I could be knocking down bitches left and right, but I'm here with you, son."

Jasiah smiled slightly, amused by his father's antics. He took a deep breath and clenched his crutches, grateful to have his father during his early adulthood. Since they'd became acquainted, Big Siah had always made Jasiah feel like a priority in his life, even when he didn't have anything to offer but perspective.

Jasiah cleared his throat but didn't have anything to say. He knew his father's points were valid, but the reality of the pain made him frustrated and irritable.

"You'll be okay, Siah," his father placed his hand on his shoulder. "I got you every step of the way."

The words from Big Siah instantly changed Jasiah's mood. It was the second time his father told him that, the first being during the sleepless nights when he had to kick his addiction to pills. He hung his head for a moment, trying to let the little boy in him, who never had a supportive father, heal.

"You, okay?" Big Siah asked.

Jasiah simply nodded. He knew that if he opened his mouth to talk, he might shed a tear. So, he stayed quiet. There was a part of him that always thought his father was in New Orleans to escape something in D.C. But at that moment he felt his father's genuine concern. He needed a moment to process that someone cared about his well-being besides Destiny. She had been the only person worried about his mental health for so many years, it had been hard to conceive that someone else genuinely cared if he was 'okay.' In that moment, Jasiah settled with the notion it wasn't too late to receive what he needed during his adolescent years. His father's love and support.

Later that night, as he watched Tiffany and Ava spoon one another in his bed, he started to analyze what he really wanted as he moved into his next phase of life after graduation. He picked up his Blackberry and went through his instant messages with Destiny over the last few days. He chuckled at their mindless conversations about R&B songs and episodes of *Everybody Loves Raymond.* He let out a frustrated sigh, knowing that he would welcome an actual phone call with her just to use her as a soundboard.

But instead, he dropped his phone back in the drawer and looked over at his girlfriends. He felt like being in a throuple no longer served him in his current situation. He still wanted Tiffany to himself, as he did when he first met her. But she was a package deal that he knew he didn't want to maintain long distance.

Jasiah had his mind set on having a fresh start in New York City with no distractions. He felt as though the best way to do that would be no strings attached. He just didn't know when or how he should let his girlfriends know about his plans. He didn't want the news to end things abruptly either.

In the darkness of his room, Jasiah pulled Tiffany over to his chest where she came willingly, snuggling against the side of his body. He ran his fingers through her hair for a moment while he enjoyed the warmth of her body against his. Staring up at the ceiling, he debated on whether how to tell his lovers that he was moving to New York immediately after graduation. He couldn't picture their response. Then, feeling Ava shift in the bed and Tiffany instinctively placing a hand on her hip, Jasiah was reminded that they truly didn't belong to him, so he didn't have much to worry about.

Jasiah planted a kiss on Tiffany's forehead. He had to admit that she had been an amazing partner, understanding of his schedule with school, not complaining about the hours he spent at practice or his downtime in the casinos, and quenching all his sexual desires. But he knew that he couldn't quench all of her sexual desires. He glanced over at Ava and saw her as a symbol of what he couldn't provide for Tiffany. Witnessing them together, not just the way their bodies reacted to one another, but how they wanted one another to be happy, Jasiah knew he couldn't compete. Nor did he have the desire to do so. He just needed to figure out how much longer would he keep up the charade of being a part of their relationship.

"Get some rest," Tiffany whispered, as she rubbed her hand across his chest.

"You keep touching me like that, neither one of us will sleep," he warned, tilting her face up by the chin.

Her eyes glimmered like diamonds from the streetlights that shined in his room. The soft gaze between them made Jasiah move in closer.

He kissed her softly on the lips and slowly pulled her on top of him. She hesitated initially, giving some resistance to his advances. But when he reached over and gripped her ass, she straddled him willingly.

"I don't want to wake Ava," she whispered, before darting her tongue into Jasiah's ear.

"Then be quiet," Jasiah insisted, as he reached between her legs, feeling her jewel box.

She moaned lightly, exciting him.

118

"Get on this dick," he urged as he kissed her neck.

"Not yet," she whispered back, planting kisses all over him.

Jasiah caressed the slit between her legs as their mouths met again. Tiffany released a melody of her faint moans in his ear, until his fingertips were covered in her wetness.

"Now," he grunted between his teeth as he felt himself pulsating, his manhood begging to be used.

Ava suddenly shifted in the bed, like she was reaching out for someone. They both froze and looked at her. Tiffany reached over and touched Ava's hand. But that only made Ava's eyes shoot open. Jasiah started to kiss on Tiffany's cleavage, signaling to Ava that they were in the midst of something. She just gripped Tiffany's hand and stared at them in the darkness.

Jasiah didn't look Ava's way as he guided Tiffany onto his shaft.

She moaned out, her face covered in pure ecstasy. After a few steady pumps, Tiffany let go of Ava's hand and planted both of her palms on Jasiah's chest as she grinded her body against his. He relished in the sensation, watching her intently as their bodies collided. He felt Ava shift in the bed again. He wanted to tell her to go back to sleep, but instead, he watched her start to fondle Tiffany's breast, then pull Tiffany's lips toward hers.

In that moment, he felt like the fun between the three of them had dwindled. He had no desire for Ava to be

119

there, mainly because of his limited mobility. As he watched them, he remembered the first time something like this happened. He had been turned on immensely. But now, the fantasy was conquered and watching Ava coax Tiffany into an orgasm while she rode him only made him feel like a tool.

He gripped Tiffany's hips as she rocked her body back and forth on top of him. Her warm, moist flesh sending him into another dimension. But it was Ava who had one hand on Tiffany's throat, kissing her and inhaling every breath she released. It was her hands playing with Tiffany's clit or groping her breasts while she moaned out, "Yessss!"

Jasiah closed his eyes, voiding the reality before him. He started to imagine the nurse on top of him. Her full attention on him. His imagination caused him to pump into Tiffany vigorously. He could hear her sounds of ecstasy but in his mind, they had a new face. When he felt Tiffany clench around him as she reached her peak, he met his as well. His eyes shooting open to both women staring at him.

"What?" he asked bashfully, as he released Tiffany's hips, realizing he had dug his nails into her skin as he came. "Did I hurt you?" he asked.

"Where were you?" Ava asked.

Both women stared at him for an answer. He didn't have one. "I'm right here," his fingers trailed the outline of Ava's body while Tiffany dismounted him.

"Selfish," Tiffany mumbled as she headed for the bathroom.

Jasiah laughed off her comment. "That's rich coming from you, Tiff," he responded.

She turned on her heels. "Were you thinking about your homegirl? Was it... Destiny?"

Jasiah laughed again and sat up, moving to the edge of the bed. For once, Destiny wasn't at the top of his fantasy list.

"Jasiah, you know Tiff is—"

"Spoiled," Jasiah cut Ava off. "I wasn't thinking about Destiny," he responded, as he leaned over and picked up his shorts.

Tiffany disappeared into the bathroom.

Ava fell back against the pillows and mumbled, "We've created a monster."

Jasiah stared at his view of Common Street from his bedroom window while he slipped on his shorts. *What am I doing?* He asked himself when Ava started massaging his shoulders. But to make sure she didn't feel rejected, he turned and kissed her pouty pink lips.

He didn't try to control Ava's movements. And soon, she was straddling his lap. Rubbing her body against his.

Tiffany came back into the room and slipped into bed behind them.

"I'ma go out for a smoke," he uttered, breaking free from his embrace with Ava. "You cool?"

She nodded and moved to continue spooning with Tiffany.

Jasiah grabbed his Marlboro Lights from an end table in the living room and headed out to the balcony for a smoke. The humid night air did not provide the relief he imagined. But the bustling on Common Street, was the distraction from his reality that he needed. Taking a seat, Jasiah lit the cigarette and took a long drag as he tried to figure out if he would miss New Orleans. The vibration, the food, the culture, the people – it had all been love at first sight for him. But in his heart felt like it had to be a love lost. Just like Destiny. The feeling of separation and hard decisions made him instant message her – They gave me three more weeks in this cast.

After his third drag from the cigarette and no response from Destiny, he felt like it was a sign for him to move on from New Orleans too. Sitting deeper into his chair and fumbling through his phone, he knew that in his last month in New Orleans he needed to take in all the Crescent City had to offer. He decided to call Amelia. "Boy, do you know what time it is?" she asked after he introduced himself on the phone.

Jasiah looked at his phone and just realized that it was after midnight. "This is Nawlins, I know you not making dodo," he joked.

"I work twelve-hour shifts; I need my rest."

"Definitely keep up with that beauty rest," he uttered as he heard something moving in his living room behind him. He looked back through the glass pane at his father telling a young lady to make herself at home. "I just wanted to connect with you. See how your day went."

"Seeing you again, getting this phone call, I'd say I had a pretty good day."

Jasiah smiled.

"But I'm going to sleep, Jasiah."

"Understood," Jasiah easily complied as he saw his father approaching the balcony door. "Dream about me."

"Bye, Cher," she giggled and hung up.

Removing the phone from his ear, Jasiah watched his father open the balcony door.

"Son, I have plans out here," his father whispered. "I'ma need you to go in your room and stay in there."

"Are you serious?" Jasiah looked at his father with a twisted brow.

Big Siah looked back at the young lady sitting on a bar stool. "I'm serious as a muthafuckah."

Jasiah smashed out his cigarette and stood. His phone started vibrating. It was a response from Destiny – *Just do what they tell you so you don't end up with a gimp leg.*

Jasiah smirked at Destiny's comment and reluctantly entered the apartment.

"This is my son, Lil Siah," Big Siah introduced but didn't give a name for the girl.

Jasiah smiled at her. "Nice to meet you."

"Son?" the young lady looked puzzled. "That's your son?"

Big Siah nodded proudly.

"Shit, now I think you may be old enough to be my Daddy," the young lady commented.

"Girl, I'ma be your Big Daddy before it's all over with," Big Siah responded flirtishly, moving toward the kitchen. "Let me get this cripple son of mine a bottle of water so he can get out of our hair."

Jasiah stood still and waited for his father to meet him with a bottle of Deer Park water. "Thanks, Pops."

Jasiah went back in his room and sat on the edge of the bed with his back turned to the two sleeping beauties in it. He debated whether or not he wanted to turn on the television. But he opted for grabbing the iPod on his dresser. Slipping on his headphones, he settled on an old playlist. Next's "Too Close" beat dropped, and Jasiah was transported back to 1999, when he was homecoming king at his high school. At that time, he thought he would be attending Harvard with dreams of becoming a defense attorney. He hadn't even heard of Xavier University. A smile crept across his face as he thought about the next chapter in his life.

Meanwhile, in Boston's South Shores, Destiny was caught in the same whirlwind of thoughts about her life. As she showered in an exquisite hotel, she still grappled with the fact that someone had attempted to violate her.

Leaning against the cold tile in the shower, Destiny tried to process the horror of the attempted rape for the hundredth time. Did she lock her room door? Was the predator already in her room? How long was she followed? Was her predator still on the loose because he was untouchable with connections on Harvard's campus?

Along with her questions, she played out various scenarios. What if she had slept with a gun under her pillow? What if she had grabbed the taser and shocked him instead of reaching for the knife? What if he'd never decided to flee and instead opted to fight? What would her quality of life be as a murderer? And the number one question plaguing her brain... Who was he?

Destiny had searched TheFacebook.com for countless hours trying to find the assailant to no avail, causing profile pictures to run on a continuous loop in her mind. She figured he was connected to the campus because he gained access to Adams House undetected. And if he wasn't affiliated with the school directly, he was definitely affiliated with a student who resided in Adams House, that was keeping quiet about their predator guest.

Destiny got out of the shower, wiping the steam from the mirror to have a look at herself. She knew that because of everything she was into, she wouldn't be able to determine who the violator was without some professional help, other than the police. She applied light makeup around her eyes, in attempt to cover the dark circles and bags from sleepless nights. Dressed in a mock neck blood red dress with matching 4" stilettos, she felt like she had on the armor needed to get the job done.

"Where the fuck are you going?" Ron questioned, as he looked at his cousin combing down her long hair in the dresser mirror once she stepped out of the bathroom.

"I'm going to see a man about a dog," Destiny answered sarcastically, giving herself a once over before remembering she needed lotion.

"What's wrong with you?" he asked.

"What?" she looked at her cousin like he was crazy.

"You going out on a date while your attacker is still on the loose," Ron shook his head. "You got a death wish?"

"You keep trying to locate the IP address of where those messages originated, I'm going do my part," Destiny retorted.

"You need to stay where we can see you," Jax suggested, as he came in from the balcony.

"We don't live in fear," Destiny reminded her brother as she slipped on her trench coat and grabbed her purse. "Don't wait up."

Destiny was relieved that a cab was in front of the hotel because she forgot she needed to call one. Destiny hoped her cousin's IT expertise stretched beyond Harvard University Police Department and that he could use his backdoor channels to find the culprit. In the cab, Destiny looked down at her red ensemble and knew it was the wrong color choice as it prompted thoughts of the bloody knife in her hand in her dorm room.

Her eyes shifted to the historic buildings she rode by. Usually, they looked straight out of a fairytale. Now, Destiny felt like the entire Boston metropolitan area was the setting of her private horror film. Each dark window represented eminent danger. A tear welled in her eye as she tried to swallow the anxiety growing within her. "We don't live in fear," she mumbled in the backseat of the cab, reminding herself of the mantra that helped her push past trauma for years.

And she convinced herself that she had to do what it took to find justice for herself. With the backed up at the crime lab, Destiny had no idea how long it would take to determine any DNA match on the knife. According to police, no one with stab wounds fitting her description had shown up in any emergency room in the area. She hoped that when he fled her room, he slithered off into the hole he came from and died. But until she had confirmation of that, she had to do all that she could to bring the predator to justice. So, with her brother and cousin working one angle, she rode to meet Antonio and hoped he could help her with another angle.

It didn't dawn on Destiny to get Antonio involved in her problems until he came to her after her brief moment on the news. He told her, "You let your lawyer speak for you, one day you could be entitled to punitive damages for your mental anguish." That was the moment she paid him a dollar to represent her and divulged the troubles she was experiencing with a stalker. She was going to take full advantage of not only Antonio's attraction toward her but also the dollar she'd finally paid him to represent her. She knew his investigator was the best in this area, but she needed to use him pro-bono.

As she grew closer to the restaurant to meet Antonio, Destiny started to think about what she would do if she did find the perpetrator before the police. Immediately, her mind was filled with visions of violent acts until she saw Antonio standing outside of the restaurant. Just seeing his disposition, her fiery red mindset started to cool down. He looked relaxed in his slacks and sports jacket. She wanted to match his energy after he greeted her with a bright smile while assisting her out of the cab.

"Well, I hope I'm not too late," Destiny mentioned as she stood on the curb.

"You're right on time," he leaned in and kissed Destiny on her jawline. "You smell divine," he whispered into her ear as his left hand delicately cradled her face. He inhaled the scent of her again. "As always," he added.

Destiny closed her eyes, enjoying Antonio's gentle embrace. She took in his scent as well, her nose trained to the familiar smell of Creed cologne. She turned her face slowly, opening her eyes and allowing theirs to meet. They owned one another's air for just a second longer than expected. Destiny would have accepted a kiss from him, right there on the sidewalk, if he had tried it. But he didn't. In the blink of an eye, he had moved away and was going toward the door. "Let's get a table before the kitchen closes," he suggested.

As Destiny followed him, she started to rehearse her fragility in her head— reminding herself to be soft spoken but don't avoid eye contact.

"Any updates?" Antonio asked, after they ordered drinks and appetizers.

Destiny shook her head no. "I need your help," she blurted out – forgoing her intentions to be subtle.

"If I help you, how are you going to help me?" Antonio asked, as he sat back in the u-shaped booth.

"I don't work that way," Destiny admitted, knowing that she didn't want to lose control in their budding relationship.

"Well how do you work, Miss Peay?" Antonio asked.

"With more tact," Destiny stared directly into Antonio's steel gray eyes.

They engaged in a staring match for a moment. Destiny's golden eyes permeated Antonio's silver glaze until Antonio chuckled and looked away.

"Destiny, you intrigue me," he admitted.

Destiny started to draw imaginary circles on the white tablecloth with the pink-painted nail of her index finger. She started to think about the night Antonio spent with her in the hotel room that the university moved her into. How they'd slept on the bed fully clothed. How he held her after she'd awakened from a nightmare.

Be a rose and not the thorn – Destiny told herself as she leaned her head back. She knew her approach was too direct. But she knew she couldn't just turn into a softer young lady immediately. She had to melt before his eyes. She slouched a bit in her seat, making it seem as though her confidence had left her. Then she turned away and started fidgeting with her fingernails.

"I'm just trying to figure out if I should still come back here," Destiny acknowledged, looking at Antonio. "Maybe I would be better off at Columbia or Howard."

"There's nothing like a Harvard Juris Doctor," he retorted.

"I've battled with my self-esteem long enough on Cambridge's campus... and to add being violated," she sighed. "I left D.C. for this very reason."

"Then don't go back there either," Antonio placed his arm over her shoulders.

"Sometimes it better to tussle with the monster you know," Destiny's hand landed on Antonio's upper thigh as she stared in his eyes. "How can I return to a place that doesn't take my safety seriously?" Destiny questioned.

"Destiny... this is just—"

"With all of the DNA... camera footage... I just can't figure out why the police can't locate him. I know he's connected to the campus somehow." Destiny conjured up a tear as she talked over Antonio. As the tear rolled down her cheek, she finally looked away from Antonio, as if she didn't want him to see her pain. "This is just madness to me."

"Let me see what David can do," he referred to the firm's investigator as he squeezed her shoulder.

"The police should really be handling this," Destiny wiped her face with the corner of napkin as she thought *hook, line, and sinker.*

Chapter 9 – Attraction

Jasiah sat at the bar of Dragos in Metairie with his frat brother, Big Dave, and his latest 'girlfriend', awaiting Amelia to join him for dinner. Anticipation coiled in his chest as he swirled his Hennessy, each late-night conversation with her replaying like a favorite song. Jasiah had patiently waited two weeks to see her again and now, their union was moments away.

"She better show," Dave told Jasiah as they toasted their second shot of Hennessy.

"No bullshit," Jasiah agreed.

"Eat one of these charbroiled oysters, get that thing ready for later," Big Dave joked.

Jasiah laughed and looked over at the door again. He instantly smiled when he made eye contact with Amelia. Amelia returned the gesture, a shy warmth in her eyes, and gave a small wave. Jasiah nodded toward her, subtle but deliberate. Beckoning her over with a head nod.

"They getting thicker and thicker, homeboy," Big Dave mumbled. "That's more my speed, bro."

Jasiah elbowed Big Dave before standing to greet Amelia as she grew closer.

"Hey," Jasiah spoke, as he reached out for a short embrace. As he wrapped one arm around her shoulders for a quick church hug, he enjoyed her softness and the scent of sweet vanilla surrounding her.

"Hey," she spoke back. "I hope you weren't waiting long."

"Naw, you cool," he motioned for the hostess. "I'm ready to be seated."

"We can just sit at the bar," Amelia recommended.

"Naw, I don't need this nigga listening in on our conversation," Jasiah nodded toward his frat brother. "Unfortunately, I can't drive so... you know."

"We're making it work," Big Dave extended his hand to Amelia. "I'm Dave."

They exchanged pleasantries before heading to their table. Despite the difficulty of Jasiah navigating the restaurant floor on crutches, he admired Amelia's voluptuousness as her hips swayed from side to side.

She was even more captivating than he remembered. Her natural beauty shone through, the subtle makeup she wore only enhancing the delicate features Jasiah admired. Still, her style didn't quite hit the mark for him. Her hair was neatly tied in a tight bun, and he couldn't help but imagine how soft, bouncy curls would fall around her face, begging to be touched. The colorful dress she wore was bold, loud even, but it clung to her body in all the right places—tight around her curves in a way that made his pulse quicken. Jasiah gave Amelia a slow, deliberate once-over, already picturing how he could help refine her look, if things between them progressed.

Once they were seated, they began chatting like old friends. Jasiah found the conversation refreshing. She had a great sense of humor and loved smiling. But when Jasiah ordered his second Long Island Iced Tea, Amelia told the waitress to hold on the drinks.

"What's the matter? I'm not driving," Jasiah asked. "Are you afraid you're going to take advantage of me or something?"

Amelia laughed. "I won't take advantage of you tonight," she winked at him. "I just know you're on pain meds and it's not healthy to mix the two," she touched his hand. "Think of your liver."

Jasiah blinked a few times before responding. "You sound like you care."

"Of course, I care," she said with a soft smile.

Jasiah smiled back but didn't know how to respond. He just hoped she was being honest.

"So, what are you doing after graduation?" Amelia asked, as their fingers intermingled. "Are you fleeing the great state of Louisiana or are you sticking around for a while?"

Jasiah shrugged, "I have a few options."

"It's always good to have options," Amelia nodded. "I'm actually going to transfer to a hospital in New York this summer," she informed him. "So, you better have fun with me while you can."

"Really?" Jasiah's eyes widened, thinking what a coincidence.

"There is an offer at an ER in New York City that is too good to pass up," Amelia confessed.

"So, nothing is holding you down here?"

"Nope," Amelia shook her head. "No children, no man," she shrugged. "I already told you about all of the family I have over in the Graveyards, but they are up to no good."

Jasiah sucked in a sharp breath. The last thing he needed was for Amelia and Tiffany to be connected in any way.

"What's that look for?"

"Nothing, I just know a few people over in there, that's all," he admitted.

"I stay clear of that nonsense," she shook her head.

Jasiah nodded, "I understand."

"So, what are these options?" Amelia inquired.

Jasiah cleared his throat. He had been avoiding telling Amelia about his plan to move after graduation. He didn't want his plans to get in the way of them getting to know one another, but most importantly he didn't want to miss out on the chance of feeling her softness inside and out. But since she had just revealed her plan, he felt at ease about his own. "I play poker professionally," he admitted. "So, I'll probably go to this tournament right after graduation in Florida."

"Texas Hold 'Em is my game," Amelia proclaimed. "Maybe we could head down to the casino after this."

Jasiah had not been in a casino since his accident. And he didn't want to go to Harrah's. He was more fearful of exposing her to his seriousness in the game than running into Ava. He wanted to keep his attention on Amelia. Therefore, Jasiah simply replied, "Maybe."

"You don't think I'm any good. Do you?"

"Any woman that says Texas Hold 'Em is their game, I can believe it's her game," Jasiah nodded.

Amelia started to blush.

"You're beautiful, you know that?" Jasiah complimented her.

"You don't have to lie to me," Amelia snatched her hand away from Jasiah and folded her arms across her chest, as if suddenly she wanted to hide who she was.

"I just believe a woman should be complimented," he sighed. "I didn't mean to make you feel uncomfortable."

"It's just been so long since anyone has looked at me the way you do," she confessed, placing her hands in her lap and looking down. "And then the compliments... it's just a bit much for me, that's all."

Jasiah was shocked. He would think anyone could see her beauty. He admitted to himself that the man he was two years prior wouldn't even look at her size 14 twice. He would silently recognize her beauty but pass her by. But there was just something about her that made him want to sink his teeth into her thick thighs and snuggle into the softness of double D breasts.

"Well, I hope it's something you can get used to," Jasiah simply stated as he stretched his leg from under the table.

Amelia looked up and met his gaze.

"Amelia, you are beautiful," Jasiah reassured as he looked her directly in her brown eyes. He admired the beauty mole on her chin, her perfectly shaped eyebrows and thin pink lips.

"You're too young to know how to talk the panties off a lady like this," Amelia responded in jest.

Jasiah laughed.

"You over there giving me those bedroom eyes, I see what you're doing," Amelia continued.

"No, I just know what I like," Jasiah replied. "You're trying to deflect the conversation... but it's cool. I don't want my compliments to make you feel uncomfortable, Amelia. I just want to make sure you know that I truly like you."

There was a pause between them. But Amelia laid her hand back on the table, fingers outstretched toward Jasiah. He took her hand and lightly squeezed it. She smiled at him and assured him, "I like you too."

Jasiah felt something move within him. It was something he had not felt in years. He had to admit that he wasn't just drawn to her curves; it was everything about her—the warmth in her laugh, the way she spoke with both candor and charm, her smile that lingered in his mind. Their conversations about real life events and current news had been the highlight of his days over the phone and getting the same level of conversation in person was refreshing.

"So, let's see what you're like on the table," Jasiah suggested not wanting their time together to end there. "If you don't mind driving."

"No, not at all."

He focused on Amelia, who he started to think could fill the void within him for a real relationship. She seemed strong enough to take on his mother's wrath and sweet enough that he felt the need to protect her- even with their age difference. Once Jasiah paid the check and bid farewell to his friend at the bar, they headed to Harrah's Casino. Jasiah told himself that he just needed to stay away from Masquerade, the nightclub within the casino that Ava worked at, to avoid confrontation. Jasiah and Amelia went over to the regular Texas Hold 'Em table, and he laid down two hundred dollars for chips. He gave them all to Amelia.

"Let me see what you're made of," he told her.

"You sure?" she looked at him with a twisted brow.

Jasiah gave her a reassuring nod.

Jasiah watched intently as she played her first hand. He fought every fiber in his being that wanted to indulge in the game. *Let her shine* – he told himself. Soon, without warning, someone came over with a wheelchair.

"Mr. Sheffield, take a load off," the floor manager urged him. "We can take you to the high stakes area."

"My lady is playing here," Jasiah informed him as he sat down. "I'm following her lead."

Amelia didn't turn her attention away from the cards, but Jasiah could tell she was listening.

"Are you comfortable, Mr. Sheffield?" Amelia questioned, still focused on the game.

"I'm fine, Miss Dubois. Enjoy yourself," Jasiah assured her as he watched her hand.

Within moments, a waitress came over to take drink orders.

"I think I'm with something like a big deal," Amelia mumbled.

Jasiah laughed. "They just want to get you liquored up so you can spend all of my money," he replied casually, as he tipped the waitress.

Jasiah was content with watching the way Amelia played. She knew the game pretty well. A few hands he thought she could have played differently. But once she doubled the money Jasiah had given her, he was confident in her abilities. When she got up, Jasiah thought she was just stretching but she turned and asked was he ready to leave.

"You're hot," Jasiah told her as he tried to blow his cigarette smoke away from her. "Don't stop now."

"It's getting late," she yawned. "And I would have rather spent this time with you beside me," she took the cigarette from Jasiah's fingertips and put it to her lips. "Let's cash out," she blew smoke rings.

Jasiah bit his bottom lip as he looked up at Amelia. He had a good feeling about her. She was different. He was confident that they were about to have a good time together. For the first time in a long time, he started feeling a connection with a woman that wasn't just physical. It felt refreshing; and he couldn't wait to see how far they could go together. He was ready to bet it all on Amelia.

Chapter 10 – Relief

Destiny sat at her desk and slowly opened the file given to her. Within a matter of three days, the Rossi and Associates investigator, David, had found the culprit. As soon as she opened the manilla folder, her perpetrator's face popped out at her. It was him, the nameless familiar face. The attacker. The harasser. The predator. And he wasn't familiar because they knew one another, he was familiar because he was a white face that could blend into any crowd. And he did. He was the janitor at 14 Plympton Street, *The Harvard Crimson*'s headquarters, who picked up overtime cleaning dorms.

She cringed, thinking of how no one at the Crimson reported him as a suspect. He clearly fit the description, including the markings she left on his face from their tussle. She was sure he was walking with a limp. Destiny turned her head to the side and squeezed her eyes shut, trying to control the sense of vulnerability coming over her that caused her to shiver.

Destiny quickly closed the folder and composed herself. She kept her eyes closed as her fingers sat on top of the folder and tried to picture her interactions with the guy taking out the trash, vacuuming or mopping. There were none. She spent minimal time at 14 Plympton Street. Her pleasantries in the office were slight with anyone since she spent more time working at Rossi and Associates during her senior year. And she was right the entire time – her series on police brutality and law enforcement's microaggressions on campus toward people of color sparked his hostility

141

toward her. Or maybe it was the fact that he was invisible to her. Destiny took a deep breath, thinking what kind of household he'd been raised in to assume defiling a woman would be a response to speaking up about inequality.

She took another deep breath and opened the folder again. However, before she could get into the details of George Mason's life, there was a tap at her door. She looked up to see Antonio standing there. He was dressed in gray pinstripe single breasted suit, fitted white shirt and his shiny cufflinks. Even without a tie around his neck, he still looked as much like an expensive lawyer as she had ever seen.

"You got what you need?" he nodded toward the folder.

"Thank you," Destiny smiled, masking the fury growing within her.

"David has given the information to the police. Mr. Mason should be apprehended by the close of business today."

Destiny's smile faded. A part of her wanted to dish out her own revenge. She wanted him to feel violated like she did.

"You're not pleased," Antonio recognized the change in her disposition.

"No, I am. Thank you. I feel like I can breathe again," Destiny lied. "I was just wondering when a detective will contact me for the lineup."

"Don't worry, I'll be with you," Antonio assured her. "You're not alone in this. I'll make sure of it," he turned to leave.

She wanted him to hug her. She wanted to feel his soft, thin lips on her forehead. She wanted him to whisper those words into her ear as his large hands held her firmly.

"Ant—Mr. Rossi," Destiny called him before he was out of ear shot.

"Yes, Ms. Peay?"

Destiny was stumped. She wanted to say something clever. Something inconspicuous, that only the two of them would get. But all she could do was wink. Antonio smiled and winked back. He stuttered in his step as he left the office, almost doubling back but instead, he gripped the door jam on his way out of the office. Destiny imagined that he wanted to kiss her as much as she longed to feel a sense of security.

She looked through the file again, thoroughly. She picked up her the phone and dialed her mother. But when a male's voice answered the phone, Destiny was confused.

"Jasiah?" she questioned.

"You rang?" he asked.

She looked at phone and noticed that she had inadvertently dialed Jasiah's number on her work phone.

"I'm sorry, I didn't mean to—"

"It's okay, Shawty, you were on my mind too," Jasiah cut her off. "How are you?"

"I'm better," Destiny admitted. "What about you?"

"Life is interesting," Jasiah admitted, as he sat outside of his lecture hall to talk to Destiny. "I'm just trying to solidify my plans after graduation."

"No more interning at Netaspend, McMillian and Associates?" Destiny asked jokingly.

"Those days are long gone," Jasiah sighed. "But really, how are you?"

Destiny looked at her predator's photo sitting on her desk. She couldn't find the words to say how she was feeling. Destiny took a deep breath, trying to swallow the rage growing within her. Her mind started swirling from being held at gunpoint as a teen to being under a stranger's weight just a few weeks prior. She shook off the uncomfortable memories before they could consume her.

"Destiny, you're okay," Jasiah tried to convince her. "Stop crying."

Destiny didn't recognize her tears were falling. She was amazed that Jasiah could hear them through the phone. She wiped her face and turned in her seat so no one could see her tears through by her door.

"Destiny, you just have a few more weeks," he assured her, his tone even and smooth.

"You have no idea what I've been through," Destiny whispered revealing her pain to Jasiah.

"You want me to come there? Just tell me you need me, and I'll be there," Jasiah urged her.

"You have finals, just like me. You have your life, and I can't—"

"You can, just tell me you need me, and I'll be there," Jasiah assured her.

Destiny held the line. She wanted to tell him to come but she also didn't want to divulge everything she had been through. She took a deep breath and regained her composure. "Jasiah, I didn't mean to call you," Destiny cleared her throat. "I shouldn't keep imposing on your life like this, I'm sorry."

"Destiny—"

"Jasiah, I don't know why-," she hesitated, cutting herself off from saying she didn't know why bad things kept happening to her. "I just—"

"You just needed to hear my voice. I know. We've been playing this game for years."

He hung up before Destiny could respond. She held the phone to her ear, listening to the empty dial tone, her mind racing. She wished she could've been honest with him, told him to come. She longed for the comfort of his embrace, more than any fleeting fantasy of Antonio. But it was Antonio who had been there when she identified George Mason in that lineup. It was Antonio who had opened a bottle of champagne, trying to convince her that good days were ahead. And under Antonio's steady gaze,

Destiny had managed to set her mental anguish aside, if only for a moment.

In the mist of their chatting in Antonio's apartment, with the city lights of Boston in the background, Destiny felt compelled to write another op ed piece for *The Crimson*. They had finished two bottles of champagne before Destiny started to proofread her piece on cyber bullying. However, by the time she came out of Antonio's office, she was only met by Antonio curled up on his sofa, fast asleep. She didn't know whether she should wake him, or just gather her things to leave. She dropped her notes and floppy disk in her bag and grabbed her heels to go quietly.

"Where are you going?" Antonio asked, his eyes still closed. "And how are you going to get there at this time of night?"

Destiny stood up. "I was going to call a cab from the lobby."

"Just stay," Antonio urged, finally opening his eyes. "I'll stay on the couch. You can have the bed."

Destiny looked at Antonio in shock. "It's been a long day; I would really like a shower."

He sat up on the sofa and rubbed his eyes.

"I'll just go. I know you have a trial in the morning," she concluded quickly.

"No, no, no," he stood. "I'd love to have breakfast with you in the morning."

Destiny stood there, feeling like this was the moment she had been prolonging. Antonio had been patient and respectful. He had helped ease her worries. She knew she owed him. And now, they were in an overnight scenario by no fault other than her own. She should have left after dinner if she didn't want to take the next step with Antonio. She picked up her glass and started to gulp down the rest of its contents, wishing it was something stronger.

Antonio removed the glass from her fingertips, grabbed her by the crook of her neck and kissed her passionately. It took Destiny by surprise as she dropped her shoes and bag onto the floor. She moaned lightly, enjoying the sensation of his tongue intertwined with hers.

"Let me get you a towel," Antonio insisted, as he pulled away, taking her by the hand and guiding her toward the bedroom of the apartment. Along the way, he stopped at a closet and took out a towel and a washcloth. "I'll get you something to slip into," he added.

Destiny bit her bottom lip as she followed him into the bedroom, contemplating if she was ready to actually give herself to Antonio. A part of her wished she had curled up on the sofa next to him and just be enclosed in his arms. But with all of the champagne she'd drank, there was another part of her that was ready to feel him inside of her.

"You can shower in my bathroom," he informed her as he turned on the lights to his immaculate bedroom.

Destiny had visited his apartment many times, but she had never been in the bedroom. She admired the aesthetic – the all-white linens on the bed, the barren dresser, adorned with only an Aztec printed vase on the corner. It was surely the most mature bedroom she had entered. Different from Jasiah's with his mementos, or the dorm rooms on campus. All of Destiny's sexual encounters to this point had been with boys. She suddenly became nervous to be with a man. However, there was a part of her that needed it.

With liquid courage, Destiny started to undress in the bathroom with the door slightly ajar. She wanted Antonio to see her. She wanted him to fantasize about her. She intentionally didn't look in his direction as she dropped her black panties. But her eye caught the bruise on her shoulder from the attack in the mirror. She touched the still tender spot as her mind flashed back to her hitting the floor in her dorm room. She shook off the memory, with a slow breath and entered the three-sided glass shower. Destiny cursed to herself when she thought of her hair. She was so busy trying to be sexy, she'd forgotten to be practical. She hated to get it wet. She decided to braid her hair into two braids and tuck them into one another.

With the steam surrounding her, Destiny exhaled, feeling the relief of her stalker being behind bars. She inhaled the scent of Jo Malone English Pear body wash and felt the tension in her body be released by the decadent scent. As she lathered her body, she felt like she was washing away all of the anxiety that had been eating at her soul for months, if not years. Just as she was turning off the water, she heard the door open wider.

"Can I wash your back?" Antonio asked.

Destiny looked through the fog on the shower glass and saw him standing in the doorway shirtless, dark silky hair covering his chest. His pants button undone.

"Sure," Destiny agreed.

He dropped his pants quickly. She turned away, not wanting to stare too hard.

Antonio slipped in the shower behind Destiny and pulled her small frame into him. "How do you feel?" he asked in a whisper.

Destiny exhaled, feeling like it was a loaded question. "I don't know," she answered honestly.

"Tell me what I can do," he requested, as he ran his fingertips down her spine. "Tell me what I can do to make you feel safe with me."

Destiny closed her eyes, wondering if she could feel safe with anyone. She exhaled. "Just keep doing what you're doing," she responded, as she relaxed under his touch.

He initially ran his hands along her slender shoulders. She tensed up, feeling his breath on her neck. She told herself he wasn't a stranger as his hands trailed her arms lightly. She took a deep breath when he grabbed the body wash and lathered his hands. She braced herself against the shower glass, as his hands roamed her body including her buttocks and back up. He massaged her shoulders, easing the knots that had developed there. "You're so tense," he mentioned, as he rubbed deep into her back.

"This hasn't been an easy time for me," Destiny admitted.

"I'll take care of you," he volunteered, pulling her closer to the water. As the suds washed away from her upper body, he kissed the crook of her neck. "I've been wanting you for so long," he enveloped her small frame into him from behind, his hands cupping her breast.

"Now you have me," she whispered back, as all of her common sense suddenly left her. She closed her eyes and enjoyed the sensation of his fingertips trailing down to her most sacred place.

Antonio turned her around and Destiny stood on her tippy toes for them to share a kiss. The sensation of their bare skin touching along with the passionate kiss sent a flurry of emotion through Destiny. She reached up to wrap her arms around him, but he pulled away suddenly. Destiny eyes popped open to see what his next move was. "Say it again," he requested, as his mouth moved down to her neck and then his tongue trailed down to her breast.

"You have me," she whispered, enjoying the sensation of his mouth all over her wet torso.

She watched him get down on his knees, lift her leg over his shoulder and start to devour her. She moaned out and grabbed for something to hold on to as his tongue pushed inside of her. She placed her palm on the steamy glass pane and braced herself again. When she leaned her head against the wet shower wall for a moment, she thought about her hair but said go for it and enjoyed the sensations running through her body as he consumed her.

For a moment, she looked down at the scene before her. There was her boss' boss, twice her age, down on his knees pleasing her. She felt powerful. It heightened her arousal. She threaded her fingers through his smooth, dark hair and then grabbed his head to bring him in closer, slightly grinding against his mouth until she came. She shuddered and moaned and tried to pull away, but Antonio kept going.

"Antonio, please," she found herself saying as her knees weakened. "Let's go to the bedroom."

He stopped and kissed her inner thigh. "You taste so sweet," he assured her, standing up. He placed his head under the water stream. Destiny watched the hot water penetrate his hair, cascade down his face, over his thin lips, along his broad shoulders, run down his toned abdomen serving as a spout to his hardened genital and on to his muscular, hairy legs. His erection begged to be stroked, so she did. Their eyes locked on one another. She moved closer and kissed his chest. He grabbed her hair and started to fumble with her braids.

"No," she protested by placing her hand over his. She could feel the tendrils around her face curl under the steam, but she couldn't imagine unleashing her entire straightened mane and allowing it to transform into the opposite of what Antonio had always seen.

"Shh," he kissed her mouth. "I'll send a stylist to the house in the morning."

Destiny took a deep breath and tried to convince herself to stay in the moment. Antonio sensed her reluctancy and turned her around.

"I am going to take care of you," he assured her as he continued to unbraid her hair. "Let me take care of you," he murmured, his voice low and insistent.

Destiny pressed herself against Antonio, giving into him.

He released her hair under the water stream, slowly edging Destiny under the water until her head was tilted back and the water was up to her hairline. Her straight mane started to show its natural wave pattern under the water. All Destiny could think was that her hair would take forever to dry. She felt Antonio move from behind her. When she opened her eyes, she noticed Antonio standing in front of her, stroking himself.

"You should be touching me," she reminded him.

"I want you so bad," he admitted.

Destiny wondered if she was a fetish for him as she placed her hand over his and helped him work toward his climax. They shared wet sloppy kisses as their hands worked together for him to reach his peak. As she felt him start to pulsate in her hand she looked down to watch the explosion at their feet.

"I want to feel you, Antonio," she assured him as she rinsed her hands under the shower head.

He grabbed her, bringing her up to his mouth to kiss. His hands sliding over her firm buttocks and down the crease until he touched her from behind. Destiny moaned, feeling as if she was suspended in air by his hands. When she felt the rise of his member between them, she pulled away.

"What's wrong?" he asked.

"Nothing," she assured him as she made a swift exit from the shower, grabbing her towel and walking out of the bathroom with Antonio's eyes glued to her as if he was in a cage and couldn't follow.

Destiny went into the bedroom and found smooth jazz playing and a single candle burning on a nightstand. She went to the hall linen closet to get a towel for her hair. When she re-entered the bedroom, Antonio was just coming out of the bathroom with a towel around his waist. Destiny started to rub the excess moisture out of her hair with the hand towel.

"Do you have conditioner?" she asked.

"Girl, you better get your ass over here," Antonio replied as reached in his nightstand for a condom.

Destiny looked around the bedroom and decided it wasn't the atmosphere she wanted. She had been confined to single spaces every time she had sex. Whether it be a bedroom, a dorm room, or a car. But now, she could enjoy a living room or a kitchen counter if she wanted to.

She shook her head. "I want all of Boston to watch this," she stated as she did an about face to head to the living room. When she heard Antonio's footsteps behind her, she dropped the hand towel and slowly released the one around her body as she felt him approach. First she showed her lower back, and then the cease of her buttocks, before dropping one side from her fingers and then the next. She heard Antonio groan from behind. Looking back, his lips immediately met hers while his hands gripped her waist. He spun her around.

Destiny closed her eyes as their bodies intertwined. She allowed Antonio to guide her where he wanted to have her. Feeling her calf brush against the back of the couch she was slightly disappointed at the safe option. But as he slowly laid her down, his mouth trailed different paths on her body. He began by kissing bruises and old wounds until he was back between her legs to consume her again. Destiny moaned freely, reclaiming something that had been stolen from her – her sexuality. But when she thought she would reach her climax, he turned her over and devoured her from behind. She grabbed a pillow as she muttered, "Oh my God!"

She didn't know when he got the condom on but soon, Antonio's mouth moved to her shoulder before he pulled her up on all fours and attempted to enter her from behind. She pulled away, triggered by his weight on her back.

"Did I do something wrong?" Antonio asked.

Destiny shook her head as she tried to mask her trauma. "Lay back," she instructed.

Antonio laid back and Destiny straddled him. They shared a kiss while she maneuvered for him to enter her. She pulled away to watch him. His expression of ecstasy almost looked painful on his face as he clenched his teeth. Destiny held in her amusement as she enjoyed their togetherness. Their pace quickened and she became even more aroused. Their sounds of passion coming to a halt when he let out a grunt with his explosion.

Antonio fell back against the sofa, panting as Destiny raised off of his fading erection and sat on her knees next to him.

"You're amazing," Antonio declared, leaning over to plant kisses on her breast.

She smiled bashfully as she retreated from his touch. She glanced at the city view before retreating toward the bedroom without saying a word.

"Where are you going?"

"To bed," she replied, strolling through his hall like it was her second home, picking up her damp towels along the way.

But the pair had their way with one another again, Destiny laid in the darkness of Antonio's bedroom, watching the single candle still flickering in the room. The liquid courage had evaporated, and her anxiety resurfaced as the pain from her bruises started to throb.

"Destiny, are you okay?" Antonio asked, his eyes still closed.

"I don't know," she responded, her fingers lightly trailing his jawline now that she knew he was awake.

"What's wrong?" he asked, pulling the comforter up further on to her body, nearly to her neck.

"My body is just sore," she didn't want to be honest with her emotions.

"I'm sorry," he kissed the exposed bruise on her shoulder. "You want me to get you something for the pain?"

"No," she snuggled into his chest. As she listened to his heartbeat, she found herself saying "I just want to feel safe," she whispered.

Antonio hugged her and kissed the top of her head. "You're safe with me. I promise."

Destiny closed her eyes and drifted off to sleep as she tried her best to believe him. But when the darkness of the night lifted and the aureate sun shined through the bedroom window, Destiny felt foolish. She woke up alone in the bed. She turned to the alarm clock on the nightstand but found Antonio's boys staring at her through a photo. She felt like his two young sons in the frame had watched them all night from a perfect angle on Antonio's nightstand. She covered her head with the comforter in shame for a moment, blocking out everything around her. She sat with the weight of her sin- she had given herself to a married man.

"Good morning, baby," Antonio spoke, entering the bedroom.

"Morning," Destiny replied, as she uncovered her face from the covers. She suddenly felt ashy and dry. She felt on her hair and imagined Antonio was staring at a mega curly bush. She cringed, imagining what she looked like in the mirror.

"What's wrong with you?" he asked, as he reached under the plush comforter and tickled her toes from the edge of the bed.

"I feel crazy," she admitted as she blew a curl out of her face. "With this hair and my same clothes from yesterday, I feel like this is a terrible walk of shame," she admitted.

"You look gorgeous... I love the curly hair," he assured her as he picked up his Blackberry and started typing. "What time is your class today?"

"Eleven."

"I don't think the stylist can get here before ten," he made a face. "Sorry about that," he looked at Destiny. "But after class, you can come back here, and we can have lunch. I'll have the stylist come around 2 p.m.."

"I'm scheduled to be at work at one, Antonio."

"Call out," he shrugged.

"We have a meeting to go over the Grant vs Pope discovery again," she reminded him.

"It can wait until tomorrow," he laid back on the bed with her. "If I didn't have a trial this morning, I would roll around in the bed with you all day."

Destiny shook her head and tried to figure out what she was getting herself into. This was a side of Antonio she didn't know existed. "At the least, I need some conditioner," she contended.

"I'll get Mike to bring you some right now," he referred to his driver. "What brand?" he asked, as he started pulling the white sheet away from Destiny's body.

"Paul Mitchell," she grabbed the edge of the sheet to keep her body covered.

"No, let me see," he insisted. "Let me see you in the sunlight."

"Antonio, I need some lotion," she protested.

"All you need is me," he still tugged on the comforter. "Come on, let me see."

Though his actions were playful, there was a seriousness in his tone as well. Destiny looked away, telling herself that she couldn't get caught up in a married man's web.

He reached under the covers and tickled her toes again, bringing her attention back to him. Their eyes locked for a moment. "Don't over think this," he urged. "I meant what I said... you're safe with me."

His words allowed her to drop her guard. She allowed him to uncover her body and then he crawled between her legs and kissed her on the inner thigh.

"Good morning, delicious," he spoke to her lady parts before giving it a kiss.

Destiny giggled. But soon, her giggles turned to moans as he used his tongue to arouse her into a frenzy. His tongue lashing made her feel stimulated in a way she had never felt before. Nothing had brought her to complete ecstasy the way Antonio did in far too long.

Antonio had her on such a high, she didn't feel nervous calling into work from his apartment as his chef served them omelets. She didn't care about the walk of shame as she ran through the lobby of the hotel Harvard housed her in for the rest of the year. She felt relieved when Antonio sent a car to take her to her regular salon in Dorchester to get her hair straightened. And then she was back to his apartment.

Destiny had so many secrets locked away that she compartmentalized the arrest of her attacker and her affair with the man who signed her paychecks. She was able to move around the office the same way she always had. Even when a bouquet of exotic flowers came from "God", she only chuckled to herself, reminiscing on Antonio's comments of thinking that was his nickname considering with how many times she'd called out for God over their weeks of intimacy.

"I trust you have discretion, Destiny," Antonio had told her that evening when she entered his apartment.

"Well, hello to you too," Destiny looked at him.

"Hi."

"Hi."

An uncomfortable pause stretched between them.

"Am I missing something?" Destiny asked.

"Emmanuel was in your office right after the flowers arrived."

"Yes, from God," Destiny laughed. "So creative, Antonio."

"I just hope you have discretion," Antonio repeated.

"The flowers were a lovely surprise," Destiny looked at Antonio. "But if gestures like that make you nervous, don't do them," she asserted.

"Calm down," Antonio grabbed a bottle of Moet from the fridge.

"I'm calm," she rolled her eyes. "I'm the epitome of discretion. And don't pop that. I want to go out," she stated all in the same breath.

"We have time for a glass or two," he popped the cork anyway.

Destiny rolled her eyes when he handed her a filled glass.

"You need to loosen up," he winked at her.

"I need to find somewhere to live," she mumbled, as she sat down on the edge of the sofa and took a sip of the bubbly, thinking about returning to her parents' house in a few weeks.

Antonio didn't say anything as he went over to the record player and played a Frank Sinatra album. As the horns started to blare, Antonio glided over to Destiny and held out his hand.

"Come on, baby," he coaxed her.

Destiny drank the entire flute of champagne and joined him for a close dance. She held on to his shoulders as they glided around the room as Old Blue Eyes sang "The Way You Look Tonight." Destiny swayed with him to the melody and enjoyed being in his arms. He held her lightly around the waist and sang along with Frankie.

"I have an idea," Antonio told her suddenly.

"Let me guess? Take out?" Destiny responded.

He laughed. "We could definitely have takeout, but I was thinking, you could work at my brother's firm in New York," Antonio twirled her around. "He is always looking for good employees. People are still shying away from the city since 9/11."

Destiny glared at Antonio. Though she had been smitten with the Big Apple on her few visits, she wasn't going to jump at the chance of being in an unfamiliar city that was still on high alert after the horrific terrorist attack that rocked the nation.

"I have an apartment there that you could stay in until you're ready to come back to me."

"Come back to you?" Destiny stopped dancing.

"I mean back to the firm."

"Antonio, what if your wife comes to New York?"

"She will stay at the Plaza, where she normally stays," he shrugged. "It's a corporate apartment for clients but I can put them up somewhere else while you are there."

"Antonio..." Destiny didn't know what to say but she had plenty of questions.

He grabbed her around the waist again. "We can go check it out this weekend and you'll have a chance to meet Anthony."

"Antonio..." she called his name again.

"I'll come visit you, you'll come visit me," he kissed her. "I'll miss you in my bed every night, but absence makes the heart grow fonder, right?"

She kissed him back but wondered how he made it seem so easy. "Antonio... this seems easier said than done."

"Just trust me, baby," he picked her up, wrapping her in his arms.

Destiny exhaled, feeling protected against the warmth of his body. She wrapped her legs around his waist, not caring that her pencil skirt was bunched up around her waist as she planted a kiss on him.

"You trust me, don't you?" he asked, as he held her by the buttocks for support.

Destiny nodded, relinquishing any doubts that started forming in her head. "Theme From New York, New York" start in the background. "I'll even take that as a sign." Destiny pointed in the air, a nod to the tune now filling the room.

Antonio smiled as he sat Destiny on his kitchen island.

"What are you doing?" she inquired, as the coolness of the quartz touched her skin.

"I'm about to have my appetizer," he confirmed as he kneeled.

Chapter 11 – Proxy

Jasiah watched the cleaning lady vacuum the nearly empty apartment. He wanted to ensure the space was in the condition he received it in before he handed the keys over to the leasing agent. Closing the door behind him, he felt like he was turning the page and starting a chapter in his life. He had experienced living on his own and living with his father. He had achieved his goal of receiving his degree in Economics. Though he was disappointed about missing the tennis championship with his teammates, but he would be listed as a 2004 Tennis Champion at Xavier all the same. Jasiah felt like New Orleans owed him nothing. The city had awakened Jasiah's senses and unlocked abilities he never knew existed within.

"You good?" Amelia asked once they were in the elevator.

"I'm good, baby," he smiled at her. "Are you ready for our adventures ahead?"

Amelia smiled as Jasiah's fingers intertwined with hers.

"I'm ready," Big Siah interrupted with a playful giddy grin.

Jasiah laughed. "Pops, you're not coming with us."

"I'm just fucking around," he laughed. "But you know your muvha coming into town tomorrow, right?"

"How do you know when my mother arrives?" Jasiah looked at his father with cocked eyebrows. "I haven't heard from her since I asked her to cosign for me to get another car."

"You can pay cash for a car, Jasiah," Amelia interjected as they exited the elevator.

"Naw, this gambling money ain't tax free, I need some type of tax write off. And I want it to be under her insurance."

"Listen to this momma's boy," Big Siah commented.

"The way he cuddles under me at night, I can tell he misses his momma holding him," Amelia added.

"Hey, hey, hey," Jasiah stopped walking, his boot making a loud thud against the floor as he came to a halt. "You going too far now."

"I'm just joking, boo," she gripped Jasiah's hand to make him continue walking.

Big Siah shook his head. "I believe you."

Jasiah decided it was better to be quiet than feed into their shenanigans. He was feeling apprehensive about the next few days ahead. Not only was he breaking the news to his mother that he was moving to New York to pursue a new dream of being a hedge fund manager, he had to introduce Amelia. He didn't know how his mother would react to the woman who was eight years his senior and his soon to be live-in girlfriend while he was in the Big Apple.

Jasiah had started to fall hard for Amelia after she'd become his driver, chef, physical therapist, gambling partner, and lover. Amelia was the multi-faceted woman that intrigued him and satisfied most of his whims. He didn't care if he had just jumped out of a three-way relationship by ghosting the women and into another. Big Siah continually asked his son if moving with Amelia was what he truly wanted to do, considering they'd just started seeing one another exclusively. Jasiah was steadfast in his idea that she would make a good companion in New York City.

"What time does Lafayette's plane land?" Amelia quizzed, looking at her watch.

"Soon," Jasiah responded, as he opened the driver side door of his rental car. "I'ma pick him up and get something to eat."

"I have some links and red beans and rice," Amelia informed Jasiah.

"I thought you had an evening shift?"

"Night shift," she corrected him.

Jasiah hated when she swapped with someone on the schedule to take a night shift. Not only did he worry about her safety, but he also missed the warmth of her body next to his.

"I'ma head to the hotel. I'll see you later, Siah," his father interrupted as he walked toward his car.

"A'rite Pops," Jasiah watched his father walk away. He secretly worried about his father going back to D.C.. But

Jasiah insisted that when he left New Orleans, his father needed to leave too. And Big Siah continually told him that New York City wasn't an option for him. Jasiah rotated his neck as he watched his father drive away. For some reason, the thought of them no longer living together started to raise some tension within him.

"Hey, earth to Jasiah," Amelia waved her hand in front of Jasiah's face.

"My bad," he turned to open her car door before adding. "Baby, you don't have to worry about me and La... I'ma catch up with my cousin... let him have his time on Bourbon. We can figure out something to eat over some Hurricanes."

"It's no trouble," she insisted as she got into the car.

Jasiah closed the car door and slowly treaded over to the driver's side. His walking boot clinking against the pavement, irritating him with every step he took. He lingered outside of the car for a moment, attempting to get his thoughts together. He knew he couldn't tell his girlfriend that he would never take anyone to her modest abode that she shared with a cousin. It wasn't just the worn, secondhand furniture that made him uncomfortable in her home, it was also the altar they had erected. Jasiah didn't believe in the power of their chants, candle lighting, and rituals. He had learned to overlook it to some degree because she wasn't the first woman he'd dealt with that believed in Iwa- the spirits of New Orleans voodoo.

"Be nice," he muttered before opening the car door. "Amelia don't worry about us," Jasiah repeated once inside the car. "I just want you to pack a bag and join me at the Hilton when your shift is over."

"You sure?"

"Positive," Jasiah looked over at her and ran his fingers through her hair. "Don't worry yourself," he reiterated.

Amelia leaned over and kissed him on the lips. She placed her hand over the front of his pants and rubbed.

"Baby, don't start nothing you can't finish," he warned.

"I know what I want," she insisted.

"I know you do," Jasiah acknowledged, cherishing the moment.

But that didn't stop him from continuing his normal routine when his cousin visited New Orleans. The pair headed straight to a strip club as soon as Lafayette touched down.

"Man, I'm surprised you're leaving here," his cousin admitted as he sipped his Blue Motorcycle cocktail with a stack of ones in his hand.

"Why would you say that?" Jasiah sat up with his left leg outstretched on the sofa.

"You never came home during breaks except for Thanksgiving," Lafayette pointed out. "Especially after Destiny stopped checking for your ass."

"You act like I spent that time in New Orleans," Jasiah shook his head, ignoring his cousin's statement about his ex. "Once I got into those high-stake games, I had to keep rolling with that."

"I'm just saying, New York though?"

"That's where the money is. I'm telling you…. My first economics course changed my whole perspective on how to get to the money and New York is where the action is."

"So, you're never coming back?" Lafayette asked, looking over at his cousin.

Jasiah shrugged as a dancer finally approached him with an offer for a lap dance.

"You have to at least come with me to the D.C. takeover in Miami, it's gonna be epic."

"I have to move," Jasiah declined, as he squeezed the dancer's ass and slid a ten in her g string.

"Come on, cuz, you gotta take one trip before you become a corporate nigga."

Jasiah tuned his cousin out as he admired the dancer's petite frame. He didn't want to talk about D.C., or anything related to it. He felt like there wasn't anything there for him. When his accident happened, he longed for the comforts the DMV offered him by way of family. But he had managed without them through the entire healing process, which only gave credence to him being able to manage in New York City with Amelia.

For a split second, he thought about his initial plans in life – get a degree in political science, go to Harvard Law School, marry Destiny, and go work with his stepfather as a criminal defense attorney. And in his current reality, none of that was happening. He changed his major to economics and he was headed to pursue a new dream of being successful in the stock market. He still had going to Harvard Law School in his back pocket, but he hoped his position as a junior analyst would open doors for him while he studied to get his broker's license.

He bit his bottom lip as the young lady grinded on his lap seductively. When she turned around, for a split second, he thought she looked familiar. But it was her eyes. Her hazel eyes sparkled even in the dimness of the club. Another faint thought of Destiny biting her bottom lip seductively flashed through his mind.

"Nigga, you look like you're in love," Lafayette joked from afar.

Jasiah continued to ignore his cousin and pulled the dancer to him to tell her that he wanted to go into the backroom for a private dance.

She quickly stood and held out her hand to lead him to the back. Jasiah was frustrated that he struggled to stand to his feet with the boot on but as he looked at the dancer, he felt aroused.

"Where are you going?" Lafayette asked, with a dancer bent over his lap.

"I'll be back," Jasiah told him as he followed behind the young lady. He watched the jiggle of her ass, with the pink string from her floss sitting on her back. He could imagine pulling on her long weave to make her arch her slender back. She occasionally turned around and made eye contact Jasiah. "How private you want it to be?" she asked, when they entered a hallway only illuminated by a pink light.

"How far do you go?" he asked, intrigued by her.

She licked her lips and looked Jasiah up and down slowly. "We can negotiate in the champagne room," she responded, holding out her hand.

Jasiah took it.

Once they were in the dark room, lit only by candles, Jasiah felt like they had warped into a different atmosphere. The room didn't smell like musk, it had a pleasant cinnamon scent. The dark navy sofa blended into the wall color. Jasiah sat down, leaning against the plush wall backing.

"How much for some head?" he asked, not wanting to play around with the matter.

"Two-fifty," she answered.

Jasiah reached in his pocket and pulled out three one-hundred-dollar bills, "Here's three if you promise to not take your eyes off of me," he laid the money beside him on the sofa.

She got on her knees and pulled his manhood out. As she went to work, Jasiah played in her weave. He stared at her back, imagining it was his first love. He remembered the tenderness he felt inside of her. He recalled the way she touched him. The way she moaned out for more of him. He thought about the last time they were together, when all her inhibitions seemed to be out of the window. He held the nameless proxy's head down for her to gag on his member as he relieved himself. As he exploded, he intended to drain himself of his lost love.

But the more Jasiah and Lafayette partied and talked, the more he reflected on the shift in his life's trajectory. Laying in his hotel bed alone, he felt like something was missing. Initially, he thought of Amelia and how they would be entangled in one another's arms. But when he started to call her, he really didn't want to talk to her. It was someone else at the forefront of his mind. Instead, he opened his laptop and started an email to Destiny, quoting from Shakespeare's *Sonnets* –

> *Love is not love*
> *Which alters when it alteration finds,*
> *Or bends with the remover to remove:*
> *O no! it is an ever-fixed mark*
> *That looks on tempests and is never shaken.*

He watched the blinking cursor, debating on whether or not to hit send. He didn't even know if she still appreciated Shakespeare anymore. He had used lines like that to woo her in high school. But now, four years later, he didn't know whether or not she would give a damn. They both were graduating in two days, and he was certain he would probably never see her again if he didn't pop over to her parents on a Federal Holiday.

He held his head in his hands and convinced himself that everything he felt was an effect of the alcohol he had been consuming away from Amelia.

"I'm tripping," he concluded aloud and looked over at the rushing Mississippi River outside of his hotel room window.

At the same time, Destiny was sitting in a hotel room alone, looking over the Charles River running through Boston. As the full moon reflected in the indigo waters, Destiny felt foolish. There was a sinking feeling within her that was familiar. Antonio had promised a celebratory dinner and night on the town before her family arrived for her graduation. He had failed to come through on either of those promises, as he continually updated Destiny with lies.

She refilled her glass of merlot and looked around the luxury hotel room in sadness and resentment. She had left the graduate reception on campus early to satisfy his schedule, yet she was alone. When she looked at the artwork over the bed in the hotel room, she saw a quote from Shakespeare's Hamlet- *To Thine Own Self Be True*. For a split second, she thought about her first love. His knowledge of Shakespeare while in high school connected them as she studied the late poet. She rolled her eyes, remembering it was Jasiah who had also left her feeling foolish so many times during the spring of their senior year of high school. She closed her eyes and sank into the emotion – her disappointment in Antonio triggering unpleasant memories of Jasiah.

The summer before they were to part for college, Jasiah started to become extremely poor with time management. He was always late or cancelling. Initially, Destiny thought there was someone else. She knew that she had been mean for months after having an abortion as she battled depression. She had cut off sex, fearing another condom would break.

Jasiah never wavered in their routine of weekday dinners and weekend library dates. But it seemed as though as soon as she opened herself up to him again, he became flaky. At the same time, she knew his biological father had just come home from prison and they were trying to secretly build a relationship. So, she gave him grace when his reasoning involved his surreptitious meetings with his father. But when Destiny's oldest brother, Junior, told her that he had lost some money playing Tunk against her boyfriend in some random house on Georgia Avenue, Destiny lost it. She thought she would say things to convince Jasiah that he didn't belong in afterhours spots, but somewhere along the way, she convinced herself that it was better for him to go live his life and she wouldn't have to worry about him.

Destiny opened her eyes and looked at the alarm clock by the bed – it was nearly midnight. She looked at her phone and there were only two instant messages. One from her brother, Jax – *its lit in here. We need you.* And then another from Emmanuel – *they are still asking for you.* Destiny had not been to the members' only club since the

174

attempted rape. But at that moment, she thought she could reclaim her power and independence and have a ball with Emmanuel one last time.

She slipped out of the burnt orange mini dress she was wearing and admired her body in the satin and lace teddy she wore underneath. The once black and blue bruises were healed. But the memory of them was still there. She sighed, running her palm over her flat stomach and told herself "You could use some unadulterated fun, Destiny Peay." Just as she tied a tight knot in her trench coat, the hotel room door opened.

Antonio entered with two dozen red roses in hand, a large, wrapped box and his Louis Vuitton duffle bag on his shoulder.

"Hey," he spoke with a joyful smile, placing the deadbolt on the door without taking his eyes off of Destiny.

Destiny clenched her teeth, thinking about her lost chance for some normalcy in her life. She had been on a whirlwind romance with Antonio since she gave herself to him. He decided when their workday ended, chose where they ate or found entertainment outside of his apartment. She didn't mind it most days, being taken care of was a relief to her. But tonight, after waiting on him when she could have indulged in so many other things, Destiny felt like she was close to her wits end. She wished she had a leather whip with her. She pictured herself wrapping it around Antonio's neck.

"What's wrong? I got here as soon as I could," Antonio kept a smile on his face as he sat the roses and box on the bed.

"I was just leaving," Destiny retorted as she stuck her hands in her pocket. "You have a nice night."

"Come on now, Dee," Antonio sat his bag down and came closer to her. "I bought us a nice bottle of champagne and your favorite sushi," he wrapped his arms around Destiny who didn't budge. "I have a surprise for you that I was working on."

"Oh yeah?" Destiny eyebrows raised at the mention of a surprise but also a fragrant floral scent that lingered on Antonio's coat. "Where were you? Like for real," she pushed him away by adjusting her elbows and took a step back.

"It started with a late ruling. And then I had to rush to parent-teacher conference night —"

"The teacher wears Chanel?" Destiny questioned. "Or does Victoria?"

He smelled his jacket and then started to take it off. "I mean we hugged to greet one another, but it was nothing more than that."

"Antonio, you could have just cancelled."

"But I wanted to see you," he went over to his bag and pulled out a disposable bag with a covered tray. He started opening the packaging as he continued to explain.

176

"Don't stand there all upset, Penelope," he jokingly called Destiny by her middle name.

"You're not funny, Michelangelo," she did the same to him.

Antonio looked at Destiny as he stuffed a piece of salmon sashimi in his mouth. "Where are you going? Take your coat off, Destiny. Relax."

"I just told you I was leaving," she reiterated as she went over to the full-length mirror and took a look at herself. She played with the curls framing her face and watched Antonio simultaneously.

He wiped his hands with a napkin and came closer to her again. He spun her around to face him and pulled on her coat belt. Destiny, wanting to taunt him, allowed the coat to open, revealing her ensemble. She watched his eyes widen before he tried to make eye contact with her.

"Where were you headed?" he questioned with a twisted brow as he helped her out of her coat and let it fall to the floor.

"Out," Destiny shot back as she stepped over the coat and went over to her nearly empty glass of wine.

"Shittttt," Antonio sang out as he started to unbutton his shirt, following in Destiny's footsteps. "Don't play games like this, Dee."

"It's not a game, Antonio," she sipped her wine. "Parent-teacher conferences or taking your nearly grown sons out for pizza doesn't take until midnight."

Antonio took the wine glass from her fingertips and sat it on the table before scooping her into his arms. He kissed her deeply as his hands wondered over her curves. Destiny didn't resist. It was the attention she craved from him.

She found herself helping him remove his shirt, running her hands over the ripples of his muscles in his deltoid down to his biceps. Antonio's mouth trailed her neck as he pushed the teddy straps from her shoulders. He exposed her breasts and placed her hardened nipple in his mouth. Destiny moaned out as she felt his fingers pushing her teddy downward. She picked up her glass and gulped down the contents as she stood fully exposed in front of Antonio.

He stood up straight, their lustful glares meeting as he unbuttoned his pants. She backed up against the glass of the window, not caring who could see them along the Charles River. Antonio kicked off his Loro Piana loafers and walked out his slacks as he stepped toward Destiny. He kissed her again. Pressing his hot stiffness against her. He grabbed the back of her head, running his fingers through her hair to grip it. He moved to her ear and whispered, "Don't play with me, Dee."

They were so close, Destiny reached up and bit his bottom lip. "Get a condom," she instructed.

Antonio quickly did as told and came back ready for them to be one. Destiny accepted him, moaning out as she felt his body temperature inside of her. She held onto his shoulders as he buried his face in the crock of her neck. His motions were short and fast as he braced himself against the window.

"Stop," Destiny told him as she pushed his shoulders. "You have to slow down," she insisted.

He gasped for air as if he couldn't keep his composure. She pushed harder until he released her thigh and she landed on both of her feet. She immediately turned around on her own, ready to watch her own reflection in the glass as he entered her from behind. She enjoyed the view of the tug of war between their bodies. Each stroke seemingly more enticing than the previous. She watched his facial expression, the biting of his lip, the pleasure in his hazy eyes. With her hands on the glass, she pushed back against Antonio violently. The slapping sound of their skin against one another seemed to echo in the room until Antonio grunted loudly, his hold on her waist turned to a pinch as he gripped tighter. Destiny felt him starting to throb inside of her and pushed away. Antonio backed away slowly and fell into the chair, Destiny once sat in. Seeing him sitting there, panting heavily, his hair now disheveled, satisfied Destiny in a way.

It was silent between the two as Destiny kicked off her heels and went to shower. She quickly pulled her hair into a bun and placed a shower cap on it before getting under the rainfall shower. She felt like the water stripped away the built-up resentment enabling her to convince herself that it was better to just go to sleep then stay mad. When she came out of the shower, wrapped in a hotel robe, Antonio was back in his slacks. A bottle of champagne was popped, and a glass was poured for her.

179

"Antonio, I can't —"

"Let's toast," he interjected, holding up a flute for her to take. "I want to congratulate mi amour for accomplishing her goals and toast to our adventures together in the future."

Destiny took the glass, never taking her eyes off of Antonio as he clinked his glass against hers and started to sip. She took a sip of the champagne and sat the glass down. Without a word, she went over to the bed and sat down.

"What's this?" she inquired, running her fingers over the edge of the box as she smelled the roses.

"It's for you. Open it," he coaxed, clicking the chopsticks he enjoyed the sushi with.

Destiny slowly unwrapped the box to expose the brown Louis Vuitton box. Destiny eyes widened as she revealed a duffle bag inscribed with her initials. Her mood instantly lightened as she inspected the luxury piece of luggage. A smile crept across her face as she ran her fingers over the stitching.

"You like it?" he asked.

"Thank you, baby," she squealed.

"You're going to need it when we go to Miami for a long weekend to really celebrate your graduation."

Destiny's mouth dropped open. "Just me and you?" she came over to him and eased on to his lap.

"Yes, of course," he sipped his champagne with his free hand while he rubbed Destiny's lower back. "I have a little business to attend to while we are there, other than that, I'm all yours."

Destiny kissed him, hoping she could keep her anger suppressed. As her tongue tangled with Antonio's, she had to remind herself that he was not Jasiah. She told herself that he wouldn't continue to put her on the backburner, that this was a one off in their love affair.

"What were you saying you can't do?" Antonio asked, caressing her face gently, "Before I interrupted with the toast."

Destiny rolled her eyes in response.

"And I still want to know where you thought you were going with no clothes on?" he added, as he removed the robe from her shoulder and kissed her bare skin.

His gentle touch made the fine hairs on her body stand up. She exhaled and ran her fingers through his silky hair. "Doesn't matter," she whispered as she turned to straddle him.

As Antonio kissed on her neck, she sipped the champagne to cleanse her palette. "It's getting late, I think we should go to bed," she suggested.

"I'm not sleepy," Antonio told her as he sat back in the chair.

"I didn't say we should go to sleep."

Chapter 12 - Visions

Destiny rubbed her index and thumb over her eyes as she cleared imaginary irritants from her eyes in the shower. A mischievous smile crept across her face as she recounted the day's events. She was officially a Harvard graduate. Just watching her family cheer for her, while they were supposed to hold their applause to the end, filled her heart with joy. The feeling overshadowed the hopelessness she felt the previous morning when she learned that George Mason had posted bail.

Destiny leaned against the shower and recounted how she nearly flipped a table over when Antonio broke the news to her. She didn't understand how they would release a man who had committed such a heinous crime. She immediately thought the man was well connected to the town in some way, and she wanted to uncover who his benefactor was. But when she shared the news with her family, everyone assured her that justice would prevail.

It wasn't until Junior shared polaroid photos of a brutalized George Mason laying on a linoleum floor that she felt relieved. She didn't ask any questions, assuming her brothers had figured out a way to talk to the streets of Boston the same way they did in D.C. She just hoped that the people Junior hired to do the job were meticulous in covering their tracks.

"You've been in there a long time," Antonio yelled into the bathroom.

Destiny cut her eyes at the door, trying to process how one man could disappoint her and also be a knight in shining armor at the same time. It was by happenstance that Destiny saw Antonio before the commencement. She avoided getting too close, but she could see him ushering his wife and sons to their seats before he joined the rest of the faculty in his academic regalia. No matter how much he celebrated her behind closed doors, including paying for her celebratory lunch with family, it didn't diminish the fact that she didn't have a significant other to celebrate with her in public. The ability to pop bottles of prosecco in a private room at Smith & Wollensky, didn't lesson the discomfort of continued questions of where her man was or comments about Jasiah not being able to attend.

Destiny turned off the water, feeling revived from the hot shower. The first thing that caught her eye in the hotel room was her cap and gown thrown over a chair. Her heart smiled. Despite everything she had been through, she had made it. She felt like a testament to Black excellence as an ivy league graduate.

"You're glowing," Antonio mentioned as he pulled Destiny close to him.

She massaged his muscular arms and pressed her lips against his. "It's been a long day," Destiny uttered. "And you missed it all."

"I was there with you, baby," he laid her on the bed, gently caressing her body. "Wishing I could touch you and kiss you," he slid his hand between her legs and kissed

Destiny fervently. "And tell you that you're embarking on the best part of life."

"Tell me now," Destiny cajoled, as she reached for him.

"Baby, you're remarkable," Antonio confirmed. "Remarkable in so many ways."

His sentiment reminded Destiny of Jasiah's stepfather giving her accolades earlier that day when she called Jasiah with her family on speaker phone to congratulate him on his big day as well.

"*What you and Jasiah have accomplished today is remarkable and a testament to Black excellence,*" Destiny recalled Roy Netaspend's words as Antonio's tongue circled her breast. She was sure that the two men were using the adjective differently.

"You're so giggly tonight," Antonio commented, and he moved upward and kissed her slender shoulder.

"I'm just happy," she affirmed, as she placed her hands behind her head.

They stared at one another, their eyes like twinkling stars in the darkness that canvased the room as Antonio's hands trailed her body.

"There are so many things I want to do to you," Antonio uttered, as he leaned his forehead onto hers and grinded himself against her. His hardness against her softness, teasing and pleasing both of them. "So many things I want to do for you."

Destiny moaned, resisting the urge to touch him as she felt like his skin begged for it. Her most intimate parts pulsated against his as he slid his hands behind her head and took her hands into his, their fingers entwined. "Are you ready?" he asked Destiny. "Are you ready for all that we can be together."

"Are you ready?" Destiny asked back. She kissed him before he could answer. She didn't want to hear his fragile promises, his unintentional lies. She was well aware of how quickly circumstances changed in his world. She nibbled on his bottom lip, wanting him to feel just the tinge of pain. It was nothing compared to the mental anguish she often felt burdened with. But hearing him moan sent a surge of unspoken desire within her. She fought against her desire to tell him how much she wanted it to just be the two of them. Instead, she left their questions in the air as if they were rhetorical.

The next morning, Destiny bid her family farewell while Antonio stayed in their hotel room reading the newspaper.

"How are you getting your stuff home?" her father asked, as Destiny made a cup of coffee in the hotel lobby.

"It's taken care of, Daddy," Destiny informed, not wanting to tell her father that her personal items had already been shipped to the apartment in New York City that Antonio offered.

"With all that you've been through, Harvard should take care of much more," Mrs. Peay's older sister, Georgia, uttered as she stirred her coffee.

"All those nice-looking white boys I saw at that graduation yesterday, how come you ain't get you one of those?" her paternal aunt, Doreen, interjected.

Destiny chuckled and shook her head. She wanted to tell her aunt that she had a white *man* that took good care of her, but she couldn't, not at that moment.

"She keep picking the wrong black ones, that's for sure," Mrs. Peay commented.

"Ma!" Destiny exclaimed.

"My niece came up here for an education. The husband will come later. Right, boo?" her Uncle Cookie, Doreen's husband, added.

"Thank you, Cookie Man," Destiny smiled.

"Don't nobody want Destiny's mean ass," Jax interjected from his perch at one of the tables nearby.

"This is not gang up on Destiny morning," Destiny frowned. "I'm more concerned with becoming a lawyer. Not somebody's wife," Destiny affirmed.

"You tell'em niece, you gonna get your coin," another paternal aunt, Diane, added from her seat. "Now let's get going before we miss our flight."

Destiny exhaled, feeling blessed to have so many people come to celebrate her and a little guilty that she had to hide her relationship from all of them.

"Auntie, we will be at the airport with plenty of time to spare," Junior assured her. "I don't understand why we are leaving here without you," Junior looked at his sister.

"Because there *is* a man that she ain't ready to say goodbye to," Aunt Diane guessed. "Destiny, you're not slick."

Destiny tried not to blush as she laughed off her aunt's comment. "Y'all get to the airport, I'll be home soon so we can continue celebrating."

"You get that coin," Aunt Diane reiterated.

Destiny thought about her family until she boarded her first-class seat, headed to Miami, with Antonio that afternoon.

"You've been quiet since your family left," Antonio recognized as he touched Destiny's knee.

Destiny looked down at his olive tone hand on her bare skin. Usually his touch thrilled her, but in that moment, she felt a bit of shame, even if they were nearly the same complexion. After listening to her family comment about how Destiny had triumphed against years of systemic racism, she started to question whether she was dishonoring herself by being a white man's mistress. She chuckled aloud, acknowledging that those were questions she should have asked herself months ago. But at that moment, after hiding her entanglement all weekend, she started to question it all.

"They left me with a lot to think about," Destiny admitted as she turned to Antonio.

He smiled gingerly. "We're going to have an amazing time," he gave her knee a pat. "Two meetings, that's all I need to step away for."

"You said one meeting," Destiny recognized. "Antonio, am I going to be spending a lot of time alone on this trip?" she questioned.

"Of course not," he leaned over and kissed her.

Destiny continued to look at Antonio even though he had turned to the flight attendant to order two glasses of champagne.

"I'll have water," Destiny corrected him.

"Two waters, and two champagnes," Antonio requested, looking at Destiny. "What's wrong?"

Destiny bit her bottom lip, a habit she thought she'd outgrown. She didn't know what to say. She didn't know where to start. "It's nothing," Destiny faked a smile. "Just thinking about the sunshine, the beach, the clubs."

"Oh, I thought you were thinking about the news report this morning about that brutal attack on Garden Street," Antonio looked at Destiny.

"What happened on Garden Street?" Destiny asked, as if she didn't know it was where George Mason lived.

"George Mason was attacked; he is in ICU."

"I still can't believe he posted bail," Destiny shook her head. As far as Destiny was concerned, George Mason should just be grateful his life was spared. "But that definitely wasn't on my mind."

"Interesting," Antonio turned to take the champagne from the flight attendant.

"I just want to leave it all behind me," Destiny declared as she accepted her flute from Antonio. "I'm ready to breathe new air."

"I'm all the air you need baby," Antonio smiled and winked as he rubbed her thigh.

"You don't have to smile so hard, Antonio," she rolled her eyes.

"I'm just wondering if we could join the mile high club," he whispered in her ear.

"You're going to have to take me further away than Miami for me to risk being put on the no-fly list, buddy," Destiny shook her head.

"Noted," he reached over, cupping the back of Destiny's head in his hand before he lightly kissed her. "But remember you know an amazing attorney... the no-fly list should be the least of your worries," he stared at Destiny in the eyes.

Destiny nodded, feeling like there was more to what he was saying.

"I'm serious, Dee, I'll take care of things for you," Antonio insisted.

Destiny searched his gray eyes for some context. She figured he already had it in his mind that she had something to do with George Mason's attack. So, she sat up, leaning in closer to Antonio and told him, "I'll let you know what I need from you."

"You don't have to hide yourself from me," Antonio assured her.

Destiny sat back, her mind now wondering what more could he be talking about. She sighed, releasing herself from a tense moment and decided to deflect. "Antonio, who does Victoria think you're with this weekend?"

Antonio shook his head and sat back as well, not bothering to answer the question. Destiny slowly sipped the champagne, knowing that mentioning his wife would stop his prying. Closing her window cover, she leaned her head on Antonio's shoulder, and drifted off to sleep before he could start another conversation. When she woke up, she hung on his arm until they checked into their room at The Ritz-Carlton South Beach.

From the bar at the same hotel, Jasiah thought he saw Destiny entering the elevator, but he quickly dismissed the idea of his ex-girlfriend hanging on the arm of a greasy-looking white man in South Beach. To his knowledge, a tall, older white guy wasn't Destiny's cup of tea. He shook off his thoughts of Destiny and called the bartender over to order another round of shots to for him, Lafayette, and his frat brother, Pete, who had returned to Miami after graduation.

He decided to join Lafayette for D.C. Takeover weekend in Miami on a split-second decision when his graduation turned into a whirlwind of female emotions. Jasiah started the day on a natural high. He dressed in all black and adorned himself with his diamond pendant chain and diamond earring. He felt like he was on top of his game, slipping into his Gucci sunglasses and taking off his orthopedic boot against doctors' orders to put on a new pair of Gucci oxfords. He was admiring himself in the hotel lobby mirror when Destiny called with her family on the phone. Hearing them cheering him on from Cambridge made him feel like he was still a part of her large family. In retrospect, Jasiah had to admit that moment was probably his first strike with Amelia for the day.

He had no idea that Tiffany and Ava would show up after they hadn't spoken for nearly a month. When Tiffany explained to Amelia that they were Jasiah's girlfriends, Amelia ran away, refusing to speak to Jasiah. His mother immediately started discussing non-disclosure agreements with the women.

Avoiding a pleading moment with a girl he barely knew, Jasiah wrote Amelia a letter, telling her she was still welcome to join him in New York and he hopped on a plane. But now, Jasiah was sitting at the bar wondering if his mind was playing tricks on him.

"Man, I swear that was Destiny," Jasiah admitted to Lafayette.

"You gotta stop this, Siah. This obsession is not healthy," Lafayette shook his head.

191

"Nigga, I'm not obsessed," Jasiah refused to think it was his imagination. "I'm just saying."

"Yeah, okay," Lafayette drank his shot quickly. "Man, we need to get in somebody's pool or ocean," he declared.

"Yeah, you're right," Jasiah turned to Pete who had the hook up at the hotel. "You think we could use the pool?"

"Man, we might as well head back to the Clevelander for that," Pete retorted.

"A'rite, I'm going to get us a cab."

"Hold up, I have the concierge working on getting us a discount on a boat with jet skis."

"That's what's up," Jasiah tossed back his shot of Hennessy before glancing at the shiny elevator doors, hoping the woman that resembled Destiny exited the doors and assured him that Destiny didn't have a Sugar Daddy.

Chapter 13 – My People

Destiny tried pulling her hair up into a messy bun. An irritated scowl on her face as she ran the brush over her sweated out roots, the result of being entangled in Antonio's arms since they'd arrived in Miami. She slammed the brush against the marble countertop as she huffed in frustration, knowing that matters would only worsen when the humidity really hit her hair. *If I ever get out of the hotel room,* Destiny thought. Antonio appeared at the bathroom's doorway, on the phone, his finger over his lips – motioning for her to be quiet.

Destiny's eyes narrowed at his reflection in the mirror as she became even more annoyed. She abandoned her frustration with her hair and started out of the bathroom; however, she caught a glimpse of pill bottles in Antonio's open toiletry bag on his side of the sink. She paused in stride and looked at the number of pills thinking she didn't recall seeing the medications at his apartment. Seeing the combination of pill bottles, she felt like a she was vacationing with her dad. She read the labels – atorvastatin, amlodipine, and atenolol. Her eyes widened when she read Cialis. Destiny shook her head, wondering if he'd needed medical assistance every time they'd had sex. She dismissed the concern, allowing the level of pleasure she received to overshadow any doubts about his capabilities. However, she pondered if he was at risk for keeling over on top of her like Celie's dad in *The Color Purple.*

Destiny took one more look in the mirror attempting to convince herself she wasn't a songbird locked in a cage.

Armed with a bottled water and the latest copy of *Cosmopolitan Magazine*, she padded over to the balcony, opting to enjoy the fresh air. Shielding her eyes, she cast her gaze to the cloudless, bright blue sky. At 1 p.m., she should've been sitting on the beach edge, her toes buried in the sand. Instead, she was wrapped in a hotel robe, feeling captive. They'd arrived, made love, ordered room service, and made love again before Antonio was fast asleep. She'd spent her first night in Miami sipping prosecco on the balcony, yapping to Bria on the phone.

As Destiny sat on the under the scorching Miami sun, a smile crept across her face at the thought of Antonio's attempt to wake her for early morning sex before they hit the gym, instead, she had pulled him to the balcony so they could watch the sunrise together. It was a peaceful moment between them where they shared childhood memories of traveling to beaches where the water definitely wasn't as blue as what they were staring at under the horizon.

It was a moment she would cherish. But when Destiny looked back at Antonio in his makeshift office, the euphoric feeling evaporated like the condensation on her bottle of water. She frowned at the papers and folders in disarray on the sofa, remnants of his room service lunch on the coffee table. She thought he would catch on to her stare and notice that she was eager for him to get off of the phone; eager for them to make memories of their own. But he didn't. He was just as focused on work in their hotel room as he was in a conference room.

Destiny studied Antonio silently, through the closed glass door, as she did often. Admiring his chiseled chest, peeking from his v neck shirt, that she now knew he got waxed in the summer. She licked her lips when her eyes settled on his thin pink lips, she loved the texture of them – always soft and moist. However, none of his sexy attributes could take away from her current annoyance. She stood and opened the glass door separating them.

"Antonio—"

"Hold up, babe, one more call... I almost have this deal closed."

"Antonio, I'm leaving this room—"

He held his finger up as the phone started to ring. "Not now, Dee," Antonio dismissed her.

Destiny sucked her teeth and sat down in a pout, leaving the balcony door open. She hoped to annoy him by allowing the air conditioning to turn off as she turned back to her magazine. She flipped through the pages, her eyes rummaging through the words aimlessly. None of the salacious articles were usually entertaining and often educational, caught her attention. She threw the magazine down on the teak wood table and after one more glance at the bright outdoors, decided to get dressed. Without a word, she went to the closet and retrieved a fitted white dress and a pair of open toe 4" mules. She thought to herself that at least she would enjoy the beach club downstairs. She felt Antonio watching her, but refused to look his way, moving about the room as if she were the only one there. By the time Antonio was ending his call, she was in the bathroom vanity mirror, adorning herself with a gold choker.

"I picked you up something," Antonio told her as he started to shower and quickly jumped in, regardless of the water temperature.

"What's that?" Destiny questioned, as she looked at Antonio, he was fully lathered up. She smiled to herself, watching the water glide across his toned body, knocking the fragrant suds to the shower floor. Destiny eyed him from head to toe – admitting that regardless of his age, he looked like he could grace the cover of any magazine.

"It's on the bed. I want to see you in it today," he informed her, quickly glancing her way. "We're leaving in twenty minutes."

Destiny looked at her hair again in the mirror. She groaned as she kicked off her heels in frustration and removed her necklace. Before she knew it, Antonio pulled her by the arm. His strong tug bought her under the water with him. She gasped and he laughed.

"Antonio!" she hollered, trying to push him away, stretching her neck so that the water wouldn't ruin the messy bun she'd just perfected.

He clobbered her with kisses. "You know I love your hair wild and curly," he admitted, as he groped her body, his wet hands and body saturating her dress.

Destiny heaved in her wet clothes as she continued to push away.

"Come on, loosen up a bit," Antonio coaxed, holding her tightly. "Please, Dee."

"You know I don't play about my hair," Destiny warned, glaring into his eyes.

"Just relax," he insisted – pressing his lips against hers. She continued to resist, turning her head to the side. He willingly kissed her cheek and then jawline. "Be in the moment with me," he whispered, his head resting on the side of her face.

Destiny still fought to get away from him. But Antonio was relentless as well, holding her firmly, water splashing off of his back.

"Come on, baby, just be here with me," he whispered seductively.

Destiny took a deep breath and stared into Antonio's eyes. His steel stare met hers and he smiled – like he knew she would cave. He squeezed her tighter and attempted to kiss her again, this time, his tongue slid into her mouth. She stopped pushing him away, allowing his words and touch to subdue her. He didn't hesitate to gather her wet dress in his hands and pull it over her head. She cringed as she felt the trickles of water on her hair, knowing she had no recourse after that.

"You know there was a better way than this," Destiny told him.

"We're here now," he started to unpin her hair. Once he unleashed her long, bra-length mane, he smiled. "Can I wash your hair for you?"

"Later," Destiny replied, knowing she didn't want to delay leaving the room any further with that action.

"Fair enough," he kissed her again. Destiny kissed back and tried doing what he requested – being in the moment with him.

Just as Destiny's hands started to roam his body as well, he pulled away and ran his fingers over her decolletage, then downward, as he started to back her against the cold shower wall. His fingers slipped between her legs, rubbing against the fabric of her thong.

She gasped at the sensation his touch caused.

"You like that?" Antonio asked, his tongue trailing her collarbone.

Destiny moaned, not wanting to admit that his movement turned her on with actual words.

He bit her lightly and allowed his tongue to trail down to her exposed breast as he rolled the wet panties off her hips. His tongue kept going and Destiny watched intently as she ran her fingers through his hair. He came back up and kissed her again in the mouth. She wrapped her arms around his shoulders, and he lifted her up. Destiny didn't miss a beat, wrapping her legs around his waist. He stepped backwards and Destiny cringed as she felt the water cascading over her head. But she kept going with him. Their kisses became tainted with shower water as he held on to her with one hand and the other gripping the back of her head until her hair was completely saturated. Then

Antonio backed them against a wall and attempted to enter her.

"No," Destiny wiggled out of his arms.

"No, what?" Antonio looked confused pulling her toward him.

"No," she pushed him away and exited the shower, grabbing a towel and heading for the bedroom with Antonio following her.

"What's wrong?"

"You need a condom," she shook her head.

Antonio laughed. "I thought you said you have an IUD," he groaned, as he continued following her around the room, dripping water over the floor with his member at attention. Destiny didn't care if she was on year three of having a Mirena. She had always been steadfast in using protection.

"No," Destiny protested.

"It's just me and you... why do you—"

"As long as you have a wife, it's not just me and you," Destiny pointed out as she toweled off her body and then started with her hair.

"I'm not sleeping with Victoria," he retorted, as if he were confessing something, snatching her towel from her to use for himself. "You know that."

"I know nothing," Destiny replied as she thought back to just a week ago when he showed up to their hotel room three hours late with a floral fragrance lingering in his suit jacktjacket. She snatched her towel back from him but couldn't wrap herself in the now damp cloth. She dropped the towel with frustration and headed for the drawer with her underclothes. "I'm getting out of this room," she declared.

Antonio came up behind her. He pressed himself against her.

Destiny froze. Her mind involuntarily going back to the night of the attack.

"Relax," Antonio urged as her body stiffened in his arms.

Destiny blinked, trying to ease her anxiety but she ended up trying to use her elbows to put some distance between the two of them.

Nevertheless, Antonio came in closer. Holding her from behind in a bear hug. "Destiny, you know I can't get enough of you," he whispered in her ear. "I'm just excited to be away with you," he kissed her neck.

"Antionio, you are away with your Blackberry, not me," she grumbled.

"I thought we had a pleasant evening yesterday," Antonio turned her to face him. "Just thinking about hearing the waves crash as I made love you makes me want to taste you right now," he leaned her into the dresser. "I'm becoming obsessed with you — having you in my arms, in my bed," he whispered.

Destiny accepted his affection, but suddenly, she couldn't help feeling like a toy. She wanted him to tell her he was falling in love with her. She wanted him to compliment her brilliance like he had in Andy's Diner on that dreary day in March, not talk about just having her in his bed.

"Antonio, where is this going?" she found herself asking, as his tongue trailed the curve of her neck.

"Can we keep going like this? Easy and carefree?" he asked. "I give you what you want, you give me what I want," he pulled himself away enough to stare into her eyes, his hand firmly cupping her face before diving in for a kiss. "I'll give you everything you want and so much more if you we can keep going just like this."

Destiny sighed. She liked the idea of being taken care of. But she didn't know how long she could continue giving herself to a man that belonged to someone else.

"That's not the response I was looking for," he admitted.

"I'm sorry," Destiny apologized, her fingers trailing his bare chest. Except, she didn't know what she was apologizing for. "Of course, we can keep going like this," Destiny met his gaze. "I just want to have a clear understanding before I move into *your* New York apartment."

"I'll hold up my end of the bargain," he kissed her face. "I promise; as long as you remain all mine."

Destiny faked a smile. "I'll be just as much yours as you are mine."

Antonio laughed. "You're a cunning one," he replied, her sentiment clear to him. He merely took her by the hand and pulled her over to the bed.

Destiny didn't fight him. Grabbing a condom from the nightstand, she obliged his sexual desires, hoping he got what he wanted so they could move on with their day. It worked, but stepping out into the hotel hallway, adorned in a white metallic string bikini and matching sarong he'd dressed her in. Her reflection in the mirror near the elevator disturbed her. She felt more like a video vixen ready to go on set than a Harvard graduate.

"This isn't me," she admitted, releasing his hand.

"It's Miami, baby," Antonio stated with a smirk. His cream linen collared shirt was unbuttoned halfway, exposing his chest, paired with a matching pair of drawstring linen pants.

"This isn't me," she repeated. "I need to put on another cover up."

Antonio's Blackberry rang. Checking it, he rushed out a clipped response. "I'll meet you in the car downstairs in ten minutes," he dismissed, pressing the elevator button to go down.

Destiny simply turned to change. Re-entering the hotel room, she immediately kicked off her block heel sandals, surveying the mess they'd made. Deciding she couldn't wait for housekeeping, she rushed through the room, gathering the used glasses, settling on an area to leave them for collection when Antonio's open briefcase and scattered files grabbed her attention. Curiosity got the best of her as she searched through the file tabs, wondering if she'd recognize any cases she'd worked on before she left. A file marked D.P. caught her eye and upon opening it, Destiny was immediately met with photos of herself.

She thumbed through photos of her going to class, talking to Jax, meeting with the editor-in-chief at *The Crimson*. Her breath hitched as she flipped to photos from the last party she'd hosted with Emmanuel and her brother. The night of the attack. There she was, her leg cocked up on a man's shoulder, and another photo of her with the whip around a nameless guy's neck as he stuffed a twenty-dollar bill in her bustier. She threw the folder into the briefcase and slammed it shut, her heart pounding in her chest. She instantly regretted it because it locked, and she had no idea what information the other files could have held.

What the fuck, Destiny thought, slipping into a backless tan linen slip dress she had hanging up in the closet. Throwing the sarong into her straw bag with her necessities for the day, Destiny's mind raced. Numerous questions swarmed in her head while she made a swift exit: *Were those photos a part of the investigation that led to finding George Mason? Did Antonio have her followed the entire time they have been dating? Why did he bring the file to Miami? Did he intend on blackmailing her to stay with him?*

She stared at herself in the hallway mirror as she waited for the elevator. If there was one thing she'd learned from her family, it was that she couldn't show her anger, anxiety, or confusion right away. She had to play it cool. She reapplied her lip gloss, tossing her drying curls side to side as she figured out how she looked best. The elevator came and she slipped on her Prada sunglasses, coaching herself to stay calm. In the elevator, she let it sink in, she wasn't fooling Antonio. He'd been fooling her. Her mind turning over the possibility that he knew more about her, and maybe even her family, than she'd realized. That his request of the plane to *let him take care of things* started to have new meaning.

She adjusted her face as she approached the car in front of the hotel. By the time the driver opened the door, Destiny was able to pleasantly smile. The curves of her mouth being held up by the strings Antonio had attached to her. Her plane ticket home, all of her worldly possessions in an apartment he supplied, and her gap year job. The evidence in his briefcase could be enough to take before the ethics committee at Harvard to get her offer for admission to law school rescinded.

To her dismay, Antonio was still on the phone, but managed to greet her with a kiss on the cheek like they were seeing one another for the first time that day. To drown out Antonio's voice, she quickly pulled out her iPod and allowed Smokey Robinson to soothe her worries. Antonio's hand abruptly landed on her knee, starling her. She stared at it, wanting to knock it away but quickly remembered she was left to his tutelage.

Riding through the palm tree lined streets, she contemplated returning to her hometown and starting over. But she couldn't imagine going back to D.C. with just the clothes on her back. How could she explain to her parents that she'd let all of her job opportunities in D.C. go for a job in New York that no longer existed?

She felt Antonio's fingers inching her dress up. Placing her hand over his, halting his intentions, and she met his gaze.

"I'm just trying to make sure you're not asleep," he smiled.

"I'm well rested," she took the ear bud out of her ear. "What are you working on?"

"A few things," he looked out of the window.

"Anything to do with me?"

"Your stuff has arrived at the apartment safely. Your employee file has been transferred to the New York office and your start date is after the holiday."

"The first week of June?" Destiny asked with a smile, assuming he was referring to Memorial Day.

"Independence Day," Antonio corrected her.

"That's over a month away, Antonio," Destiny replied in shock. At her informal interview, while in New York viewing the apartment, his brother acted like he needed her in the Manhattan Office immediately. She immediately started to wonder if the job offer was a rouse.

"Well, I thought you'd like to get acclimated to the city, get in the rhythm of traveling back and forth to Boston;

plus, I have plans for us," he leaned in, cupping her face in his hands and kissed her.

"Such as?" Destiny questioned pulling away.

"Just wait and see," he pushed forward peeking her lips, then her neck. "You're perfect," his hand slipped up her dress and he squeezed her hip.

"Antonio, you are never out of the office this often."

"Baby, you have not been around in the summer to see what I do," he cautioned as the vehicle came to a halt. He immediately sat up straight and opened the door.

Destiny waited for him or the driver to open the door as she surveyed her surroundings. They were at a marina. She took a deep breath and swallowed the trapped feeling washing over her. The driver opened her door, but Antonio was waiting with his hand extended. They walked the dock, passing the large yachts and opulent sailboats, Destiny started to realize she was out of her league.

"I have a few business associates joining us, nothing major. Really casual," Antonio informed her.

Destiny stopped her stride.

"Everyone is cool," Antonio assured her.

"Antonio, you could have prepped me a little sooner."

"You're right," Antonio shrugged. "But I'm sure this will be great... let's have lunch, maybe ride some jet skis, and we will return at sunset."

Destiny shook her head. "Is this what a vacation is like with you?" she inquired, continuing to walk alongside him.

"You're not enjoying yourself?"

"I don't know yet," she answered honestly. "This is the first time I'm getting out of the room and now I feel like I'm going to have share your attention more than I would like."

"With how good you look, trust that my attention will be on you," he stopped in front of a boat Destiny could only compare to the Spirit of Washington back home. "This is it, baby, take your shoes off."

Destiny felt a flicker of embarrassment for assuming they'd board a simple cabin cruiser. They were greeted with glasses of champagne upon arrival as they boarded the Custom Line Cruising Yacht. Destiny was in awe of the private vessel. If it weren't for the nagging irritation of finding a file on herself, she would have been overjoyed. But instead, she was annoyed to find that there were already two couples aboard. Both couples similar to Destiny and Antonio – an older man with a younger woman, however, she was the only African American aboard. Destiny was immediately consumed with the thought of being at a mistress meet up. She wondered if each of these women were oblivious to a surveillance file on them as well.

"Patricia," one of the young women introduced herself.

"Destiny."

"Honey, you can leave your stage name behind and give me your government," Patricia arrogantly stated, swinging her blonde hair.

Destiny's welcoming façade instantly dissipated. "My name is Destiny but if you want to be one of my subjects, you may address me as Madame."

"Whoa!" the gentlemen next to Patricia interjected. "Antonio, you lucky dog!"

"And you are?" Destiny turned her attention to the enthused gentlemen.

"Robert," he shook her hand.

The other couple introduced themselves as well — Jessica and Codwell.

"So, Destiny, are you from Miami?" Robert seemed intrigued.

Destiny smiled, "No, I'm a native Washingtonian," she responded. "Antonio and I met in Cambridge."

Everyone's eyes widened.

"Would you like something to drink?" Antonio asked Destiny.

"I'll walk with you to the bar," Destiny suggested.

Antonio signaled for a staff member as he pulled Destiny close to him. "Would you like more champagne or something else?"

Destiny thought she needed something stronger. "A cosmopolitan," she requested, as she moved away from Antonio and the group. "Excuse me," she uttered, once she noticed how abrupt her movements were, but she told herself that she needed to get her attitude in check. Leaning on the railing, her eyes scanned the scenery, from the deep blue water to the clear blue sky. The surroundings were beautiful but after the first glance she could no longer see it. She tried to remember what else was in the file but the photos. Her knuckled turned white as she gripped the railing tightly as she wondered if Emmanuel set her up.

For a moment she looked back at Antonio chatting with his guest. They resembled a group of faculty members chatting to her. She wanted to make a swift exit off of the boat and escape the awkward feeling of being the only Black person in a space. She had dealt with it many times for academic reasons but never in her true leisure time. She didn't want to be guarded or have to put on any airs. But then it dawned on her that this would be her reality as long as she was with Antonio.

Turning back to the water, Destiny rotated her neck, trying to ease the tension within her. Releasing the railing, she hoped the onset of flutters in her belly would start to subside.

"You, with this backdrop, is stunning," Antonio complimented as he slid his arm around her waist, holding her requested drink out in front of her.

Destiny faked a smile and accepted the drink. "Thank you."

"You seem deep in thought."

"I am," Destiny admitted, as she sipped her cocktail. "I want to feel comfortable, but my anxiety is getting the best of me," she admitted.

"You're in good hands, Dee," he spoke lowly, trailing his fingertips along her arm. "Let's join the others... lunch will be served soon."

Destiny sipped her drink again and convinced herself to swallow all of her apprehension, along with the lingering questions plaguing her mind. After another sip, she set her gaze on Antonio, "Lead the way."

Antonio took her by the hand, continually kissing her fingertips as he guided her into the cool interior of the boat.

Destiny looked around, attempting not to ogle the lavish décor. She only wished she had a camera to capture the moment and share it with her mother. As a staff member handed out damp cool towels to wash their hands, Destiny noticed the staff continually consulting with Antonio. When they asked him if he was ready for the first course, it dawned on her that he was the owner of the vessel.

Destiny smirked to herself, realizing she didn't know Antonio as well as she thought. She quietly ate the tuna tartare and listened to the men talk. She studied Antonio under a new setting. His hand movements, the rhythm of his words. He was a different person to her. When the men started to discuss the new assault weapons ban as if

210

infringed on their 2nd Amendment right, she quickly deduced he was a gun enthusiast.

"Why do you need a semiautomatic weapon?" Destiny interrupted. "What on earth are *you* at war with?"

The men paused their conversation.

"Oh, honey," Patricia laid her hand on the table delicately. "Why don't we go out to the bow and enjoy another cocktail before the second course and let the boys discuss their toys?"

"I'm fine where I am," Destiny told Patricia, turning to Antonio. "So now you need more than two rounds?"

The table laughed. "That's a loaded statement," Robert chuckled.

"We all have the right to bear arms," Codwell replied. "The founding fathers—"

"Let's be honest, for a regular civilian, there is no reason to have a magazine," Destiny scanned the table. "The right to bear arms was something needed while war was on American soil. When America was trying to get its footing as an independent Nation. But today, as one of the world's superpowers, there is no reason why any red-blooded American, in the comfort of their homes, needs a SAW."

"Baby girl—" Robert started.

"Destiny or Madame... you choose," Destiny snapped in response.

"I think I may have forgotten to mention Destiny is my *outspoken* colleague," Antonio faked a chuckle as his hand landed on her thigh, giving it a slight squeeze.

Everyone chuckled along with him to lighten the mood.

"I may be from a metropolitan area, but I'm familiar with rural America as well. If you need a semiautomatic weapon to catch your prey, you're not much of a shot." Destiny ignored Antonio's action to shut her up.

"Little lady-" Codwell started.

"Destiny," she smiled as she corrected again while watching Antonio whisper in one of the stewardess's ear.

"I think I'd like to call you Madame," Codwell replied, a grin etched on his face. "You may be—"

Suddenly the music was turned up. Nat King Cole's "Sentimental Reasons" drowned out Codwell's voice.

Antonio stood. "Excuse us for just a moment," Antonio extended his hand to Destiny.

Destiny took his hand, and they went in the middle of the living room. Antonio pulled her close to him, the way he did nightly in his apartment.

"I know this isn't your crowd," Antonio mentioned, directing the way he wanted to sway her body to the music.

"Mildly put," Destiny admitted, as she stared into his eyes and wondered how long she could keep up the charade with him.

"But, this is *my* crowd," Antonio added as he spun her around. "And where is all of this Madame stuff coming from?"

"I'm sure you know," Destiny sniped, the photos in his possession still heavy on her mind.

Antonio didn't respond, continuing their dance as if no one else was in the room. But Destiny could clearly see all eyes were on them.

"I feel on guard," Destiny admitted into his chest.

"You have to relax," Antonio taped her hip, prompting her to move toward the right before he brought her back center. "Dee, it's your approach," he twirled her on his fingertips. "Your tone."

She rolled her eyes.

"And that... the eye rolling," he whispered into her ear once he drew her closer to him.

Destiny stopped dancing. "I'm feeling a little nausea," she stated loud enough for everyone to hear. But the truth was, she couldn't relax. She couldn't turn off her persona. It was embedded in her and she didn't know how to express that to Antonio. She made a swift exit out to the deck. Welcoming the heat that took her by surprise in contrast to the cool interior of the yacht. Sucking in a deep breath and centering herself, the sounds of Chuck Brown and the Soul Searchers blared from speakers at a distance, filling her with instant relief.

Without a second thought, she ran to the edge of the boat and looked over the handrail trying to catch a glimpse of the boat that was playing go-go music from her hometown. She smiled, bobbing her head and singing along to "Wind me up, Chuck." The steady beat of the cow bell grounding the rhythm was the reprieve she didn't know she needed. As the horns entered the song, she studied everyone intently, from the girls dancing to the guys smoking cigars, searching for a familiar face. Even though her eyes initially landed on no one she knew, just the sight of the young black people having fun brought her some joy. It was the type of fun she hadn't realized she longed for until she saw it. If she could swim, Destiny would have dived off of the side of the yacht and joined *her* people.

Then her gaze landed a familiar slender figure - Lafayette, Jasiah's cousin—and her former arch-nemesis. Decked out in Sobiato swimming trucks, he stood on the top deck, surveying the scene until he locked eyes with Destiny. Shock was mirrored in each of their gaze. Destiny had no idea that she would be so excited to see Lafayette, but his familiar face was refreshing.

"Yo, Destiny!!!" he yelled, pointing at her. "I see you, girl!"

Destiny pointed back at him and laughed. Feeling some relief, she ended her laughter with an exaggerated sigh.

"You know those people?" Antonio questioned, as he came to her side.

"Small world, right?" she turned to him. "Wow," she looked back at Lafayette on the passing boat, but he had disappeared from the top.

"Would you like to invite him or her or whoever over for a drink so you can catch up? We can dop the anchor."

"No," Destiny protested, as she laid her hand on Antonio's chest. Her hips still swaying with the base guitar and beat. "Not worth the trouble."

"I want you to be comfortable," Antonio proclaimed as he took her hand and kissed it.

His actions weren't enough to soothe her worries. She stared at Antonio for a moment, a part of her wondering how she didn't recognize that she was being followed. She came to terms that keeping her head on a "swivel" wasn't working out for her on any account.

"Dee, baby...," Antonio voice trailed off as if he were trying to find the right words to make her loosen up.

"Go back to your guests Antonio," Destiny suggested, turning away from him.

"I want to be with you," he didn't let her hand go. "I want you," he confessed as he pulled her into his chest.

"You don't want me; you want a version of me that doesn't exist."

"If you're going to be my partner—"

"We're just having fun right?" Destiny reminded Antonio. "Just easy and sexy and—"

"Destiny—"

"I can be professional. I can be charming. I can be alluring. But I will not be belittled. I'm no one's baby girl, little lady, or any other demeaning name you or your friends want to use to hide your condescending nature," Destiny warned.

"But you will be *Madame*? Someone can refer to you as Madame?" Antonio questioned with a smirk on his face.

Destiny rolled her eyes. "Antonio, what's your end game?" she asked as she crossed her arms across her chest.

"I just want you to open up to me, Destiny. Be honest with me."

At that moment, Destiny couldn't hold her tongue anymore. She wanted to see how honest Antonio would be with her. "Why did you have me followed?" she questioned.

"Mr. Rossi, the next course is being served," a deckhand interrupted. "Would you like Olivia to serve you and Miss Peay under the awning?"

"Yes, please," Destiny answered for Antonio without a second thought.

"So, you're done with the group." Antonio concluded, delicately moving strands of hair out of Destiny's face.

"Antonio, you know this classifies as a fight right?" she informed him, as she smacked his hand away, dismissing his care.

"If this is a fight, I know we will do well together for a long time," he smiled.

Destiny rolled her eyes and shook her head.

"I guess you'll never stop doing that."

"Why are you having me followed?" Destiny asked again, as she looked over at a lingering deckhand, fiddling with some ropes. "Excuse me, is it possible to refresh my cocktail?"

"Andrew, if you could tell Olivia please," Antonio ordered, without looking away from Destiny.

"Yes, Mr. Rossi."

Once the deckhand left, Antonio responded, "I need to know who I'm in bed with."

"I don't even know who I'm in bed with," Destiny mumbled.

There was silence between them. Destiny stared off at the water and passing boats. She watched people on the jet skis at a distance. Then, as the doors to the cabin of the yacht opened, she could hear Patricia's laughter. It felt like everyone was having fun, everyone except her. She sulked, feeling burdened by the reality of her relationship with Antonio. She was his arm piece and bedmate.

She thought she was in Miami to celebrate her accomplishment. That Antonio wanted to spend time with her uninhibited. She had imagined them laid out on the beach, reading poolside, and enjoying Cuban food.

"This isn't fun," she found herself saying. "Sitting quiet while you're on the phone. Sitting quiet while you and your good ole boys make ludicrous comments about antiquated laws that should be amended."

Destiny watched Antonio's jaw flinch as he held back what he wanted to say.

"Go back to your guests," Destiny suggested.

Antonio didn't move. He just stared at the water with Destiny.

"Mr. Rossi, I have your lunch set up under the awning," Olivia announced, approaching them with a martini in hand.

"After you," Antonio motioned toward Destiny, stepping to the side.

Destiny thanked her for the martini and followed the steward to the back of the boat to a table that could seat eight, set for two. There was a seafood tower with assorted cold shellfish and a bottle of champagne on ice.

"Destiny, no one means any ill will," Antonio mentioned once they were seated. "It's okay to let some things go."

"I can't," Destiny shook her head in opposition. "That's part of the reason why my people have been subjected to years of oppression, too many nig—too many people letting condescending comments go."

Antonio sipped his champagne and looked out into the distance.

"You wouldn't understand," Destiny concluded.

"Each one, teach one. Right?" Antonio stated, as he looked back at Destiny.

Him quoting an infamous black statement made Destiny frustrated. She didn't know if he was mocking her culture or believing the quote. She covered her face with her hands and let out an exaggerated sigh of frustration.

"Dee, relax," he removed her hands from her face. "Let's enjoy this time together," his voice was calm and even.

Their gazes met and he smiled at her. Destiny took a deep breath and figured that she needed to accept his soft approach. She returned the gesture.

"Come here," he pulled her closer and came in for a gentle kiss that slowly grew into a passionate one. He cupped her in his arms and pulled her so close to him that she was nearly on his lap by the time she pulled away slowly. "Are you okay?"

Destiny nodded. A gesture that was only lying to the both of them.

"Good let's eat," he peeked her on the forehead and then released her to pour the both of them glasses of champagne.

Destiny picked up a slice of sourdough bread and started to nibble on it.

"I still feel as though you're too young to be so serious," Antonio spoke as he handed her a flute.

"I'm sorry, but mass shootings are on the rise, and I don't take—"

"These clients pay me a lot of money to ensure their interests are protected," Antonio cut her off to get to the bottom line. "Your clients' values will not always align with your own. Sometimes, you have to be knowledgeable and pacify them."

"All money isn't good money," Destiny uttered.

"All money is green and spends just the same," Antonio touched her thigh.

"What about your integrity?" Destiny looked at Antonio.

"Do I look like I'm compromising anything?" Antonio chuckled. "Let's just pacify their interests. Can we agree to that?"

"You should have warned me about the type of role you expected me to play today," Destiny sipped the champagne. "You're doing a terrible job at communicating with me."

"For some reason I imagined you being the life of the party, vibrant and carefree. Not caring about particulars."

"You've never seen me that way."

"I have evidence portraying you that way," Antonio uttered.

"That's what you want from me?" Destiny cut her eyes at him.

"I want everything from you," Antonio admitted.

"That's genuine coming from a married man," Destiny replied sarcastically, as she picked up a shrimp.

"What's going on, Dee?" Antonio questioned. "I'm here with you and you keep bringing up Victoria."

"I never expected to be in a situation with you where you expect me to be seen and not heard," Destiny glared at Antonio.

"I never said that," Antonio dismissed her statement. "I know you have a voice, Destiny, you've made that perfectly clear," Antonio slurped on an oyster. "And I didn't ask you to be quiet, just appeasing."

"Antonio, I want to be a lawyer. It's fun for me to have a debate on a difference of opinion. I don't have an issue with that type of conversation. It makes me cringe to be called baby girl, little lady, or any of those micro aggressions," she sipped the remains of her flute.

"Understood," Antonio threw his hands up. "I don't want to censor you. I merely want you to be aware of your mannerisms."

Destiny rolled her eyes.

"There it goes again," Antonio uttered.

"I'll work on it... if you can work on correcting people before I have to with how they are speaking to me. You say you want me to be your partner—"

"You are my partner," he told her as he held her hand. "I can see us having all type of adventures together."

Destiny smiled. "Then stand up for me," she requested. "Not usher me away to attempt to correct me."

"I didn't know which way the conversation would go," Antonio admitted. "I thought I was doing damage control."

"Damage control should have started when Patricia assumed Destiny was my stage name," she sucked her teeth and rolled her eyes.

"I can see that now, but you didn't help matters by offering the call name Madame *and* you doubled down on it."

Destiny simply gave Antonio a side eye.

A quiet moment lingered between the pair as Destiny tried to process her current position. She was at Antonio's disposal and there was nothing she could do at that moment. She was a kept woman and she figured she needed to keep her mouth shut.

Antonio pulled Destiny close to him and fed her an oyster. When some of the juice ran down her chin they both giggled as Destiny tried to catch it with a napkin.

222

"You are so messy sometimes," Antonio commented.

"You like it," Destiny whispered seductively.

"I do," Antonio kissed her on the temple. "Let's get on the jet skis."

Destiny shook her head. "No sir, you should have started me with some swimming lessons first."

"You can't swim?"

"I could never let go," Destiny admitted.

"You just haven't had the right teacher."

Turning in his direction, she beamed up at him. She was amused by the idea that he could be the right person to help her let go.

"I'm going to tell the captain to drop the anchor," Antonio stood.

"And check on your clients," Destiny added.

"That too," he stood. "You have that dress off by the time I get back."

After having her fill of the crustaceans on the platter, Destiny decided she needed to freshen up. She wandered back inside, following the steward to the owner's cabin. Her fingers trailed the shiny lacquer, touching everything as she traipsed into the bathroom, vividly imagining daily exposure this level of luxury. She thought that maybe she could learn how to be quiet, or at least control her eye rolling.

223

After using the amenities in the full ensuite of the cabin, she spied her tote bag, neatly placed on the bed. Checking her Blackberry, Destiny noticed a missed call from Jasiah. Her heart skipped a beat, the call a clear indication that he was in Miami as well. She immediately returned the phone call but had to abruptly end it when Antonio came into the cabin with her.

"What do you think about staying on board tonight?" Antonio asked, as his hand grazed her hip.

"Just us?"

"Everyone," he whispered, as he hands wandered her body.

"Antonio." Her tone questioning his motives.

"Everyone is intrigued by you," Antonio ran his hand into the knap of Destiny's hairline. "Robert called you witty and feisty."

Destiny rubbed her temple with her thumb as she tried to determine if that was a compliment. She felt like she had turned into Antonio's show pony.

"Are you okay?" Antonio questioned as he rubbed her back.

"I have a slight headache," she fibbed. "Let me just chill out here for a second."

"I'm looking forward to you holding me tight, and screaming in my ear on the jet ski," he admitted.

"Antonio, I'll watch," she dropped her hands from her face and looked at him in the eye.

"I'll settle for you as my audience," he quickly obliged.

Destiny was relieved to take a seat on the yacht's swim platform, allowing her feet to dip into the cool ocean water with a martini glass clinched between her fingers. The salty breeze kissed her skin while her eyes followed Antonio and Codwell, their laughter echoing over the waves as they zipped playfully through the water. She brought the cosmopolitan to her lips, its tart sweetness grounding her in a surreal moment of escape. Everyone else's chatter melted into nothing as she slipped in her earbuds, letting Vivian Green's "Emotional Rollercoaster" flood her senses. She closed her eyes for a second, overwhelmed. How did I get here? A brown girl from a city once deemed the Murder Capital, now lounging at the edge of a yacht, toes in the Atlantic, drink in hand, music in her ears. It felt like a dream she never dared to dream.

And then, it happened. A moment so unexpected, so unreal, it almost knocked the breath from her lungs.

Jasiah.

He rode past her. Her heart stuttered. She blinked hard, rubbed her eyes—was she imagining him? Was it just the sun playing tricks oner mind? No. The creature on the jet ski was no mirage. She knew. She knew. She would recognize that body anywhere—those arms, those legs, that smooth, bare chest, and his face... that impossibly bronze face that always soothed her worries.

He hadn't seen her. His eyes were locked on the yacht's upper decks, unaware that she was right there, feet dangling in the water, breath caught in her throat, heart threatening to break if he didn't just look at who was right in front of him.

"You should come in, ma'am.. you don't know what these thugs will try on the water," the deckhand suggested.

Destiny rolled her eyes and waved her hand, hoping she could catch Jasiah's attention.

"You do know that's not Antonio. Right?" Patricia stated.

"I know him," Destiny responded before she started to call her ex-boyfriend's name while waving both of her hands to get his attention. Finally, with her voice carrying across the water, he stared ahead. Grabbing his attention sent the butterflies fluttering. Watching him glide on the water toward her, Destiny's heart quickened. Miles from anywhere either of them called home, their paths had crossed. To Destiny, it had to be kismet. The chasm that was always keeping them a world apart somehow closing.

"What are the freaking chances?" Jasiah exclaimed, eyeing Destiny as he rode closer to the docking area.

"I know right," Destiny smiled, immediately comforted at the sight of her friend. He looked as good to her in that moment as he always had. She bit her bottom lip nervously as her eyes scanned his molded chest and broad shoulders. Under the bright sun, everything about him shimmered. The diamond in his ear glimmered. The small

226

beads of water clung to his skin, glistening. To Destiny, he was a bronze god. In an instant, she wanted him closer.

"Don't bite your lip like that," he urged, as he did a small donut, playfully splashing her with water.

Destiny jumped back and laughed. Any other time, she would be furious about her hair, but she was too excited seeing Jasiah to even care.

Jasiah turned the jet ski back around to face her. He leaned forward on the handlebars, admiring her beauty. There his love was, with her same amazing petite frame that she always had. But the lustrous curls that framed her face made her look so carefree, which Jasiah knew she was not. She instantly knew she wasn't the same girl he last laid eyes on six months prior. She was a new woman that he wanted to know.

"There is so much I want to say to you," Jasiah admitted.

"Words, words, words" she quoted Shakespeare's *Hamlet* with a smile beaming across her face that made her radiant to Jasiah. She knew everyone was listening to her conversation and didn't want them to send the wrong message back to Antonio.

"Are you going to introduce us to your friend?" Robert interjected from behind Destiny.

"No need," Destiny refused without taking her eyes off of Jasiah.

Jasiah chuckled at Destiny's candor and replied "Okay, Hamlet," before doing another donut splashing Robert who didn't move fast enough.

Destiny laughed and reached for a towel to hand to Robert. "Refreshing right?"

Robert wiped his face.

"Robert, you don't have to stand guard over me... I'm fine," Destiny stated firmly.

Jasiah stared at Destiny in awe. He couldn't believe the company she was in and how she was dressed. Her string bikini took him by pleasant surprise. He shook his head thinking this was nothing like the Destiny he thought he knew. But instead of dwelling on it, Jasiah asked "Are you staying at the Ritz?"

"Are you stalking me?" Destiny retorted.

"I told Lafayette I saw you getting on to the elevator yesterday, but he told me I was tripping. And then he told me that while I was out riding around that he saw you on a yacht. I was like what? Destiny... on a yacht?" Jasiah rested his chin on his arms, giving Destiny his full attention. "I had to come see for myself."

"Here I am," Destiny knew she was smiling too hard.

"Yes... there you are," Jasiah shook his head.

The affection between them was evident. They were communicating with each other without speaking. As they sincerely looked at one another, time and space paused, like it had done for them on a sidewalk in Georgetown,

228

when they'd shared their first kiss years ago. Gazing at one another, neither uttered a word nor made a move, though they were both secretly longing to be closer.

"I have so much to say to you," Jasiah broke the silence with the same thought. He wanted to tell her that life still didn't taste the same without her. But as he watched a woman serve Destiny a fresh martini while a man mopped around her, he felt like the sentiment was too little too late.

Destiny knew this wasn't the time nor place for him to say whatever it was on his mind.

"You look surprisingly good for someone who came close to death," Destiny remarked, unable to stop her gaze from lingering on his dimples.

"Yeah?" Jasiah eyebrows raised. "You think so?"

She nodded.

Then, without warning, Antonio came in hot on his jet ski, nearly crashing into Jasiah. Destiny was relieved that Jasiah was quick with his reflexes, grabbing his handlebars and putting his foot to the pedal to move out of the way. Their actions caused a surge of waves, splashing the turquoise water on her thighs. Destiny gasped, watching Jasiah circle back around. Relief washed over her at the realization that he wasn't ready to leave her.

"Everything okay, baby?" Antonio asked, as he climbed aboard the watercraft with the aid of a deckhand.

"Perfectly fine," she stopped smiling at Jasiah and looked at her lover. "Jasiah this is Antonio. Antonio, this is Jasiah."

"High school pals?" Antonio assumed.

"You remember me telling you about why I chose Harvard? Well, here he is," Destiny informed Antonio.

"Oh, the boy you were chasing after," Antonio laughed. "The one that ended up someplace else."

"Xavier," Jasiah spoke, his dimples that Destiny had been enjoying, faded quickly. "I ended up at Xavier."

"Your loss," Antonio antagonized, his eyes scanning Jasiah. "Would you like to come on board, have a drink and catch up?"

Jasiah looked at Destiny for confirmation on if it was okay. She grabbed a towel and began helping Antonio dry off. He quickly realized that watching Destiny attending to another man was jarring for him. Jasiah took that as a signal for him not to join them. But he felt himself staring at Destiny's figure in the bikini. He wanted her to hop on the back of his jet ski and ride off with him. To stop staring, Jasiah diverted his eyes to his bad leg and decided it was best not to limp around a yacht.

"I'm good," Jasiah declined. "It was nice to see you, Destiny."

"It was good to see you too," Destiny admitted, looking back at Jasiah. "Maybe we'll run into one another again on land."

"Maybe," Jasiah winked at her, knowing he would love to make that happen. "You take care of her," Jasiah instructed, as he looked at Antonio. "That's precious cargo."

"I know," Antonio looked down at Destiny.

Destiny smiled at Antonio, though she really longed to see Jasiah standing before her. She looked out of the yacht's portal, hoping to get a glimpse of his smile, instead, she was looking at the waves he had caused by riding away.

Chapter 14 –Moved

When Jasiah stepped into his Upper East Side apartment, he had to look at the number outside of the door to make sure he was entering the right unit. He expected to be greeted by darkness and boxes, yet the lights were on, Dirty Dozen Brass Band music swarmed the air, and he could smell food.

"Hello!" he yelled out, prepared to use the umbrella by the door as a weapon.

"You're early," Amelia showed herself. She smiled brightly at Jasiah, which confused him.

"Amelia? I haven't heard from you in a week," he closed the apartment door and dropped his keys on the small table by the entrance.

"I needed time to process everything," she admitted as she disappeared again.

Jasiah walked down the narrow hallway lined with mirrors, to take a look around. He felt like he had stepped into the perfect bachelor pad, but now, there was Amelia. He watched her in the kitchen, dressed in a fitted cotton mini dress that hugged her curves effortlessly. He licked his lips, admiring her perfectly rounded behind. Then he looked back at his home for at least the next six months. He pulled in a deep breath, happy to have the same ceiling to floor windows that he'd enjoyed in his apartment in New Orleans, though the view wasn't as grand. Without saying anything to Amelia he went out on the small terrace and looked down at the bustling boulevard below. He couldn't wait to get out in the New York City streets. He felt like announcing himself, the same way Prince Hakeem had in *Coming to America*, but instead, he retreated into his apartment and looked back at the woman that ran out on him. Amelia peered back at him with puppy eyes, as if she didn't know what to say. But it was clear to Jasiah - they needed to talk.

When Jasiah got close to her, he couldn't resist hugging her. He had to admit to himself that he initially missed talking to her while in Miami. Enveloping her in his arms, he smelled her hair. He was hoping to capture a sweet scent reminiscent of his childhood, but instead, he got a whiff of reality - sweat from a hard-working woman.

"How long have you been here?" he asked.

"Three days," she answered as she turned around and looked at him. "You don't seem happy to see me."

"I'm just in shock," he admitted, staring at her. "I wish you would have called me after you read my letter and told me you wanted to work things out," he leaned against the quartz island. "You know how I feel about communication."

"I was going for the element of surprise," she brought herself closer to him and wrapped her arms around his waist.

Jasiah planted a short kiss on her lips. "I know I told you that the invitation to join me was still standing but you could have at least called to tell me something."

233

She sighed and stared up at him with the innocent eyes that he loved to stare into. "I know I over reacted," Amelia admitted. "I just couldn't wrap my head around the things Tiffany way saying."

"Your relationship is with me," he reminded her. "You should have given me a chance to explain things to you."

"I was afraid I moved too fast with you."

"But here you are," Jasiah moved away from her. "Makes me wonder if you really want to be with me or just want somewhere to live."

"I acted childish at the graduation... I'm sorry. I thought we would have the next day to talk. I didn't expect you to hop on a plane."

He sighed and pinched the bridge of his nose. He wished she had just called him or returned his phone calls once, then he wouldn't have spent a week in Miami acting as if she didn't exist. He had to admit to himself that after he saw Destiny on the yacht, he started living out his fantasies with any willing woman in South Beach during D.C. Takeover.

"What's for dinner?" he asked, burying the memory of sowing his royal oats.

"Jambalaya," she responded.

"I'ma take a quick shower," he started toward the bedroom. "My boxes are in the room I assume?"

"You have the left side of the dresser," she informed him, as she moved back over to the stove.

Jasiah knew he was walking away from the conversation too abruptly. He turned around and pulled Amelia back to him and kissed her. When their lips met, he didn't feel anything, which bothered him. The admiration he'd had for her when he was in New Orleans had dwindled. She smiled when they separated, and Jasiah forced a closed lip smile before breaking eye contact with her.

He slowly walked into the bedroom and fumbled around to see how she had put things away. It almost mirrored how he had things in his apartment in New Orleans. Amelia's attention to detail made him start to think more optimistically. As Jasiah showered, he told himself, *just make it work.*

He lathered his body and thought that perhaps their sexual connection would bring back the sparks. With that in mind, he came out of the bedroom in just his towel, hoping that being inside of her would trigger something that didn't feel like regret. Amelia was setting the table when he turned her toward him and drowned himself her aura.

"Why did you run away?" he asked, his hands already pulling up her dress.

"That was a lot to take in," Amelia admitted. "First, your ex calls and the way you were talking with her family and then your girlfriends," she shook her head. "I can't give you a polygamous life."

"Did I ask you to?" Jasiah questioned, finally grabbing a hold of her panties, yanking them until he ripped one side off. Instantly, he was aroused to an erection.

"Jasiah," she gasped.

Just as quickly he turned her around, pushing her body against the back of a black leather dining room chair.

"I'm not ready," she tried to turn back to him.

"You're ready," he told her, leaning into her soft flesh. With his left hand, he fondled her breast, teasing her erect nipples. With his right hand, he intended to coax her body into submission. After licking two of his fingers, he pressed them between her legs, massaging her sacred lips.

"I want to feel you soaking wet," he whispered into her ear before darting his tongue inside.

Amelia moaned out, clutching the black dining chair for support. Her sounds only heightening Jasiah's desire. His towel dropped as he grabbed her by the throat to turn her head to the side. They shared a sloppy, passionate kiss. Still Jasiah couldn't find the desire, the yearning that he once had for Amelia. He sucked in air, holding her face and stared into her eyes for just a second.

"I—"

Before Amelia could get out her statement, Jasiah bit her bottom lip playfully. His actions causing her jewel pulsating in on his fingers.

"Open up," he instructed, feeling like he would complete his task no matter what.

Without hesitation Amelia opened her legs and leaned over the chair, ready to accept his stiff thrust.

She gasped.

He gasped.

"Jasiah, wait," she implored.

"Wait for what?" he asked, grabbing her by the hair. He pumped so hard into her, there was a slight sting as their bare skin collided. "You left me at my graduation with two crazy bitches, knowing how much I want you."

"Jasiah!" she called out. "Gottdamn."

"What do you want me to wait for?" he asked, as he released her hair and held on to her full hips. As he slapped on the ass, watching it ripple sent a surge through him. He immediately slapped it again.

Amelia moaned out, "Oh my God! You're gonna make me cum."

"Cum all on this dick," Jasiah coaxed, pumping harder. He pushed into her body, one hand circling her neck and one gripping her hip. With the trombone and trumpets flowing through the stereo speakers setting the pace, he dove deep inside of her. Her moans making a new melody while Jasiah relished in her muscles hugging his manhood. His teeth sunk into his bottom lip as he kept stroking, determined to find something within her.

He smacked her ass again before grabbing her hair. As her back arched, his knees buckled, and he reached climax. Falling onto her back as he heaved to catch his breath.

"Is that how you tell a girl you miss her?" Amelia turned to him with a smirk.

He responded with a nod, planting a kiss on her forehead. "I'll get you a Plan B pill in the morning."

"I'm on birth control," she responded, as she picked up her torn lace panties at her feet. "Remember?"

"Better safe than sorry right?" he took the panties and twirled them around his finger as he started back to the bathroom. "Let's get washed up so we can eat."

Once they got to table, Jasiah quickly recognized the awkward silence between them. The intense sex didn't fix the disconnection between them. The air was still thick with questions no one was asking. Jasiah looked at Amelia and figured he had to do something to say something.

"In my letter and voicemails, I asked you to call me," Jasiah pointed out.

"Well, I'm here."

"What if I came home with someone?"

"You wouldn't do that," Amelia replied confidently.

"You don't know what I would do," Jasiah pointed out. "And it felt like you didn't care either," Jasiah sat his fork down and turned to Amelia.

"You already know how insecure I can be," Amelia didn't look at Jasiah. "And when this beautiful girl comes up —"

"You're beautiful," Jasiah cut her off. "Tiffany might be shaped differently, but that shouldn't affect your confidence."

"Jasiah, you don't have to—"

"I left them alone to give you my undivided attention. Trust me, I know what I'm talking about."

"I don't need to be someone you use to pass the time, so you don't feel lonely in this city by yourself, Jasiah."

"And yet, you're here," Jasiah pushed his plate away from.

"Well, I did quit my job and —"

"You were already moving to New York before you knew I had plans on coming here. Don't act like you uprooted your life for me," he recalled.

"I wasn't saying that!" Amelia exclaimed.

"Calm down."

"Calm down my ass, Jasiah! You make me feel amazing, you treat me better than any other man has ever treated me. And I'm standing there looking like a fool as two bitches, one of which is my baby cousin's good girlfriend, comes up and tells me that they're with you."

"They *were* with me... And it was fun, when it was fun. But I only wanted to be with Tiffany, Ava was like bonus pussy," Jasiah answered honestly, as he tried to digest that a woman almost ten years older than him didn't have a good man until he'd come along.

"I'm not with bonus pussy."

"And I'm fine with that!" Jasiah yelled.

"That's all I needed to hear."

"I been saying it since the shit went down," Jasiah threw his hands in the air. "Amelia, we have a good thing together. Don't let your insecurities fuck that up," he warned.

"Jasiah, that's easier said than done, especially after I seen your keepsakes of you and your ex-girlfriend."

Jasiah shook his head. He couldn't even say she was going through his stuff because all she did was put it away. "Destiny is old news," he got up from the table and went over to the couch.

"No, she's not."

"You're going to have to take my word on this one," he turned on the television. Jasiah stretched out his leg on the sofa and rotated his neck, trying to stretch away the uneasy feeling building up from the nape of his neck at the mention of Destiny. In a perfect world, they would be together, but they didn't live in a perfect world.

"Amelia, you gotta have more faith in me. More faith in what we're building together," Jasiah insisted, without turning to look at her.

"I've fallen in love with you, Jasiah."

Jasiah closed his eyes and cursed to himself. A part of him wanted to laugh because he knew that her words were a fallacy. If she'd ran from him because he was involved in a three-way relationship, he knew she would certainly flee if she knew everything else he'd been through in the past.

"Come here," he coaxed.

Amelia came over and sat beside him.

"Let's table emotions for now," Jasiah suggested.

A tear dropped from her eye.

Jasiah wiped it away. "I'm not saying this because I'm not falling in love with you. I'm just saying, let's continue to respect one another, be honest with each other and see where it takes us. You running away was a big setback for me."

Amelia nodded.

"Don't cry, baby, we're in New York, the city that never sleeps. The Big Apple," Jasiah tried to lighten the mood by wrapping her in his arms. "Let's start having the experiences we envisioned when we committed to taking on this adventure together."

Amelia exhaled.

Jasiah held her. As he caressed her back, he did remember the comfort he felt with their closeness. He hated to see Amelia cry. But he didn't want to lie to her. He felt like being honest about his emotions would be the best tactic. He hoped he was right.

"I need to clean up the kitchen," Amelia pulled away.

"I'll help you," he stood up.

"No, I need a minute to myself," she declined.

"Amelia, it's me and you. Okay?" he held her gaze, hoping he could stay honest to that statement.

She nodded but he felt like she could feel his uncertainty. Jasiah sat down and hoped Amelia's love would stop his longing for a love lost.

***

Destiny threw the big joker on the table and watched Bria collect the book as they played a game of Spades against her cousins.

"Where is my man Jasiah?" Her Aunt Diana asked, as she came by the dining room table where they were playing. "He didn't make it to the graduation. I most certainly thought he would be here today."

Destiny rolled her eyes. All she could think was *if one more person asks about him*. She understood that the family was accustomed to him swinging by on holidays, but everyone was also aware that they were no longer together. "I don't know where he is," Destiny answered honestly. "And I don't care," she added as she smacked down a king of diamond and dismissing any notion of Jasiah.

"Let me get this straight... you come home from Harvard without a man? Or a job? *And* you don't care about where the guaranteed coin is?" her aunt's neck snapped back. "Have I taught you anything?"

Everybody at the table laughed but Destiny. "I have a job and I have a man," Destiny defended herself.

"Where he at?" her aunt looked around and took a sip of her Heineken.

"With his wife," Bria uttered loud enough for everyone to hear.

Destiny kicked her best friend under the table.

"Oh, I see," Aunt Diane touched the diamond pendant on Destiny's neck that Jasiah had gifted her for high school graduation. "Whoever this mystery man is... he better upgrade you."

"I got this," Destiny retorted quickly as she threw the last card on the table and stood. "I'ma get me something to drink," she announced. "Ya'll gonna run it back?"

Destiny tried to shake off her aunt's words. She wanted to reiterate to everyone that her success was not measured by what type of man she had by her side or if she had a man at all – just as she had done at her graduation. But Destiny felt some type of way about being at her graduation cookout without a date. It was just a foreshadowing of her Thanksgivings and Christmases if she kept up the charade with Antonio. It didn't matter if that morning she was entangled in his arms in the Hamptons, and they bid farewell at the airport as she caught a flight to D.C., and he headed back to Boston. It mattered that he wasn't with her at that moment.

"Did you invite Jasiah?" Mrs. Peay asked when Destiny entered the kitchen.

"Ma!" Destiny yelled. "Enough with him."

"Calm down, girl," Mrs. Peay laughed. "Don't get your panties in a bunch, it's not like I asked about Myer."

Destiny shook her head. "Ya'll get on my nerves," she uttered.

"You get on my nerves," her mother retorted.

"What's going on in here?" Mr. Peay asked, as he entered the small galley kitchen.

"Destiny is emotional because she ain't gotta man," Mrs. Peay answered in a blasé faire manner.

"She got somebody," Mr. Peay stated, giving his daughter a onceover. "Look at her, Gayle."

Mrs. Peay turned to give her daughter a once over. "Her hair is different," she recognized.

Destiny touched the ends of her curly hair. "It's the summer... I've been—"

"Shopping," her father cut her off as he pinched the sleeve of her Ralph Lauren polo.

"Ya'll act like I didn't work my way through college," Destiny rolled her eyes. "I can afford nice things."

"I was talking to Rabbit," her father referred to an old coworker, ignoring his daughter's rebuttal. "And he said the State Department is hiring," he continued. "You could get in there and work your way up."

"As soon as I get settled in my apartment, I'll have ya'll up for the weekend. So, you can see for yourself that I'm fine," Destiny ignored the recommendation of a federal government job.

"New York is more dangerous than D.C.," Mrs. Peay interjected. "After what happened on campus, don't you think it would be wise for you to come back home."

Destiny's teeth locked and her nose flared as she swallowed the anxiety that came along with thinking of the trauma she experienced in her dorm room. To everyone around her, the bruises had healed and so had she. But that was the furthest thing from the truth.

"You been away for four years," Mr. Peay added. "We thought you would come home and put that knowledge to use."

"Daddy, I got held up at gunpoint in front of this house. Somebody robbed Ma a few blocks away. And how many times has your car been stolen?" Destiny looked at her parents. "I don't understand why ya'll are still here."

"When you get mugged in New York or sexually assaulted on that packed subway, you'll understand why we're still *here*," Mrs. Peay responded, her hand on her

245

hips. "We may be victims of circumstance but one thing for gottdamn sure – we're survivors."

"You need to bring your ass home," her father added. "Your brother is not running up to New York to save you the way he did when you were in Cambridge."

Destiny's nose flared in anger; however, she had no recourse. Jax did make her stay at Harvard more palatable. But in no way had he saved her.

"Destiny, no one is telling you that you need to come back to this house, but we just worry about you. You should be where your family can protect you," Mrs. Peay urged.

"You must be using the word protect very loosely," Destiny mumbled as she leaned on the counter.

"This girl don't know nothing," her father left the kitchen in a tizzy.

Just then, gunshots rang out. She quickly tried to determine whether they were shots from a Glock-18 or a M9 as she went back to the card game. To her, the shots ringing out on a Saturday evening solidified her decision to not come back to D.C. But deep inside, she knew she wasn't making the right decision by being Antonio's kept mistress either.

Chapter 15 – Sightings

Jasiah looked over the data again. Even though the senior advisor at Butler Investment Management was pushing for them to short the stock of Peace & Presence Seeds, Jasiah was confident that they were wrong on the call. Considering the company specialized in a commodity group, he felt like his company should play it long. Jasiah was just as nervous to present his recommendation on the future of agriculture as he had been when he gave on a presentation on the antiquated mathematical education provided in public high schools to Orleans Parish School Board.

Everyone in the office thought he would fetch coffee orders and learn by being a fly on the wall. But Jasiah was always in the mix, trying to get questions answered as they raised in his brain. He knew that his research on the commodity was his chance to show his true abilities. Though he towered over most of his colleagues, he felt small as he stood before them in the whitewashed conference room. When he presented his reasoning before the trading team, he felt like his breathing was constricted. But as he observed eyes widening with interest and a few head nods, his confidence grew by the second.

Once he concluded his presentation, the sector head, James, dismissed him from the room. Jasiah gladly made an exit and only felt like he was breathing again when he sat at his small desk in the open space. He hoped he wasn't making the wrong play in his life. Watching from outside of the conference room, he started to question if his education at Xavier had prepared him for the big leagues.

He turned to his computer screen and stared at it blankly before deciding to quadruple check the facts he had just given. That only strengthened his resolve.

"Sheffield," James called from his office doorway.

Jasiah raised from his seat quickly, intentionally avoiding eye contact with anyone in the bullpen as he headed into James' corner office.

"Good work," James acknowledged, without looking away from his three computer screens. "Can't wait to see what else you come up with."

Jasiah nodded and left the office hurriedly. Everything in his life made him feel dubious since he'd opened his apartment door and found Amelia there. He needed to celebrate his small victory for his own mental sanity. He looked at his watch noticing that it was lunchtime and decided to leave the office instead of partaking in the daily catering by his employer.

Jasiah hit the street with a smile on his face. He inhaled and exhaled deeply, basking in the sun and humid atmosphere. He eagerly took in the sights and sounds around him on the bustling Manhattan Street. Just that moment alone, the simple 'good work' had confirmed that he was where he needed to be.

Jasiah dialed his dad to tell him that things were looking up for him. He was confident his father would be as proud as he was over the small victory.

"That's great, Siah! I been telling you, you're a beast with those numbers," Big Siah encouraged his son. "Take that energy into a poker club tonight."

"If I hit big, you gotta come up and celebrate with me."

"No doubt," his father quickly agreed. "I know you're living large."

Jasiah sighed. He didn't feel like he was living large. He felt like an imposter in his own life because he was only living a fragment of his dreams. He had his father, which was unbelievable. He was living in a big city instead of on its outskirts and commuting. But he had a live-in girlfriend that he didn't need as much as he thought he did.

"I definitely should have listened to you when it came to Amelia," he admitted.

"She had your nose wide open, probably put some voodoo on you."

Jasiah laughed.

"I tried to tell you boy! She was conjuring up some shit on you that probably only work in Louisiana."

"Naw," Jasiah refused to believe that. "I like having her here. Live-in pussy that can cook and clean ain't a bad deal," Jasiah tried to look on the upside of things.

"She ain't a rider and you need a rider."

Jasiah knew his father was right but refused to dwell on it in conversation. He had spent enough sleepless nights thinking about how he should not have written her that letter telling her he still wanted her in New York with him. Instead, he lit a cigarette and tried to figure out what he was going to eat for lunch. As he scanned his surroundings, his eyes landed on a small-framed woman trying to catch a cab. He blinked three times to make sure he wasn't seeing things.

"Pops, I'ma call you later," he quickly snapped his flip phone shut and threw his cigarette down. He felt like he could jog over to catch her, but his leg wouldn't let him. "Miss Peay!" he yelled her name as he moved closer. Hoping she wouldn't have any luck with a cab before he could get close to her. When he noticed her headphones, he cursed to himself, thinking that she couldn't hear him.

Jasiah admired Destiny's style as he moved closer. Her hair totally different from the carefree curly hairstyle he dreamed about since he'd seen her in Miami. It was neatly pinned up with tendrils framing her beautifully tanned face. She wore a fitted navy-colored dress that hugged her hourglass shape well, adorned with a pair of matching patent leather four-inch stilettos. Jasiah's heart thumped against his chest as he tried to get to her before the opportunity slipped through his fingers.

Destiny stood on the corner with her hand extended, attempting to grab a cab along with everyone else on the block. 50 Cent's "In da Club" blared in her ear as she masked her agitation. It wasn't just her attempt to hail a cab in New York's July heat, it was the fact that she had to go to the courthouse at all. She was used to Antonio's investigators researching jurors and a processing server filing papers. But at Anthony Rossi's office, Destiny found herself tasked with both. On top of that, she found it difficult to make friends in the office, which left her scrambling to figure things out on her own. Destiny contemplated trekking over to a hotel on the next block to catch a cab if no one stopped for her in the next few seconds. As sweat formed on her brow, she started to walk toward the hotel's cab stand. She regretted not bringing tennis shoes to work as she tripped over a crack in the sidewalk. Destiny looked back at the raised concrete with her fist balled up like she could fight it.

Jasiah watched Destiny intently as he weaved through the pedestrians. He was glad she didn't fall but celebrated the small victory that her stuttering in step gave him more time to catch up with her. But then he heard his name being called. "Sheffield!" He looked back to see a co-worker, Jayce, walking toward him.

Jasiah cursed under his breath, faking a smile as he said, "What's up?" before turning back to watch Destiny slipping into a cab and out of his grasp. "What are you doing here, Destiny Peay?" he questioned aloud as if she could hear him while watching her slump into the cab's seat as it drove past him.

"How about lunch?" Jayce suggested with a wide smile on his face. "My treat; I want to pick your brain about the research you've been doing in the agriculture sector."

Jasiah nodded, still watching the cab move down the street. "Let's get Korean BBQ," he suggested.

Destiny was oblivious to Jasiah. She was, relieved to finally be on her way to the Manhattan Courthouse. She slumped down in the seat and told herself, *'You can do this, Destiny!'* with her eyes closed, allowing the air conditioning to blow over her. As her body cooled, she reached in her tote to triple check that she had the right paperwork, pens, and a notepad. In her tote, she spotted a small seashell. She ran her fingers over the ridges, remembering the night she picked up the keepsake on the beach in the Hamptons. Her mind wandered back to the moment that Antonio walked her into his beach rental situated on an inlet.

Antonio had been so nonchalant about bringing her there, around the friends he once shared with his wife. Taking her to the restaurant where they had a specific table reserved for anyone in the Rossi family. Every weekend in June, Destiny felt like an actress named Dee. At each social gathering she pretended to be enthused in conversations jam-packed with microaggressions and inherent bias. The only time she felt like herself was on their nightly beach stroll. Under the moonlight, with the waves crashing at their feet, Antonio held her hand and thanked her for her patience. He allowed her to vent about the conversations, make jokes about his friends, and assure her that things would be different over time.

Destiny dropped the shell back into her bag. Things were different for her now. She was alone and frustrated. She felt like she was living someone else's life, rather than her own. She wanted to reverse some of her decisions and chart her course in life differently. She wanted to feel at home.

But with a sigh, she exited the cab, rambled up the courthouse steps and did her job. Once her tasks were complete, she returned to the office. Several people were leaving but there were others perched at their desks, studying case files, making dinner orders, and busying themselves with everything other than a private life. Destiny didn't want that – at least, not on a hot summer night. She kicked her heels off under her desk and reviewed her notes about the jurors. She highlighted points she wanted to raise with the lead attorney when he returned to the office.

Interrupted by the blare of her cell phone ringing, Destiny was overrun with shock at Jasiah's name on the screen. They hadn't talked in what seemed like weeks.

"Mr. Sheffield," she called out upon answering the phone.

"Hey, Beautiful," he responded. "What are you up to these days?"

"Working," she sighed heavily.

"It's late," Jasiah pointed out. "I thought we could have dinner together."

"Boy, where are you? Talking about let's have dinner together."

"Wall Street," he answered, naming the street he saw her trying to hail a cab on earlier.

Destiny cleared her throat, scanning her surroundings as if someone were watching her. "You're in New York?"

"You sound just as shocked as I was when I saw you trying to catch a cab earlier," he informed her.

"Stop playing," Destiny smiled. "You're pranking me."

"Have dinner with me," Jasiah repeated. "Let me know how you ended up in the Big Apple and didn't tell me."

Destiny bit her bottom lip. She didn't know whether or not being alone with Jasiah was a good idea. The image of him on the jet ski was still etched in her mind. Even though Antonio had awakened sensations within her that she hadn't known existed, he was still no match for the connection Destiny felt with Jasiah.

Destiny met Jasiah on Wall Street. Realizing that they worked on the same block, she felt trouble in the air. Instantly, Jasiah was no longer the friend that lived in her emails since he had seen her with Antonio. Their one-line messages full of random questions: *what's that fish place on H Street? When was the last time you dreamed about me*? There he was, in the flesh, looking like the most handsome man she had ever sunk her teeth into.

"My Shawty," he gave her a bear hug the way he always did. The type of hug she longed for many lonely nights as a Harvard freshman. The type of hug she wanted while she was being stalked. The type of hug she needed after being attacked. She couldn't pull away from it. She settled into his arms, allowing his heartbeat to match hers. Jasiah didn't let her go. He kissed the side of her head as he held her tightly. Inhaling the sweet scent of her hair. Relishing in the familiarity of *his Destiny*.

They withdrew from one another slowly, the heat rising within both of them. She smiled nervously as she realized her surroundings. She was in front of her job where someone could see them and start a round of office gossip that she didn't need. But she refused to relinquish the moment. It was a relief to be in his presence at a time where she felt frustrated and foolish for moving to New York to continue a relationship with a married man.

"What are the odds?" Destiny uttered, as she studied Jasiah in his pressed slacks and starched shirt that didn't hide his broad shoulders and muscles. He looked professional and mature. His wavy hair now a curly temple taper bush. His light mustache was now a goatee.

"Man, who are you telling?" Jasiah seized the moment again, grabbing Destiny around the waist the way he wished he could have in Miami.

She gasped and planted both of her palms on his chest. "Not in front of my job!"

"Why didn't you tell me you were coming to New York the last time we spoke?" he inquired, as he pulled her in, holding her tighter.

"Jasiah, in our last conversation all you wanted to do was make fun of me for being a sugar baby," Destiny recalled. "Besides, you didn't tell me you were in New York either."

"But here we are," Jasiah looked down at Destiny, loving the feeling of her in his arms.

"Jasiah," she pressed on his chest, attempting to put some distance between them but he didn't release her. Instead, he took one of her hands from his chest and moved it directly over his heart, holding it in place.

She felt his heart beating against her palm. The warmth of his body making hers rise. "Not in front of my job," she repeated softly. She glanced at her Movado watch "The lawyers should be coming back from the courthouse at any moment, I have to brief them."

"You think I care about those people?" Jasiah asked, not relenting.

"Jasiah, just not here," she stated firmly, as she looked into his seductive brown eyes. She found herself reaching up and touching his goatee but quickly gained her composure and dropped her hand. "Jasiah, let me go."

"I'm never letting you go... can't you tell?" he spoke plainly, reaching down to kiss her lips.

Destiny kissed him back but the cigarettes on his breath returned her senses and she pushed away. "God, you need to quit smoking."

Jasiah didn't care what she said. He kissed her again, filling his hands with her butt at the same time. His actions reigniting the dwindling flame within them. When they parted, Jasiah laid his forehead on hers. They were quiet for a moment, neither concerned with how they looked on a congested city street.

"Jasiah, I need at least an hour," Destiny bargained. "Can we meet in an hour?"

"I don't want to let you go," he admitted, planting a kiss on her forehead.

"Jasiah," she whispered, tapping his chest with her fingertips. "Please."

He slowly released her and stared into her eyes that mirrored the golden time of day they stood in. The sun was setting, illuminating Destiny's eyes.

He didn't notice she had retrieved his pack of cigarettes hanging out of his pocket as they released one another. He just smiled while he watched her toss them in a nearby trash can like she was scoring a three pointer into the basketball hoop.

"Really, Destiny?" Jasiah couldn't believe how quick her movement was.

"I told you to quit a long time ago," Destiny looked at her watch. "Do you have somewhere to be?" Destiny asked him. "Somebody to get home to?"

Jasiah looked away, not wanting to admit that he had someone at home that he didn't want to get back to. He had already been there this evening and now he was walking the streets in search of some peace of mind.

"Jasiah, we can schedule something," she suggested reluctantly, realizing his silence was the answer she did not want.

"Destiny, what are you doing in New York?" he asked, avoiding the question. His mind spiraling with regret.

She bit her bottom lip, not wanting to answer him. She didn't know what he would think of her if she admitted that she was in New York at a job she currently hated because her lover thought it was a good idea. She didn't want to admit to herself that she had given up a great opportunity elsewhere to be within arm's reach of a wealthy man so that she could live a lifestyle out of the magazines she flipped through in her adolescent years. Instead, she said, "Filling in the time at a law firm during my gap year before starting law school."

"Really?" Jasiah questioned, delicately moving a stray piece of hair from Destiny's face. "That's what landed you in New York?"

Destiny's chest heaved from Jasiah's considerate touch. Glancing at her watch again, she realized she was out of time, "We can get into the details over dinner."

"Hide Rooftop... one hour," he insisted.

Destiny swallowed hard and nodded. As she walked back into the office, she felt delirious. She wondered why Jasiah had to look so good, smell so manly, touch her so perfectly. She couldn't shake the feeling that it was yet another kismet moment between her and Jasiah. They were in the same place, at the same time, as adults. There were no more miles between them. But it was evident, the boundaries for their relationship once set by their parents, had matriculated into boundaries set by their significant others.

Antonio called Destiny as she packed her tote bag. She instantly started thinking that she had been seen with Jasiah. Someone had reported back to him that his lady was being held, caressed and kissed in the street by a man other than himself. She answered reluctantly.

"Dee, you're still in the office?" Antonio recognized.

"Just finishing up for the day."

"Was today any better?" he questioned.

Destiny bit her bottom lip. Was her day any better at work – no. But the evening's potential was so much brighter now that she was having dinner with Jasiah.

"I'll take your silence as a no," he sighed. "Should I have stayed in the office to get you a little more acclimated?"

Destiny let out a hard sigh. "I'm a big girl. I will be fine," Destiny tried to assure him and herself at the same time.

"Dee, I just want to make sure things don't get… complicated with us."

"And here I am, thinking you were concerned for my well-being," she uttered.

"I have to take a call," he stated abruptly.

Antonio ignoring her sarcastic remark stung a little. She felt like it was the perfect opportunity for him give her the assurances she needed.

"Call me once you're settled at home."

"Sure," Destiny agreed.

She cradled the headset for a moment as she thought about the possibility of her life being even more complicated or fulfilled with Jasiah readily present in it. Once she hung up, she decided she was willing to find out.

Chapter 16 - Reconnected

The walk to the hotel went faster than Destiny expected. She spent the time trying to process if her and Jasiah would be able to make space for one another in their lives. Would it be a good time or wreak havoc? But when Destiny saw Jasiah seated near the window of the upscale bar nursing a cocktail, any hesitancy in rekindling a love affair with him went out of the window. A smile spread across her face as she realized she was walking toward the man who had had helped her build her confidence when he was just a boy. The man who love and care never wavered. Jasiah stood to greet her, allowing her smile to become contagious.

"Hey, beautiful," he revealed his dimples.

"Hey handsome," she winked at him.

Jasiah swiftly took her into his arms, their lips colliding, as he caressed her smooth face. The atmosphere between them changed. No one existed in the busy bar but the two of them at that moment. To them there was no jazz playing. There was no chatter. It was just them. The sound of their breath represented their wants, their longing for one another. Their bodies synchronized, hot and heavy, creating a dynamic that neither could draw away from.

"Can we get a room?" he asked with his lips brushing against hers as he talked.

"You're not wasting any time. Are you Mr. Sheffield?" Destiny didn't budge as she responding, relishing in the delicate graze of his flesh.

"I've always known what I wanted when it came to you, Shawty," his husky voice sent vibrations through Destiny's spine.

Destiny bit her bottom lip in enchantment. She had fantasized about Jasiah since she had seen him on the water. She thought about him lingering over her, touching her, her touching him. But she also thought about them giggling together, sharing inside jokes. She could imagine herself just lying on his chest and listening to music as the day passed them by. Jasiah's unwavering glare was confirmation that the moment had arrived.

"I think I should have a drink first," Destiny responded as she pulled herself from their rapture and took a seat.

"Of course," he motioned for the waiter. "Don't sit over there," he grabbed her hand. "Come, sit with me," he gestured pulling her out of her seat as he moved to the purple high back bench with space for two.

Destiny followed his lead, feeling comfort in his arms. She ran her fingers through the nap of his soft tapered curly bush. "Your hair wasn't this length a couple of months ago," she recognized.

"Just trying something new," Jasiah informed her instead of telling the truth that Amelia asked him to grow it longer so that she could run her fingers through it.

262

"Interesting," Destiny whispered as her hand cupped his muscular jawline and gazed into his dark bedroom eyes. She had to ask herself- *why was I so mad at him.*

"You don't like it," Jasiah assumed as he brushed his fingers over the top.

She hunched. "It could grow on me," she assured him as she turned her attention toward the waiter and ordered a cosmopolitan martini as well as various Mediterranean appetizers.

"I like your optimism," Jasiah whispered into her ear.

Destiny exhaled. She felt the tension of the day leaving her body as she enjoyed the imaginary cocoon they were in. "I was just asking myself why I ever let you out of my sight," she informed him as she crossed her legs at the knee and looked him directly in the eyes. His alluring brown bedroom eyes drew her in, calling for her to plant a kiss on his lips.

"You're still a paradox," Jasiah recognized with his forehead resting on hers after the intimate moment.

"I wish I could disagree," Destiny retorted as she sat back.

Jasiah followed, placing his arm over Destiny's shoulders. "So, you're still at a law firm?" Jasiah tried to make small talk even though he wanted to pull Destiny onto his lap and do whatever it took to seduce her.

"It's where I belong."

"I wish you could be that certain about me and you."

"Jasiah... now that I'm away from Cambridge I'm not as angry... not as angry with you or just the world in general."

"Why did you stay there?"

"I'm not a quitter."

"You quit me," he reminded her as he moved in closer, running his nose against her cheek, intoxicated by her presence.

"Yet, here we are," she whispered with rosy cheeks as she blushed from his delicate touch.

They stared into one another's eyes. He was just about to lean in for a kiss when the waiter came with her cocktail.

Destiny turned and ordered two shots of Cîroc vodka before taking a sip of her drink.

"Really Destiny? You never needed to be liquored up to sleep with me before?" he recognized.

"I never had so much to lose by being close to you," she admitted sipping her drink.

"What does that mean?" he questioned.

"Nothing," Destiny sighed as she wasn't ready to tell Jasiah how much Antonio had control over her life from afar. She took another sip and looked around at the colorful bar. She had always imagined them meeting after work at a place like this- for a drink, to review their day and make plans. She took in the moment that she had daydreamed about in in high school. The reality feeling not as good as she imagined because they didn't truly belong to one another the way she imagined.

Just when she decided to bury any guilt associated with Antonio, her eye caught a pregnant woman walking by. It reminded her of a harsh reality between she and Jasiah. "To think, we would have a four-year-old," Destiny blurted out.

Jasiah nearly choked on her words. She had not mentioned her teenage pregnancy in quite some time. He couldn't believe she was bringing up what was once a sore spot between the both of them in a joking manner.

Destiny laughed.

"That was no laughing matter in 2000," Jasiah averted his glare to the view of New York City's skyline from 20th floor. He couldn't imagine having a baby back then and he still felt that way now.

"No, it certainly was not," she admitted. "But I've run down our experiences together so many times and we never talk about what if we were teenage parents."

"So many dreams would have been deferred," Jasiah answered as he looked down at his feet, trying to conceal his current worries.

The waiter came with the shots, and still no food. Destiny put her cocktail down, with the shot glass still in hand and turned to Jasiah.

"We have to look in one another's eyes while we drink or its seven years of bad sex," she joked with him.

"You better not fucking blink," Jasiah told her as he tried to push away the uneasy feeling talking about being a father brought him.

They stared in one another eyes while the warm liquor coated their throats. Their connection felt as cosmic at it had when they first met over five years ago.

"So, catch me up," Destiny urged. "Tell me about your job; tell me about graduation… tell me anything."

"I miss my friend," Jasiah admitted, as he looked back at Destiny. "These last few months have been rough."

"You can say that again," Destiny motioned for the bartender to give them another round of shots.

"You're living large," Jasiah commented. "On yachts and living in New York City."

"All of this comes with a price," Destiny looked at Jasiah. "Everything comes with a price."

They stared at one another. Destiny searching to see if he was still the love of her life while Jasiah's stare tried to confirm it.

"I'm glad you healed from your accident."

"I'm glad you survived your stalker," Jasiah touched Destiny's fringe bang, gently removing a strand of hair from in front of her face.

"Barely," Destiny mumbled as she averted her eyes, not wanting Jasiah to see the pain she tried heavily to mask daily. "I've become very guarded with the way I can be touched sometimes."

"What happened?" Jasiah asked.

Destiny started to think of a way to evade his question. She didn't want to recount what happened. She felt like she relived the moment every time she told the story. To deflect from the question, she leaned her head on Jasiah's shoulder and exhaled.

"Life happened," she answered.

Jasiah planted a soft kiss on top of her head. "You're hiding something," he whispered.

"I'm hiding so many things," Destiny whispered back. "Do you think you can unlock my secrets?" she asked, as her hand glazed the front of Jasiah's slacks.

"Just give me a little time with you... I'll get it all out of you."

Destiny's head popped up and she looked in Jasiah's eyes, "I want you to get it all *in* me," she purred with a seductive grin.

"Girl, nobody can go from sweet and innocent to sex kitten like you," Jasiah shook his head as he slipped his hand around her waist, bringing her out of her seat and between his legs.

"You like it," Destiny reminded him.

"I love it," Jasiah laughed. "But we need to have a real conversation."

Destiny sucked her teeth and leaned over to reach for her glass. "Let's just have fun tonight," Destiny suggested watching a server come with the small plates of food she ordered.

"Was breaking up with me worth it for you?" Jasiah asked as he released Destiny from his lap.

"How many times are you going to ask me that question?" Destiny shook her head, refusing to look at Jasiah. "My answer has not changed."

Jasiah went mute. He removed his arm from around Destiny and sat up to enjoy a skewer of chicken.

"It was better for us. We were changing and we were going to be hundreds of miles apart," Destiny explained anyway.

"I was growing up," Jasiah defended himself. "Not only did I stand by you through your depression after the abortion, but I was also just meeting my father and his side of the family. Testifying in Montgomery County Courts against the officer that assaulted me and then in D.C. courts against your ex-boyfriend for trying to carjack me," he added. "That was a lot to deal with. But I still wanted us, and you couldn't see it."

Destiny closed her eyes, stung by his words. But when she reopened them, all she could see was the pain still lurking behind his alluring eyes. She reached up, cupping his face in her palm, running her finger along the faint scar on his temple. She kissed his lips gently, knowing that the blemish on his skin ran deep.

"I couldn't compartmentalize it like you could," Jasiah admitted in a whisper.

"Maybe we should have made a pact to meet back up after graduation like a Hallmark movie," Destiny joked, trying to lighten the mood.

But Jasiah agreed. "Maybe."

"But we're here now," Destiny looked at Jasiah. "Feeling some type of void for one another."

"Yes, here we are," Jasiah kissed her again. "The first time in far too long that being close to you hasn't been a tug of war."

"I'm sorry," she spoke in a hushed tone, apologizing to him and herself.

A silence fell over them and Jasiah used an ice breaker question that would always lead to an amusing exchange.

"What has Freddie Bush been up to?" Jasiah asked about the man that had once saved his life.

"Locked up," Destiny responded, shaking her head. "Public intoxication and something else... my father said he's going to leave him in there long enough to detox."

269

"Oh, this just happened?" Jasiah envisioned the drunken war veteran behind bars, spending most of his time curled up on a cot sleeping.

Destiny nodded. "Maybe like last Tuesday," she responded, as she ran her fingers over his goatee. "I'm just happy to still have my friend."

"I'm more than just your friend."

Destiny diverted her eyes to a plate, as she felt a tinge of guilt for the way she acted toward Jasiah previously. "Jasiah, you went on to have some interesting relationships, and you didn't have to worry about lying to me," she tried to spin the truth to favor her actions.

"Destiny, us being right here, right now is all that matters," he grabbed her hand and intertwined his hand with hers. "Nobody knows me like you."

Destiny sighed with relief just as her cell phone buzzed. Stealing a glance at it, she was met with an instant message from Antonio – *I'll call you after my dinner.*

"This is the Destiny I know. I'm glad to have her back. I don't know who that Harvard girl was," he stated with a chuckle.

But Destiny didn't think it was funny. She knew there was so much truth in what he was saying. She was a different person at Harvard. She rolled her eyes and replied to Antonio's text – *Dinner with who?* Before turning look at Jasiah. "If you only knew how hard it was for me in Cambridge."

"Tell me," he urged. "Tell me everything so I can understand this version of you," he gulped down his drink.

Destiny took a deep breath and cast her gaze over the view of the surrounding skyscrapers and buildings lighting up the sky. She knew she wasn't ready to tell Jasiah about her transgressions. The mockery she had made of her soul to protect her pride. When Antonio was slow to reply to her message, she threw the phone back into her purse. And right then, with a string of bad memories running through her mind, she knew she couldn't go back there for law school. She cringed, not knowing what that would mean for her future.

"Hey," Jasiah touched her elbow, bringing her attention back to him. "Don't let whoever that was in your phone ruin our time... I'm not an associate, you can talk to me, Miss Peay."

There was no way she could tell Jasiah that she helped her brother run drugs through Harvard's campus or that she emceed parties, dressed like a dominatrix to entertain some of Boston's most elite. Not at that moment.

"Jasiah, how did you get here?" she asked, avoiding admitting her transgressions in Cambridge. "All of this time, I thought you were still in Louisiana or maybe back in Potomac. And you are right here in New York."

"I work for a hedge fund," he answered. "I told you I was changing my major and I followed through with it."

"I'm happy for you," Destiny commended as she popped an olive into her mouth. "My title may be paralegal

271

at Rossi and Associates, but I swear they have me being a legal assistant, investigator assistant. Just any damn thing."

"It will make you well rounded in the field," Jasiah rubbed her back. "Gotta start from somewhere."

"I don't know about that," Destiny disagreed.

"I really don't care why we are in the city," Jasiah admitted. "I'm just pleasantly surprised that we found one another in the largest city of the United States."

"It's fate," Destiny smiled, and ate another olive.

Jasiah's infatuation with Destiny weighed heavy on him. The scent of her, her smile, the way she touched him, her complexity, the way she laughed. He couldn't help but lean in to share his feelings. "I want you," he told her. "I've always wanted you."

She leaned onto Jasiah's chest and basked in his honesty.

"Come on," Jasiah stood up and motioned for the bartender to get the waiter's attention. "I was a little presumptuous when you agreed to meet here and got a room," he admitted before motioning for the waiter again.

"Just because I go to your hotel room doesn't mean anything is gonna happen," Destiny joked with a neck roll.

"Yeah, umm hmmm," Jasiah nodded even though he didn't feel like she was being honest. "You want the shot now or in the room?" Jasiah asked.

"Now," Destiny answered. "But can I eat a little more?"

Once the waiter came over, Jasiah asked for to-go boxes as he handed Destiny the shot. "Let me see those eyes, girl," Jasiah told her.

They stared at one another as they gulped down the vodka. A simultaneous wink caused them to burst into laughter.

"What happened to you?" Jasiah asked once they got into the elevator, realizing she'd never answered the question. "Just be honest with me," he coaxed.

Destiny pressed her lips to his to avoid answering but he pulled away.

"Tell me," he demanded.

"Jasiah, I lost myself," she admitted. "I started out suffering at Harvard. I allowed my insecurities to get the best of me when I felt like a pity admission. I secretly, and wrongfully, blamed you leaving me there alone when I initially applied to be there with you."

"You convincing me to embark on my own path and figure out life for myself was the best thing you could have ever done for me, to be honest," Jasiah admitted. "I can't regret going to Xavier."

"I'm not telling your story, I'm telling mine," she replied.

"My bad," Jasiah exited the elevator.

"Jasiah let's be honest. There was no way our relationship would have survived that distance."

"I don't want to admit that," he answered. "I just remember all of the hot angry sex you used to give me on breaks through our junior year," he responded, as he opened the room door.

Destiny rolled her eyes and gulped down the rest of martini.

Once the door was closed behind them, Jasiah kicked off his shoes and started to unbutton his shirt. Destiny watched him intently, as she bit her bottom lip and took off her shoes as well.

"Let your hair down," Jasiah urged, pulling off his shirt and unbuttoning his pants.

"Get in the shower," Destiny replied.

"Get in with me," he pulled her into his bare chest.

"Jasiah, you know how I feel about my hair," she dismissed the notion.

"The hair is going to be the least of your worries tonight," he warned as he scooped her into his arms with his hands gripping her butt.

His words and actions aroused Destiny. They kissed and she ended it by lightly nibbling on his lip and running her nails across his back.

"See, that's the type of shit that drives me crazy," he hissed as he slid the zipper down from the back of her dress.

"Go get in the shower," she urged again after she had his pants unzipped.

"Naw, shawty, I can't let you out of sight," Jasiah pushed her dress strap off one of her shoulders.

Destiny moved away, removing the bobby pins from her hair as she walked over to the radio in the room. With one hand, she searched through the channels on the analog radio, the other one in her hair, little by little, her hair fell until she'd unleashed it all, a long, healthy mane that dropped past the middle of her back.

Jasiah thought she looked amazing. He couldn't resist walking over and running his hands through her hair as she searched for an R&B station. In the middle of Anita Baker's "No One in the World" Jasiah pulled her hair from the nape, jutting her chin into the air. Destiny moaned. He kneeled, despite the pressure on his leg and ran his tongue from her cleavage up to her lips. Destiny moaned again as a rush of emotions surged through her body. She reached for Jasiah's pants and managed to get her hands inside. She grabbed his manhood and another gush rushed over her as she savored his girth in her hand. Jasiah's hands didn't stop working until her skintight dress was thrown over a chair and her bra and panties were tossed to the side. He pulled her close and kissed her tenderly yet eagerly until he pushed them toward the bed, his hand guiding her down until she laid gingerly across it. Jasiah stood over her, admiring her body, as he reached in his pants pocket for a condom before allowing his pants to drop to his ankles.

"How often do you go to the gym?" Jasiah asked, noticing the set of abs on her.

"You like what you see?" she asked as she reached for him again.

"I love what I see," he pushed her back with his index finger.

Destiny fell back on the bed and scooted up to the pillow.

"Open those legs for me," Jasiah urged as he stroked himself. "Let me see it."

Destiny felt comfortable under his gaze, so she did as he requested, watching him lay between her legs. She watched him intently as he kissed her sweet spot gently, like he was saying hello. She opened her legs wide for him so he could taste her arousal. His moans insured her that he enjoyed her flavor. His hands roamed to her breast. She arched her back, feeling like she could levitate off of the bed with the outpouring of pleasure his tongue provided. She couldn't control the sounds she made, nor did she want to. Calling out his name, she came hard, a release her body needed badly.

"Come here," Destiny urged- lightly tugging on his hair, drawing him away from her tenderness.

Jasiah followed her lead, just as eager to feel her as she was to be felt. When he laid between her legs and entered her, Destiny felt as though she would cum again from merely the energy between the two of them. Feeling her caving beneath him, Jasiah became lost in her aura. He

276

pulled one leg on his shoulder as he started to pump inside of her throbbing opening.

He felt as though he had something to prove as he dove in repeatedly. Each thrust attempting to reclaim what was once his. Each moment inside of her making him more eager to recover the connection they once had. Destiny grabbed his face, "Look at me," she whispered softly.

Jasiah's eyes popped open, and he felt like he could confess his love to her right then and there. He kissed her calf and ran his tongue along her hamstring instead of saying anything.

"Jasiah, slow down," Destiny coaxed, pulling herself up and kissing him. He groaned, her flexibility allowing him to dive in deeper. "Take your time," she whispered.

Jasiah grunted, still lost in the moment, and not knowing how to control himself. He was in a place he never thought he would return to. A home he thought had a new owner. But there he was, staking his claim once again.

Destiny moaned his name again, grabbing him firmly by the hip and rolling them over for her to be on top.

"Open your eyes," Destiny purred.

Jasiah realized she was a different lover when she pushed him back, her hands firmly planted on his chest. She knew exactly what she wanted. He submerged himself in her movements, her jasmine and amber scent, the sweetness of her skin, the sounds she made. She took his hand and placed them over his head as she rode him with a steady wind. Their fingers intertwined, her lips meeting his, exchanging short sloppy kisses. He gripped her hands, aching to touch her but aroused by her dominance. They moaned in tandem until Jasiah could no longer control himself.

"Destiny, I want you," he confessed as he stared into her eyes – hoping she would catch the sincerity.

"I'm right here," she replied, as she sat up and circled her hips back and forth as if she were taming a bull.

Jasiah lost it. With his climax approaching, he grabbed her hips, keeping her in place so she could feel the explosion she had caused. "Shit girl," Jasiah breathed out as his body relaxed. "Y–yo–you" he stuttered, as he tried to catch his breath, searching for the words to express how she made him feel.

Destiny peered down at him, a cocky smile hiding her excitement.

"Don't look at me like that," Jasiah blurted out as he wiped the sweat from his brow.

Destiny's eyes bounced around the room and suddenly, she felt like she'd done too much too soon. The carefree feeling from the drinks they'd downed earlier was starting to dissolve and the reality of her actions settling into her thoughts. She retreated, falling to the side of the bed and covering herself with the sheet.

"What's wrong?"

"When I said something fun, I thought we would have a couple of bougie drinks here, hit the club down the street. Get some late-night gyros, share some sloppy kisses and then part ways," she admitted.

"This would have got my vote, 100%... hands down," Jasiah laughed, as he sat on the edge of the bed.

"What I had in mind would be more palatable for your girlfriend if you got caught for sure," Destiny sarcastically stated.

Jasiah didn't reply as he stood and headed to the bathroom to remove the condom and jump in the shower.

"I knew you had a girlfriend!" Destiny exclaimed as she followed. "Is it the same girl from New Orleans? The same girl that wanted your attention when I called to check up on you?"

"She's from New Orleans but not the same girl."

"You low down dirty dog... you brought a girl with you to the Big Apple only to cheat on her within a few months?"

"I think this is the pot calling the kettle black," Jasiah retorted, as he started to the shower.

Destiny didn't think she had a boyfriend. She had a situation. But she didn't want to let on to Jasiah that she was seeing a married man that kept her on a long leash. "What a predicament," Destiny mocked John Travolta's tone in *Face Off* in a playful manner instead of confessing her transgressions.

Jasiah laughed. "I've been waiting too long for this predicament," he smacked her butt playfully as he handed her a shower cap.

"This could be fun. Right?" Destiny asked, as she pondered how she could see Jasiah again without interrupting her lifestyle.

"Could be," he responded, stepping into the shower.

Once Destiny covered her hair, she slipped into the shower behind him. They shared a kiss and then Jasiah pulled away "But the problem is... I know you're who I want to be with." he confessed.

Destiny pulled in a deep breath, knowing she felt the same.

"Are you trying to tell me I'm not what you want?"

"So, you're just gonna go home right now, like bitch you got to go?" Destiny inquired. "Cause I'ma need somewhere to live,"

Jasiah looked Destiny up and down as if he was disgusted. "You live with him?"

"He pays for my apartment," Destiny admitted. "And I work at his brother's law firm."

"And you would give that all up to fumble through life with me?" Jasiah asked.

"Hasn't that always been our plan?" Destiny peered into his eyes.

"You should have just got on the back of my jet ski and rode off with me in Miami," he responded, staring back at her.

"You would still have to go home to your girlfriend," Destiny rolled her eyes and started to wash her body.

Jasiah took a second and envisioned him coming through the apartment door with Destiny in tow to find Amelia cooking in his kitchen. He shook off the vision of the chaos that would ensue.

"Why do things have to be so complicated with us?" Jasiah asked rhetorically.

His question lingered in the air as Destiny planted kisses on his moist skin.

She searched for the flaws that drove her insane so many summers ago. She tried hard to find the gap in their connection, the entrance to the chasm that always seemed to exist between them. Studying his eyes, she realized that somehow, it no longer existed.

Chapter 17 – Duties

The smell of coffee woke Destiny out of her sleep. A hazy blue morning light peeked through the sheers in her bedroom, when she sat up in the middle of her bed and reached for her gun, a graduation present from Jax. She took the safety off as she got out of the bed and peeked into the common area, praying that it was Antonio. Relief coated her when she caught a glimpse of the back of his head, standing in front of the coffee maker. But the nervousness didn't subside. *What is he doing here?* – she asked herself.

Destiny dropped her guard and placed the gun back in the nightstand, quickly grabbing a satin robe and made an entrance.

"Surprise... surprise," Destiny sang out as she left the bedroom, trying to mask her uncertainty about his abrupt visit.

"I was worried about you," he responded as he turned to her, adjusting his tie. "You didn't answer the phone or any of my messages. I thought maybe something had happened to you."

Destiny didn't know whether he was being sincere or not. "Even the police would say give it 24 hours."

"Well, I didn't think we were on bad terms for you to ignore me," he looked at Destiny in the eyes.

"You ignored my question about who you were at dinner with," Destiny retorted. "So, I thought unresponsiveness was the name of the game."

There was a silence between them. She could see the discontent in his face. But she didn't care.

"We're not going to start the tit for tat game," Antonio scoffed.

"You said you were having dinner and then it took you until after midnight to call me," Destiny rolled her eyes. "I was too tired to talk at that point."

The memory of her and Jasiah laying in the hotel bed watching her Blackberry ring when he did call flashed through her mind. She refused to allow Antonio's call to disrupt them watching *Coming to America* and chatting about their different experiences in New York City so far while eating the cold leftover appetizers.

"When you were in Boston, we had plenty of late nights together," he intently watched her movements.

"Antonio, let's not make this a thing," she sat on the kitchen counter, knowing it was pointless to argue with him. "How did you even get here?"

"A helicopter this morning," he felt on her thigh. He leaned in and kissed her on the jawline. "I worry about you. I can hear how sad you are sometimes."

Destiny leaned into his embrace. "I've just been frustrated... its more difficult to make friends at this office, considering I'm not always the friendliest person. Often, I feel like I don't have a real role in the office. That they just have me doing anything."

"Well, that's partly my doing," Antonio informed her. "I hope you're making connections at the courthouse and starting to look at aspects of the law from different angles."

"Well, yesterday surely was a day for me," Destiny took the coffee cup from his hand. "The heat, the back and forth... I was really exhausted but you never gave me the chance to explain that to you," Destiny tried covering her tracks. "I really wasn't in a good mood."

"I understand," Antonio ran his fingers over her hair. "But I still worry about you."

"I'll make sure I send you a good night message from here on out," she assured him as she sipped the coffee. She knew that he could be just as vague in her questioning at times, and she wanted it to continue to be acceptable in their relationship.

He stared at her with his fingers playing with the ends of her hair. "I'm surprised your hair isn't wrapped up,"

Destiny's mind warped to Jasiah's hands all in her hair the night before. She shuddered at the thought of the various times he stroked or pulled it. Wrapping it up after the night she had would have been a waste of time when she was trying to get a couple of hours of sleep.

"It's wash day," she responded nonchalantly. "So, what's the plan now? I have to get ready for work."

"You're not going to the gym?" Antonio asked with raised eyebrows.

284

Destiny rolled her eyes and sipped the coffee.

"Do what you need to do," he urged as he took the coffee mug back.

Destiny moved off the counter and pulled Antonio to her. She kissed him on the lips and lied to him. "I'm glad you're here."

He smiled. "You had me worried, Dee," he ran his fingers through her hair again.

"Your investment is safe and sound," Destiny antagonized as she walked away and went back into the bedroom. She made her way to the ensuite bathroom and wondered if Antonio was still having her followed. She shuddered at the idea of him receiving photos of her embracing Jasiah on Wall Street, but she commenced to getting her day started.

Antonio came into the bathroom while she was applying her lip liner. He ran his hand over her frame and pulled her into his chest.

"You think we make a good couple?" she asked, connecting their eyes through the mirror.

"Of course," he ran his tongue along her earlobe and slid his hand into the front of her skirt to touch her. "And after you pass the bar, we will be a power couple."

Destiny grabbed his hand to stop him. "How does Victoria fit into that equation," she replied sarcastically.

Antonio turned her around to face him. "Let's not worry about the details," he insisted as he kissed her neck.

"I can't be late to work, Antonio," she whined.

"You're right," he ran his fingers along the v neck of her blouse. "You look beautiful," he complimented.

Destiny blushed.

"You know, if this isn't working out for you, you can come back to Boston with me. No harm, no foul, no judgement on my part."

"I'd like to at least give the experience ninety days, Antonio."

"Understood," he kissed her. "But we could do more traveling this summer if you weren't working."

Destiny's ears perked up at the thought of the luxury accommodations she had experienced with Antonio. Until the reality of his divided attention soured her thoughts. She tried to shift her mood as she ran her hands along his shoulders, as if she were straightening out his shirt. "Maybe we can slip away at lunch," Destiny suggested, as she fondled Antonio through his slacks.

"I'd like that," Antonio smiled.

On the inside, she cringed at the thought of being with Antonio after the night she had with Jasiah. She masked her true emotions with a light kiss to his lips and said, "Thank you for being so concerned about me."

"I hate that we're apart like this," Antonio admitted, as he wrapped his arms around Destiny and kissed her on the top of the head. "My bed is cold without you."

Destiny slowly pulled away to glare at him. He held her stare. "Antonio, you cannot keep trying to guilt trip me! This was your idea," she reminded him as she turned back to the mirror and applied lipstick.

"I was just afraid to lose you," he confessed.

Destiny stared back at him in the mirror. She wanted to admit that he never truly had her. He started losing her the moment he told her keep things sexy and easy in Miami. And after reconnecting with Jasiah, she was certain that her heart belonged elsewhere. She swallowed hard and tried to think of something cunning to say. "Mr. Rossi, you sound like a man in love," she flashed him a smile, knowing that would make him retreat.

He moved over to his side of the double sink and straightened his tie in the mirror. "I'm just a man that takes all of his investments seriously," he uttered before leaving the bathroom.

His words wiped the smile off of Destiny's face. Her own sarcastic statement backfired. A flurry of emotions ran over her. She clenched the sink to keep her balance, reeling as if he'd just smacked her in the face. *His investment* – she recounted. *He really thinks I'm his fucking investment*. Her anger started to brew. An anger that stewed in her belly while she smiled graciously until she was seated behind her desk at work. If nothing else, Destiny knew she needed to get out of the situation with Antonio. Not just because she wanted to see where things could go with Jasiah, but because she didn't want to waste any more time with a person incapable of the unadulterated love she desired.

287

She buried her frustrations until she made it to work, knowing that currently she had no recourse. Nevertheless, she looked around and realized how lucky she was. To rake in her salary and keep it all to herself was something out of a dream. The only thing she paid for was her cellular phone bill and some meals. Antonio provided her housing and a credit card non-black clothing only. She held her face in her hands as she tried to remind herself that a life with Jasiah would be better. Then her work phone rang. She immediately sat up in her seat thinking that Antonio was observing her from the distance. She answered without looking at the caller ID.

"Miss Peay speaking," she answered dryly.

"Hey beautiful," Jasiah crooned into the phone.

Destiny eyes darted around before she replied, "Hey, handsome," she held her hand over the receiver while she spoke in low tones. "When you took a business card from my bag last night I didn't expect you to call me on my office number."

"Just calling to see if you're available for lunch."

"No, I don't think I can see you today," she admitted.

"So, you're not craving me the way that I—"

"Crave is an understatement," Destiny cut him off as she leaned onto her desk with her head down. "My leg is shaking just thinking about what I could do to you," she whispered.

"I want my leg to shake," he whispered back. "Tell me."

They both giggled.

"I have a lot going on myself," Jasiah admitted. "Hopefully tomorrow is better for us."

"Hopefully," Destiny was relieved at his quick compliance.

When Jasiah hung up the phone with Destiny, he twirled in his office chair for a moment like he often did when deep in thought. Not only did he have to think of some financial strategies for today's market trends, but he also had to ensure that Amelia got an abortion.

He closed his eyes for a moment, his mind recounting Amelia showing him three positive pregnancy tests when he returned home from work the previous afternoon. He had intended on changing his clothes and then calling Destiny to see if it was possible to celebrate his small triumph at work with her. He was anxious to see if it was possible to reconnect in any way with her. The outcome hinging on whether he would continue to try making things work out with Amelia. But when Amelia gave him the news, he couldn't make it out of his work clothes.

"I told you to take the Plan B pill," Jasiah spat in disbelief. He couldn't fathom his girlfriend telling him she was pregnant, no... not after the love of his life was no longer hundreds of miles away. He thought his destiny was so close and with Amelia's revelations, Destiny would be so far away.

"I am on Depo," she retorted. "Why would I need more birth control?"

"When was the last time you had the shot?" he asked, glaring into her eyes.

Amelia looked away, nervously looking up at the ceiling as if she was trying to recall.

"Exactly!" Jasiah started to pace the floor. "Amelia, what the fuck?" he blurted out as he was at a loss for words.

"I'm going to have an abortion, Jasiah. Don't worry... I am just starting this new job, we are in this new place, in a new relationship... I can see the writing on the walls," she retorted with her arms folded across her chest.

"You sure that's what you want to do?" Jasiah asked, carefully surveying body language.

"Yes, I'm sure," she flopped down on the sofa. "I didn't make it to thirty without children because I'm eager to make permanent connections with people that could be temporary in my life."

It stung to hear her say that. He thought he had hidden his uncertainty in their relationship well. But that statement made him aware that she felt his mixed emotions about her.

"That's how you see us, Amelia? Temporary?" he tried putting the onus of her sentiment on her.

"We've been together for four months and living together for half of that time. If you were going to be in love with me, it would have happened by now," she rolled her eyes.

"My emotions don't have to move at your pace."

"In New Orleans, you were the hare and now you've turned into the damn tortoise," she uttered before sucking her teeth.

"I'm here every gottdamn day with you," Jasiah replied. "Paying this high ass rent, taking—

"Jasiah, stop!" she yelled. "None of that makes up for the fact that I'm in love with you and you're clearly *not* in love with me. The way you just responded to me being pregnant solidified that." She shook her head. "But let me guess... you're still holding back because of how much I disappointed you when I had to take a minute to think about my man being in a whole three-way relationship before me."

Jasiah shook his head. "Why was I under the impression we were getting along just fine for the past two months?"

Amelia rolled her eyes and grabbed a cigarette from the pack on the table. He watched her grab a lighter and head for the terrace.

"Amelia," he as he rubbed his hands across his face but didn't say anything afterwards.

She closed the terrace door behind her. Jasiah watched her from inside the apartment as she puffed away while in her fitted nurse uniform.

He knew he had to keep his cool, but if she wanted to leave, he didn't want to stop her – after he was certain she had aborted the baby. Jasiah got up and joined her on the terrace.

"Jasiah, this is not how it's supposed to go," Amelia uttered. He noticed how jittery she was. Her fingers trembled as she flicked the cigarette with her thumbnail even though there were no ashes to discard. He started to wonder if she was so eager to abort the baby because there was a possibility it wasn't his.

"I agree," Jasiah replied as he took the cigarette from her fingertips. "I hate that we have to go through this," he admitted as he took a drag and suppressed his suspicions. He knew he couldn't throw out accusations that would make matters worse.

"We? I'm the one carrying our child."

"How far along do you think you are?" Jasiah questioned as he glanced at his watch – 5:20 p.m. He wanted to quickly detach himself from the situation. He was determined to touch base with Destiny that evening.

"I'm sure it was from the make-up sex in June," she shook her head.

Jasiah watched her movements. She could have come to New York unknowingly pregnant by someone she slept with during their time apart. He swallowed his thoughts, again figuring it was best that he went with the flow. He didn't need anything he said to be a deterrent from her going through the procedure.

292

"So, how are you feeling?" Jasiah questioned, hoping she would say she felt normal so it would be easier for him to slip away.

"I feel fine," she spoke the words he wanted to hear. "I just missed my period and decided to take a test."

"Are you hungry?" he inquired, knowing it would be better if he left her with dinner provided. "We can order something."

"That's fine," she agreed.

"Is it insensitive to suggest sushi?" he questioned with a smirk on his face.

"Sushi sounds good," she agreed, as she took the cigarette back and took a drag of it.

Her resolve to ignore the pregnancy was refreshing, yet alarming. He went back inside and grabbed her Nokia from the kitchen island. He scrolled to her call log, then quickly finding it erased. Again, he swallowed his suspicions and used it to justify his plans for the rest of the evening.

He ordered and joined her out on the terrace with a fresh cigarette and a glass of Grey Goose vodka neat.

"It's one thing after the other," Amelia grappled, as she looked over the rail at the people bustling below.

"Definitely," he agreed, as he took a sip of his drink.

"We would make a cute kid though," she turned around and smiled at him.

"With birth deformities from our nicotine habit. I don't think that's an attribute you want your child to have, Nurse Amelia," Jasiah refused to even visualize what their child would look like.

She rolled her eyes. "I'm well aware of the things I would need to quit in order to have a healthy pregnancy."

"I'm confident that you are," he lit the new cigarette and took a drag before offering it to her.

Jasiah stared at her midsection. He felt infuriated by the thought of his life being in any more limbo. So, when Destiny bought up her pregnancy later that night, after he had escaped his home by saying he was going to a poker club, he could have nearly choked on thin air.

And now, the next morning, he knew he had to get his head back in the game.

"Sheffield, we're heading out for some lunch… do you care to join us?" a co-worker, Chris, invited.

"Sure," Jasiah rose from his seat.

Once he stepped out with them onto the bustling street, he was shocked to see Destiny getting into an SUV. He wondered how they had been working on the same block and never run into one another, but now, he'd seen her two days in a row.

Chapter 18 – Deja vu

Jasiah cast his gaze around the bleak walls of the clinic's waiting area and felt like he was experiencing de ja vu. He got up and went into the hallway. Though he was in another state, the abortion clinic mirrored the one he had sat in with Destiny, nearly five years earlier. His current feelings mirrored the way he'd felt then. He wasn't ready to be a father. Though he was relieved Amelia was on the same page, it was his burden to bear for being careless in spilling his seed. Nevertheless, he was happy to not have to wonder if it was his kid to begin with.

After noticing his leg shaking with anxiety, Jasiah stood and moved quickly toward the hallway. His footsteps echoing as he paced, convincing himself this would be the last time he'd bear this burden.

His cell phone vibrated in his pocket as he studied his watch, figuring Amelia should be about done with the procedure. It was Destiny.

"Hey," he answered in a hushed tone. "What's going on?"

"I'll take your whispers as a sign that you really can't talk," Destiny whispered back.

Jasiah chuckled a bit. "I have a quick minute," he backed away from the suite's door.

"I'm heading back up to Boston for the weekend and just wanted to hear your voice before I left."

"That means, don't call you," Jasiah shook his head. "I get the message, Destiny."

"Let's make plans for next week," she suggested. "I've been wanting to go to Coney Island, and I thought you'd make the perfect date."

Jasiah smiled. For a split second, he thought about that being one of the things on his to-do-list with Amelia, but still said, "I like the way you think."

"Just send me an email and let me know if Wednesday or Thursday works best for you."

"I'll do that," Jasiah confirmed as he grabbed the door handle to reenter the clinic. On the other side of the door stood Amelia. "I'll talk to you soon."

"Okay, bet," Destiny ended the call.

"You're smiling awfully hard," Amelia mumbled, as she brushed past Jasiah rudely.

He followed her to the elevator without a word. He attempted to take her care bag, but she snatched back. "I can handle it."

Taken back by Amelia's attitude, Jasiah retreated to the opposite side of the elevator. But he couldn't help staring at her. The sadness in her eyes nipped at his sensibility. He honestly wanted to thank her but didn't think the was the term of endearment she would appreciate. He watched a tear drop from her right eye and instinctively, he wiped it away with his knuckle.

"Are you hungry?" he asked.

"I just want to lay down."

Her words were triggering. It was the same response Destiny had given him when they played hooky from school so she could terminate her pregnancy. As they maneuvered through the small crowd of pro-lifers in front of the clinic in Harlem, he was reminded of the small crowd outside of the abortion clinic in College Park, MD. The reminiscent feeling made his stomach flip as he ushered Amelia to his car. After closing her inside he went behind the car and vomited. He felt like his body was purging all of the regret and worry that came along with Amelia's pregnancy.

But once he was home, and laying a blanket over Amelia, his mind replayed the scenes of him tucking Destiny in the same way at the hotel his mother had reserved for them. His stomach started to do flips again. Removing himself from the room, he sat on the sofa in his living room and took deep breaths, hoping to get his queasy stomach under control. Looking over at a photo of him and Amelia he started to feel worst. He knew it was time to find Amelia somewhere else to live. Still, he grappled with his conscious on parting ways with her. He looked at the healed scar on his leg. He thought that if he'd never been in the accident, he would have never met Amelia. But he still would have been in New York City and that could have made things easier for him and Destiny to see if their love for one another could withstand adult adventures.

The longer he sat there, with the walls closing in on him, his perfect bachelor pad felt like a cell. For a reprieve, he went onto the terrace with his cigarettes and iPod. As Marvin Gaye's 'Mercy, Mercy Me' played, he contemplated

297

his decision to sit out in the heat and smog. He knew he would rather be at work than at home being a supportive partner, but his conscious wouldn't allow him to be cold-hearted.

Closing his eyes, his only solace was the music and thoughts of his last rendezvous with Destiny. A smirk formed on his lips as he recalled the sound of their skin colliding while in the handicap bathroom of his building. The panting, the hurry, the heat, the lack of restraint, the spontaneity. He shook his head, trying to control the erection his erotic memory conjured. Just as he bit his lip, recalling how nibbled on Destiny's ear lobe, his cell phone vibrated, drawing him out of his momentary bliss.

Destiny's name appeared on the screen. He didn't hesitate to answer.

"Girl, you better stop calling me before you get yourself into some trouble," Jasiah joked.

She didn't say anything. The silence was alarming.

"Destiny? Hello?"

"Are you sitting down?" she asked.

Her words pulled him to his feet, dropping his iPod from his lap. He caught the headphones before it dropped through the grated floor. "Shit," he uttered. "What happened?"

"When was the last time you heard from your father?"

"This morning, why?"

"He didn't tell you he was in the hospital?"

"Destiny," Jasiah chuckled, "my father is not in the hospital."

"Yes, he is," Destiny insisted. "He got shot last night."

"I'm telling you, Destiny... call Jax, Junior, Reds, any of them back and get the fucking story straight. I talked to my father this morning."

"Jasiah, Junior is in critical condition at Howard. They brought him and your father in together last night."

"Man, I'ma call you back."

"I'll be back in D.C. later this evening," she concluded before hanging up.

Jasiah immediately dialed his father. Each ring heightening his concern. His father answered in a groggy tone.

"Pops, what you up to?" Jasiah tried to remain lighthearted as he sat back down in the chair.

"Taking a nap," Big Siah yawned. "Did things work out for you and Amelia at the clinic? Did she go through with it?"

Jasiah started to listen intently to the background noise on the phone call. All of a sudden, he heard an intercom announcement paging a doctor. "Are you in the hospital?" Jasiah questioned.

"Oh, don't worry about me, son. I'll be out by tomorrow."

Jasiah's heart dropped to his feet as he smashed the cigarette out on the rail.

"Pops," was all he could manage. He felt blindsided and neglectful all at the same time. He wondered how he'd been so caught up in his own situation that he missed the fact that his father was in the hospital.

"I'm fine, Siah," Big Siah took a deep breath. "I don't know when I'll be able to lift my left arm again, but I'm fine."

"The question is... are they looking to finish the job?" Jasiah asked.

"I guess I'll know when I hit the streets," his father sighed into the phone. "But now I definitely know I'm too old to be *that nigga*."

"I think coming to New York with me would be better for you," Jasiah suggested.

"You need to live your life, Siah... figure out things without worrying about me. This was honestly a wakeup call for me."

Jasiah shook his head. "I'ma come get you," he resolved.

"Boy, the tension so thick in your house.... You don't need to add me."

There was an odd silence between them as Jasiah pondered what he could do to keep his father safe. To him, his father only had two options, neither of which were great. Come sleep on his couch in New York or maybe a lady friend in New Orleans would appreciate an extended visit.

"Who told you I was in the hospital anyway?"

"Destiny," Jasiah admitted.

"Yeah, I should have figured," Big Siah yawned again. "Now, *she* has something to worry about."

"He a'rite… Ainta 'rite… Ain't he?" Jasiah inquired.

"I don't know about that," his father answered. "It got really heated at that dice game real fast. He wasn't breathing too good when they got him into the ambulance."

Jasiah's heart dropped with the mention of more bad news. He couldn't imagine the anguish the Peay family was going through.

"Why don't you call up one of your old ladies in Nawlins," he suggested, knowing his father would be more comfortable in the Big Easy than the Big Apple. "Chill out down there for a while."

"That's a thought. But right now, I'm going back to sleep and you running up my gottdamn minutes."

"I pay your cell phone bill," Jasiah pointed out.

Big Siah hung up.

Jasiah went back into his apartment. His mental anguish spilled out as soon as he closed the sliding door. With clinched fist, his anger echoed against the walls. He didn't feel equipped for the stress he was under. He felt like a dark shadow had been hovering over him since he left that casino in Baton Rouge. The culmination of events leading up to that moment left Jasiah thinking someone's gris gris was aimed at him.

Amelia came out of the room, "What is wrong with you?" she asked after hearing his frustrated yell.

Jasiah's eyes locked on Amelia. He thought about the altar in her New Orleans apartment. The burning candles, the photos, the flowers. "What were you working on before I met you in the hospital? What were you asking the spirits to do for you?" he questioned before he could even think about the words.

Amelia suddenly turned pale.

Her silence felt like confirmation that she had asked her God for something. "You put a fucking hex on me!" he shouted.

"Jasiah, calm down," Amelia held her hands up as if she had to defend herself from him.

Jasiah's eyes beamed into her like lasers. He questioned every plate she had made him, any drink that she'd fixed. Any ointments she used to help "heal" his leg. His mouth started twitching as his fist tightened. He didn't want to believe in the powers of Iwa. But there had to be something.

"Jasiah, what is wrong with you?" she yelled. "You look possessed right now."

With the swipe of a hand, he sent the decorative metal face on the dining room table flying across the floor.

Amelia jumped even though the object was nowhere near her. She pressed herself against the wall. "Jasiah!" she called him like an angry parent. "You need to calm down."

"My father is in the hospital, and you think I'm supposed to calm down?" he finally admitted the source of his anger.

"And you think I have something to do with that?"

"No, I'm just tryna figure out how I got myself in this situation," he pointed to the floor. "How did we get here?"

Amelia blew out a heavy breath before speaking. "Because I gave you the attention you craved when you were vulnerable," she looked at him in the eyes. "And now that you don't need me as much, you realized the infatuation was transactional and not real," she folded her arms across her chest. "I knew all of those 'you're so beautiful' lines you used on me were bullshit."

"Your beauty has nothing to do with the way I'm feeling right now," he gritted. "Everything I've ever told you; everything I've ever confided in you about was genuine or least that's the way I felt."

"And now?"

"Now we just eat, have sex, and work. It's nothing like Nawlins. You're nothing like the woman that gambled with, that I—"

"I'm the same person!" she screamed. "You're the one that made it clear there was no future in our relationship."

"Are you serious right now Amelia? I don't even know if that was my fucking baby how eager you were to get an abortion," he finally released his suspicions.

"Really Jasiah? That's' what you think of me?"

"Right now, that's the least of my worries," he flopped down on the sofa and started flickering the lighter.

An awkward silence fell between them.

"Jasiah, when we met you were committed to making the best of our time together," Amelia recounted.

"So, you knew I was committed and still had me looking like a fool on one of the most important days of my life in front of my family?" he replied in an even, dry tone as he waved his hand over the flame, hoping the warmth would draw out some anxiety out of him.

"Does your commitment keep you coming home late every evening and ignoring my phone calls on your lunch breaks?" she snapped back. "You haven't touched me since I told you I was pregnant, like I told you I had the plague or something." she sighed.

"It's just that—"

Amelia held up her hand, cutting him off, "I was just as enamored with you in Nawlins, but I saw the look on your face when I got here. That should have been my signal to start looking for a place of my own."

304

"You knew it was easier to live in New York City rent free," he acknowledged.

"True," she hunched her shoulders. "I told you, I've been fending for myself my whole damn life. And you come along with your generosity and kindness. All I could do was thank Iwa for answering my prayers."

"And now?"

"Jasiah, I have been trying my best to make this work. And I'm not going to say you haven't either," she sighed. "These last couple of weeks, you've been distant. Staying out all night. Not touching me. I'm just hoping that things can get back to normal after I heal," she wiped a tear from her eyes.

Jasiah didn't feel a tinge of guilt for his time with Destiny. He didn't blink an eye or even bother to explain where he was. "We'll see," he uttered as he threw the lighter on the coffee table and fell back against the sofa cushions.

"I'm about to get back in the bed," Amelia announced when she realized that Jasiah was shutting down.

Jasiah watched Amelia as she walked back into the bedroom. He followed her, heading straight to the closet. Without an explanation, he grabbed a duffle bag from the top of the closest.

"Where are you going?" Amelia questioned.

"I'm going to see about my dad."

"Don't you think that I need you here?"

"My father is in the hospital, you're lying in our king-size orthopedic bed with a heating pad, you will be fine."

"It's that easy for you to walk out on me? Like right now?" she fell back against the pillows. "You can't even wait until the morning."

"Do unto others as you want done unto yourself," Jasiah uttered, continuing to pack his things.

"You still haven't let it go about your graduation?" she shook her head.

"You're here. Aren't you?" he glanced at her for just a second. "I've done a damn good job of letting it go."

Chapter 19 – Confessional

Jasiah was nearly blinded by the bright sun as he pulled out of his building's garage headed towards his hometown. He thought of calling Destiny to see if she needed a ride South, but quickly concluded that he could use some time to think. He had said some things to Amelia that he didn't know if they could come back from. And her response to his lack of trust in her only deepened his resolve to forgo the relationship.

As the natural rhythm of the Manhattan Streets faded and Jasiah finally made it to the New Jersey turnpike he decided to call his cousin and fill him in on his life over the last few weeks. Jasiah had intentionally been vague with Lafayette, not wanting his ridicule, but as he headed southbound, he felt like Lafayette's brutal honesty is what he needed.

"That gottdamn Destiny," his cousin cursed.

"Come on, La, you know how I feel about her," Jasiah sighed as he hit traffic, the highway bursting with people heading to the Jersey Shore. "Maybe I should have tried a train ticket."

"Maybe you should have stayed your ass in New York and tried to make it work with Amelia, she's a good woman."

"That bitch put roots on me."

Lafayette laughed.

307

"I'm telling you! She probably was saying some spells for a good man, and I showed up in that hospital bed. Then she —"

"Siah, come on, man. Shut up!" Lafayette didn't want to hear it.

"Man, I still don't think that was my baby. She was too eager to get rid of it."

"Does it matter at this point?"

"Yeah it matters... I been raw dogging her ass."

"You're being a ... a .... Man... what's that shit called?.... Starts with an H?" Lafayette stuttered trying to find the right adjective.

"Are you trying to call me a hypocrite?" Jasiah questioned.

"That's it!" Lafayette exclaimed. "That's exactly what I'm calling your ass. You've never been faithful to that girl."

"I've had some hiccups... but I've done right by her," Jasiah protested.

"So, Destiny is just a hiccup?" he laughed. "You just told me you were burning her ass up every chance you get."

Jasiah sat quiet as he had no recourse.

"This is your life. Do what makes you happy cuz," Lafayette sighed. "I'ma give it to you. She's developed into a bad shawty, I ain't gonna lie. You saw something in her I couldn't see."

"She's who I want," Jasiah admitted. "I just hope she can accept that I can't put her on yachts just yet."

"My mother just told me that Roy settled your civil suit with the Mo County Police, so you might be able to charter a yacht even if you can't buy one."

"You think he owns that boat?" Jasiah questioned, wondering what he could offer Destiny in comparison to someone who owned a mega yacht.

"Who cares?" Lafayette responded. "Shouldn't you be more concerned about your settlement check?"

"I ain't heard from my mother since I told her I couldn't go on the family trip this summer," he recalled.

"Well, you should check in with them about your dough," Lafayette suggested.

"I certainly should," Jasiah agreed. "It's been damn near five years since we filed suit against that cop."

"Our senior year was wild," Lafayette started to reminisce. "Who would think that I would end up fatherless and you would get a father?"

"Let's leave that behind us," Jasiah coaxed, hearing the sorrow in his cousin's words.

"My neck still fucked up because of that nigga," Lafayette continued.

For a moment, Jasiah's mind flashed back to the brutal night Lafayette's father nearly beat him to death because he intervened in one of his parents' fights.

"I bet that pain don't stop you from going down on bitches," Jasiah threw out a joke to change the mood of the conversation. "I bet it ain't hurting then."

"Naw, its certainty doesn't," Lafayette laughed in agreement.

The pair continued their lighthearted banter until Jasiah stopped to get gas and something to eat at the Pennsylvania/ Delaware line.

By that time, Destiny was walking through the door of her parent's house, catching the tail end of a family conversation that included her father, Jax and her cousin, Squeak. Avoiding eye contact with anyone, she took a moment to look around the small rowhouse that she'd grown up in, thinking about how her lifestyle had changed drastically. The only thing that had changed within the walls of her childhood home was the artwork over the years. The walls were still painted an odd pale yellow. The furniture, still comfortable and worn.

"Mrs. Peay, your daughter is home!" her father yelled.

Destiny rolled her eyes upon hearing her father's announcement.

"What you doing here?" Jax asked, as he stuck a Glock in his waistband.

Destiny stared at her brother. His face was flushed and his eyes were red. Stress was written all over him. "I thought it was the right thing to do when my brother is in critical condition," Destiny answered as she dropped her duffle bag in her father's recliner.

"Uncle Ray, Destiny got that cash... do you know how much that bag cost?" Squeak joked.

"He's stable now," Jax updated Destiny on their brother's condition.

Mrs. Peay finally showed herself from the kitchen. Destiny could instantly tell her mother had been crying. She ambled over to her, and they embraced.

"You shouldn't have come," her mother whispered to her.

A tear dropped from Destiny's eye as she clung to her mother. But she refused to break down with others watching her every move. She just took a moment to inhale her mother's soothing aroma and bask in comfort of the embrace.

"Destiny, I think you could help," Jax interjected.

"Keep her out of this," Mr. Peay demanded.

"Destiny can handle this," Jax continued. "Destiny, tell your father that you found your gangster in Cambridge."

"Shut up, Jax," Destiny pulled away from their mother and turned her stare to Jax, shooting daggers at him.

He shook his head, ignoring the anger in her eyes. "Give her some heat," Jax continued. "Or did you bring your own, Destiny?"

"I know you don't have a gun, Destiny Penelope Peay," Mrs. Peay assumed.

"Jax, what the hell is your problem?" Destiny clapped back at her brother as she stepped toward him.

He laughed, shaking his head but not saying a word.

"Things are a little hectic right now," Squeak interjected, attempting to break the tension between his cousins. "Once we know Junior is out of harm's way, Jax will chill out. Right, Jax?"

"Shittt," Jax cursed under his breath.

"I came here to pray with my mother and—"

"You came here to help us to set things right," Jax slammed his hand on the table, cutting off his sister. "Daddy, she can put in this work like the rest of us."

"What is your brother talking about?" Mrs. Peay asked Destiny.

"Nothing," Destiny answered without taking her eyes off of her older brother. She hoped he was just lashing out because she was an easy target at the moment.

She was pretty sure her father knew she had helped Jax run drugs through Harvard during her freshman and sophomore years, though it was nothing they'd discussed. But had Jax disclosed the gunplay that came along with it?

"Destiny, what are you doing in New York?" Jax snapped. "You should be at home with the family! We have

312

enough to worry about without the stress about your safety in New York too."

"Muthafuckah, are you sleep deprived?" Destiny fired back, quickly matching his aggression. "What the fuck is wrong with you? I have a career," she stepped closer to her brother. Not fearing him in the least bit.

"A career?" Jax took a step forward as well. "New York has bigger monsters that will send your little ass home in a box!"

"Enough!" their mother yelled, silencing the room. "What has gotten into you two?" Mrs. Peay asked.

"Aye, man, lets head out," Squeak cut in again, trying to break the suffocating tension between siblings.

Destiny was seriously perplexed at her brother's tone. When she was home for her graduation party, he did mention he missed the money in Cambridge, but she hadn't caught on to any animosity. Dismissing her brother's anguish, she turned to her mother and asked, "Are you ready to go back up to the hospital?"

"I'm driving," her father answered.

The car ride to the hospital with her parents was quiet. She wanted to marvel at the changes in the city's landscape, but her mind was preoccupied with Jax's aggression. She knew it was his way of showing concern; his way of telling her that she should be nearby. He was holding on to her secret – the extent of the attack in her dorm room.

Jax knew the fight she'd had put up to survive the entire ordeal. He previously expressed how he was riddled with guilt for not taking her back to his hotel room with him or walking her to her room. Destiny assured him that she only blamed the Harvard and Cambridge Police departments. Staring aimlessly, she wasn't able to focus on anything but the question lingering in her head – *What am I doing in New York?* Nevertheless, when Destiny entered her brother's hospital room, she wished her parents had spent the car ride preparing her for what 'stable' looked like.

Destiny gasped at her brother laying there, hooked to monitors and tubes in the poorly lit hospital room. His wife, Sarah, was seated beside him, which made Destiny wonder where their twin sons were. Destiny hugged her and took a moment in their embrace to gain her composure before turning back to her oldest brother. She gripped his hand, almost afraid to touch him, he looked so fragile. He was awake but not talking. Everyone started conversing like Junior was not lying in the hospital bed with a nasogastric tube pulling green bowel out of his intestine because of the trauma to his abdomen area.

Destiny leaned against the antiquated radiator under the window of the room with her mind racing. They had been in this situation before as a family or close family friend. Destiny wanted to start talking about her new job. She felt like she should tell her family that Jasiah was in New York City as well. But every time she parted her lips to talk, saliva pooled in her mouth and her stomach churned from the sight of the bowel in the tube running from her brother's nose.

She rushed out of the room, attempting to find a bathroom but she ended up vomiting in a trashcan at the nurse station.

"I'm so sorry," she apologized to a nurse who stared at her. "Where is the restroom?"

The shocked nurse pointed to the door a few feet away.

Destiny locked herself into the single stale restroom. She rinsed out her mouth and threw cold water on her face as tears quietly fell. She didn't want to lose her brother. Not again. Not permanently. She had missed making memories with him while he was in prison. He had only been home for four years, most of which, she'd been away at school.

She paced the dingy floor of the restroom, trying to figure out if she'd been selfish with her life choices. Was she really pursuing her career? Was her job preparing herself to be a future lawyer? Or was she living in a fantasy and wasting precious time with her loved ones?

Her quiet tears continued to fall. The fear of the unknown choking her. She stayed in the bathroom, trying to constrain her emotional anguish, not allowing bystanders or family to see her vulnerability. She didn't want anyone to notice that she was not mature enough to stay calm at a time like this.

After several minutes, Destiny coached herself to *'get it together'* as she looked at her flushed face in the mirror. She knew she had to put on a brave face and be careful not to alarm her brother about his condition any more than needed. She dried her tears, like she had been told to do by her parents many times in similar situations and exited the bathroom. With tunnel vision, she tried to ignore her surroundings and get back to her brother's room. However, she felt like someone was too close to her. When she turned, there was Jasiah. Seeing him was refreshing but it was also uncomfortable. She felt like all of the gun violence in Jasiah's life was tied to her.

Jasiah recognized the pain trailing across Destiny's face and instantly took her into his arms. He hugged her tightly and kissed the top of her head. Destiny wrapped her arms around him in return, accepting his comfort. They both exhaled. Jasiah looked around while Destiny's head was buried in his chest and thought the hospital halls had not changed at all since the last time he'd been there. He rubbed her back and continually planted kisses on top of her head, thinking of the time she had to comfort him along the dreary walls of Howard University Hospital.

"I hate this place," he uttered, recounting pacing the floor while Lafayette laid in a hospital bed after his father nearly beat him to death.

"How's your dad?" Destiny asked, as she pulled away.

"He's Big Siah," Jasiah shrugged. "Trying to play it cool."

Destiny shook her head.

"He told me that I should go check on Junior and let him enjoy his Jello."

Destiny smiled at Big Siah's playful behavior.

"How is Junior? Is he better?" Jasiah stuck his hands in his pocket.

Destiny started to rock in place. "I don't know," She admitted.

"He will be fine, I'm sure," Jasiah tried to stay positive. "Where is his room? I want to say hello."

"I don't want to go back in there," Destiny admitted as she looked up at the ceiling. "It's depressing."

"We can go to the chapel," Jasiah suggested.

Destiny looked at Jasiah. It was what she had suggested to him when he was frantic along the hospital's halls.

"Those prayers worked for my family then. I'm sure they can work for ours now," Jasiah hunched.

Ours? – Destiny questioned to herself. But didn't want to get into semantics with him. "You go speak first. I'm sure seeing you will be a pleasant surprise," Destiny insisted, knowing she couldn't just disappear.

Jasiah smiled. "I am the real golden child in the Peay family," he joked. "Which room?"

Destiny rolled her eyes and pointed to her brother's room.

"Come on," Jasiah held out his hand. "I got you."

Destiny took his hand and felt some relief. And when they went to the chapel to pray together, she started to question a number of her choices.

"Stay with me tonight," Jasiah insisted, as they sat quietly in the chapel.

Destiny didn't respond as she looked forward at the altar. Her heart was heavy with secrets. She fumbled with her fingers as tears trickled down her face, each one a reflection of the turmoil within. Without a word, Jasiah wrapped his arm around her shoulders, taking one of her hands into his. Destiny leaned into him, finding relief in his love and exhaled.

"I just don't think either of us should be alone tonight," Jasiah added.

Just as Destiny agreed to stay with him, her Blackberry vibrated, flashing Antonio's name.

"Excuse me for a second," she responded, as she dried her face with the back of her hand and stood.

"Don't answer it," Jasiah urged, as he held on to her hand firmly. "Don't go."

Destiny looked down at him and noticed the few tears that trickled down Jasiah's face.

Destiny sat back down. She wiped away his tears and kissed him gently.

"I gotta figure out a safe space for my dad," Jasiah whispered his worries. "I can't lose him now."

Destiny and Jasiah comforted one another, both understanding the weight of the situation within their families. And later that night, after they lied to their families and significant others about their whereabouts, they found comfort in one another's arms.

Jasiah handled her like a delicate flower, just like the first time they made love. He wanted her to know how much his heart ached for her with every kiss and suckle. Destiny willingly accepted his raw love. With so many emotions swirling around them, their familiar love provided the ease they both desired. Until Jasiah attempted to turn her over to lay on her stomach. Destiny resisted.

"What's wrong?" Jasiah asked as he kissed her shoulder. "You know you're gonna like it."

Destiny thought about playing if off like she normally did. She knew it was a position that had once given her much pleasure but now, she her emotions were so heavy she couldn't.

"I just want to look at you," she replied, pulling Jasiah back between her legs.

"I want you how I want you," Jasiah told her.

Destiny told herself that Jasiah was her safe. That he wasn't trying to cause her any harm. When she felt his weight on her back, she gripped at the crisp white hotel sheets and clenched her teeth. Immediately Jasiah noticed the tension in her body.

"Baby, I'm not tryna get any butt. Relax," he joked.

"I'm okay," she tried to convince the both of them.

"No, you're not," pressing himself against her. "It's me, Destiny," he scooped his vacant arm under her. "Feel my heartbeat," he whispered as he kissed the side of her face.

She exhaled, holding his hand. "Jasiah, I-I- I need to go to the bathroom," she pushed out, releasing his hand and turning to slide from under him.

She rushed into the bathroom, instantly feeling like an afraid teenage girl again. She didn't expect Jasiah to be right behind her, as if he knew she was lying. When the bathroom door opened, it startled Destiny.

"Boy," she placed her hand over her bare chest. "I can't pee in peace," she attempted to mask her discomfort.

"Did something happen to you?" Jasiah asked.

Destiny bit her bottom lip. Not feeling like it was the most appropriate time to disclose the details of what happened in her dorm room. To tell him that occasionally she felt this way.

"Destiny, I'm listening," he frowned. "Did he rape you?!? Why wouldn't you tell me?" he started to draw his own conclusions. "I'll kill him."

"No," Destiny shook her head. "No, I wasn't raped... but I was attacked," she confessed.

"Why did you act like he was just apprehended?

"Let's not make a big deal out of this," Destiny suggested.

"Destiny," he stared at her in disbelief. "Is that why you called me crying on the—"

"Jasiah, please," she rushed him with kisses. "I don't want to remember. Not right now... please," she felt on his body.

He slowly turned her around to face the vanity mirror. "Look at us," he insisted, resting his chin on top of her head.

He pressed a gentle kiss to the crown of her head as she stood in silence, gazing at their reflection in the mirror. Her eyes softened, and without a word, she reached back, drawing him closer until their bodies met. Their eyes found each other in the glass—an unspoken conversation passing between them. Jasiah's arms wrapped tightly around her, anchoring her to him as he placed a tender kiss on her cheek.

"I've never loved anyone the way I love you, Destiny," he whispered, voice thick with sincerity.

She turned slightly, her fingers seeking his. Bringing his hand to her lips, she pressed a kiss to his knuckles and murmured, "Just don't let me go."

"If you let me," he said, his voice low as he bent to kiss the bare curve of her shoulder, "I'll love you in every way there is."

Her hand reached back once more, finding his face this time. She cradled it gently, her thumb brushing across his skin, her silence louder than words—soft, certain, and full of feeling.

He kissed her the crook of her neck. "You bite your lip when you're trying to figure out the perfect thing to say, I just want the truth," he told her as his hands trailed to her scared spot.

Destiny moaned, delighting in his touch. "Jasiah, stop," she expressed.

"Do you really want me to stop?" he whispered in her ear.

Destiny closed her eyes and braced herself against the sink.

Jasiah hooked one arm over her shoulders, across her chest, to bring her close to him as his fingers played in her rawness. "Open your eyes, Shawty," he urged.

Destiny did as she was told, only for them to lock eyes through the mirror again.

"It's me," he told her as he tilted her face to the side and kissed her mouth. "Don't you want me the way I want you?"

Destiny was caught in Jasiah's rapture as he fondled her harden nipple.

"Jasiah," she moaned out between his lips. She became weak in the knees but Jasiah's hold on body wouldn't allow her to crumble.

322

"I love the way you say my name," he assured her.

"Jasiah, please," she gripped the edge of the sink tighter, and her head dropped. He turned her around to face him and lifted her up on the sink.

"Hold on to me," he implored her as he positioned himself between her legs.

She wrapped her arms around his neck. Jasiah pulled her to the edge of the sink and took the opportunity to enter her. They both inhaled sharply as their bodies collided.

"This isn't right," Destiny uttered.

"If it's not right, tell me to stop," he responded without leaving.

Without another word spoken, he lifted her off of the counter and moved her toward the back of the bathroom door. Gripping her ass, he continued with his mission. Each thrust feeling better than the last. Each staggered breath only heightening the moment between them. Destiny held on to him, relishing in how powerful he felt against her in this position. Jasiah held on to her, his hands roaming the slender of her back, her cinched waist, and the curve of her hips. Destiny took all of him, grinding herself against him rhythmically, until he had no more to give.

After it was over, they stared at one another as he held her still against the door. Both of them panting and throbbing against one another.

"I'll start the shower," he spoke as he peeled himself away. "And you figure out how you're going to tell me *exactly* what happened to you."

"Jasiah," she whispered, her hands gripping his forearm.

They looked at one another.

"I'm not going anywhere," he confirmed as he wrapped his other arm around her and gave her a light squeeze. "I promise."

"Don't make promises you can't keep," she moved away and sat on the toilet. "Don't make promises that you don't even need to keep."

Jasiah started the shower and waited for the water to get hot. "You're the only woman I trust; you're the only person that understands me. You're—"

"You're living with a woman," Destiny reminded him. "And I'm in a situation."

"Are you telling me you don't want me?" Jasiah spat, obviously offended.

"Of course, I want you," Destiny proclaimed.

"Then tell me what happened to you," Jasiah quickly deviated. "We made a promise to—"

"Okay, okay okay," Destiny wiped herself and flushed the toilet. Jasiah slipped into the shower while she quickly washed her hands and grabbed a shower cap.

She stepped into the steaming shower feeling like she had entered a confessional. She made Jasiah face the showerhead, with his back to her, while she divulged details of the night George Mason tried to rape her. Her hands trembled as she washed his back, as if she could scrub away the lingering feeling of George Mason on her back. She disclosed the triggering feeling because that's how she was awakened. Her movements were slow and gentle as she explained how Antonio's private investigator found the culprit.

Destiny stopped washing as she confessed how oblivious she felt to know that her violator was right under her nose in a building she frequented. She leaned into Jasiah as she admitted she was concerned about Antonio having her followed and she still hadn't figured out how much he truly knew about her life.

"What do you have to hide?" Jasiah questioned.

Then, Destiny told the secret that she had been holding in for years. She revealed how she helped Jax run weed and pills through Harvard. How she had become complicit in a narrative she once reviled. She explained that she emceed exclusive parties in Cambridge. Jasiah listened to Destiny bare her soul. Though he was shocked she turned to a lifestyle she despised, Jasiah was relieved that Destiny was human just like him. Once she finished, he told her it was his turn.

Jasiah rinsed off and made Destiny face the showerhead. He began to wash her back and tell her about his addiction to Adderall. He admitted how his father came and brought some normalcy to his life. As Jasiah moved down to her hips and buttocks, he disclosed how his gambling habit almost got him killed more than one time. He washed her legs while he revealed how relieved he was to not have to carry a gun around with him. His hands ran back up her legs and his lips grazed her skin as he admitted he was in a throuple when he met Amelia.

"Two women, Jasiah!" Destiny exclaimed in shock. "No wonder they call you Big Brother Loverboy," Destiny uttered his frat nickname.

"I've just been searching for the type of love that I only get from you," he disclosed, as he stood up straight and turned Destiny around to face him. "You're who I want."

"What about Amelia?" she questioned. "She must have made you feel something to move her from New Orleans to New York with you."

Jasiah took a deep breath and decided not to continue his story. He didn't know if Destiny would look at him differently if he told her that he left Amelia just a couple of hours after having an abortion. Especially after they had unprotected sex for the first time ever. But he told her something that he felt in his heart, "Initially, I did think I found something that came close to what I have with you. She's caring, very considerate. We like a lot of the same things, but time has revealed that the substitute can't compare to having the real thing."

"We should get out," Destiny suggested, trying to avoid continuing the conversation. "My hands are prunes."

"Destiny, do you hear me?"

"I hear you," she answered, her voice hardly audible. She cleared her throat. "Jasiah, we're making a mess of our lives."

He shrugged, not caring about what happened next with anyone but him and her. "I've always been willing to bet on us."

"You have," she agreed. "I just have so much to work through within myself."

"I'm patient," he gently cuffed her face with both of his palms. "It always pays off with us."

Their eyes met. Destiny could feel the sincerity pouring out of Jasiah. "I love you so much," she confessed, before she could control the words spilling from her lips.

"I love you too, Shawty," he confirmed.

Chapter 20 — Trespassing

When Destiny arrived at her apartment, she thought it was odd that the top lock wasn't on. She was certain that she'd locked it. When she last spoke to Antonio before her car ride back to New York with Jasiah, he told her he was taking his sons golfing and to call him once she returned to New York. She pulled out her trusty pocketknife from her Neverful tote and flicked it open, before twisting the doorknob. Upon entering, her eyes settled on a woman sitting in the living room watching television— Mrs. Victoria Rossi. Destiny's heart pounded in her chest as she anticipated she might be in for another fight for her life.

"Victoria?" Destiny called out, placing her tote on the kitchen island and leaving the knife inside.

Destiny positioned herself on the opposite side of the island to make sure there was space between her and her lover's wife. Destiny swallowed hard as she waited for Victoria to say something.

"Destiny, right?" Victoria turned off the television and stood, showing her stout figure. Destiny admired her Van Cleef & Arpels long vintage necklace that dangled over her expensive looking floral dress. She embodied the epitome of class with her professional half up half down hairdo with the lavish furnishings of the apartment as her backdrop. She matched the custom drapery and the plush, soft tone sectional. The ambient lighting highlighted her rosy cheeks. Destiny recognized the apartment was an aesthetic for Victoria while she, herself, was standing there, in a pair of cut off shorts and a tube top with a stain on it from the McFlurry she shared with Jasiah in Delaware.

"How can I help you?" Destiny inquired, as she pulled out her Blackberry and dialed Antonio's number.

"You should worry about helping yourself," Victoria responded with a curled lip.

"Excuse me?"

"You don't know what kind of matrix you've gotten yourself into with Antonio," she cautioned.

Destiny rolled her eyes as she listened to the Antonio's voicemail pick up instead of him. She hung up and dialed again.

"He will never marry you," she stated confidently, as she moved closer to the island. "Even if we divorce, he will not marry you."

Destiny's eyebrows twisted in confusion. "I thought you two had an understanding," Destiny admitted, thoughts of all of their public appearances running through her mind.

"You didn't know he was serving me with divorce papers?" Victoria mirrored the look of confusion on Destiny's face. "I thought you put him up to it," Victoria sipped her wine and moved closer to the kitchen.

Alarmed, Destiny felt like her lover's wife was closing in on her. She tilted her tote bag on its side and placed her hand inside on her knife. She shifted on her feet from behind the island, trying to balance her weight and mask her nervousness.

Destiny's eyes narrowed in on the nearly empty bottle of Duckhorn Three Palms Vineyard Merlot next to a photo of she and Antonio in the Hamptons on the coffee table. "Why are you here?" Destiny leaned over the island, the knife firmly in her fist as she looked in the bedroom. The bed was still neatly made but she wondered if her clothes had been tampered with.

"I've always wanted to contact you — to warn you about my husband, but then he asked me for a divorce. That's when I decided this conversation would be better face to face."

Destiny took a deep breath as the word *warn* floated in her head. Her grasp on her weapon loosened as she contemplated what Victoria's intentions were.

"So, you're not pressuring him to divorce me?"

Destiny shook her head no. "We don't even express sentiments of love, let alone marriage," Destiny admitted. She wanted to tell her that she was only twenty-one. She couldn't fathom her parents approving of a relationship with a man that was forty-three, let alone marrying him.

Victoria perched her lips.

"Maybe he's just tired of living a lie between the two of you," Destiny suggested.

"Ha!" Victoria swung her hand forward, spilling wine from her glass as she let out a sinister laugh. "Antonio never gets tired as long as he can control the narrative."

Destiny tried dialing Antonio again as she wondered how long this conversation would go on. Then suddenly she thought of her heated conversation with Jax. If she were in D.C., would call a family member to witness the unfolding fiasco under the guise of 'help'? Destiny quickly concluded – No! She couldn't embarrass herself by revealing her indiscretions. She dialed Antonio again- still no answer.

"You have no idea of the complexities of marriage. The intricacies associated with being married to *that* man," Victoria gulped down the content of her glass. "But if you stick around, you will learn."

"Why are you here?" Destiny repeated.

"Tonio is on the golf course breaking it to our boys that he will miss even more Wednesday night dinners and Sunday family days."

"I've never asked Antonio to change his schedule for me," Destiny retorted. "I've always respected his wishes for quality time with the children."

"Do you think that will be your saving grace as an adulterer?"

Adulterer stung Destiny.

"You know, I pitied you after what happened to you on campus. I thought, 'that young girl; she has no idea'."

331

Destiny felt like a noose tightened around her neck at the mention of her attack. She massaged the back of her neck, hoping it would release some of the tension.

"You have no idea what Antonio Rossi is capable of," Victoria shook her head as she spoke. "No idea *at all*."

"Victoria, when you got in your car or on the plane or whatever way you got here — what was your intent?" Destiny asked as her agitation started to get the best of her.

"I've known about you since he sent flowers to his own office using our florist," she started. "The young, hot girl at the office. He's had a few of you over the years. Always discreet. Always expensive. But he's never ordered flowers. Not while standing in my kitchen flipping pancakes for our boys. Not using the florist that does my weekly arrangements."

"Victoria, I—"

"You can have a seat. You asked me why I'm here; I'm going to tell you."

Destiny took a deep breath and blew it out loudly to display her aggravation. The imaginary noose hung over Destiny neck loosely as she released her grip on the blade and went to the cabinet to grab herself a glass to listen to Victoria say her piece.

"It started with the flowers... then more time at the apartment. And then he started introducing you to our circle. And the whispers about my husband's infidelity became emails and photos," she tossed her hair over her

332

shoulder. "He threw discretion out of the window for you," she pointed at Destiny.

Destiny went to the liquor cabinet, taking a closer look into the bedroom and noticing nothing was out of place. She retrieved a bottle of Grey Goose vodka and gave herself a hefty pour.

"If I have to hear one more snide remark about Tonio's feisty young girlfriend," she mentioned with her fist clinched in frustration. "I could just explode."

Destiny instantly thought of Robert calling her that in Miami and rolled her eyes.

"You're not his typical type," Victoria mentioned, as if it were an underhanded compliment.

Destiny looked down at her Jordans and chuckled. She knew she would never dress this way around Antonio, not even on the hottest day by the Hampton shores. But then, as she listened to Victoria, she figured out it wasn't about how she dressed at all.

"I thought it would have been that Megan that's at his beck and call... but it's *you*."

Destiny moved over to the fridge. "You don't have to say it like that," Destiny mumbled as she grabbed a fresh lime and cranberry juice. On the inside, Victoria's words confirmed Destiny's assumption that she was a passing fancy for Antonio. Something clicked in her — setting her mind ablaze.

"So why did I come here? I had to see for myself the little girl that's ruining not only her own life but mine as well," Victoria added.

Destiny laughed, a full belly laugh, as she gripped the edge of the counter and leaned down in a lunge, arching her back, trying to stretch out the tension that now ran down her lower back where the ends of the invisible rope laid. But she laughed, not because Mrs. Victoria Rossi was actually funny. She laughed because she had to, before her rage took over.

"You think it's funny?" Victoria shouted.

"No! *You're* funny," Destiny looked up at her. "You think it's me that ruined your life? Me?" Destiny pointed at her chest. "Your husband has been settled into his apartment across town long before I came along. He approached me. He pursued me when he found out I was leaving the firm." Destiny shook her head. "Victoria, your anger is misplaced."

"You need to part ways with Antonio!" Victoria screamed as she shook her head, causing her hair to rattle. Destiny started to wonder if the full head of luxurious hair she had previously admired was a wig.

Instead of asking about it, Destiny used the knife to point at her lover's wife and told her "You don't need to yell."

"I'll have you thrown out of this place!" Victoria continued, her voice echoing off of the walls. Destiny watched as Victoria shouted, flailing her hands, and spilling her red wine on the soft cream carpet — unraveling at the seams. "I can have you thrown out within an hour!"

Destiny rolled her eyes at the idle threat and sucked her teeth. "If you think I didn't check New York's law on unlawful evictions before I agreed to stay here, you're a bigger fool than the whispers say," Destiny looked Victoria up and down as her lip curled with disgust. "You need to go back to Cambridge and discuss this with *your* husband."

Victoria screamed out, but this time there were no audible words. Then she flopped into the seat behind her. Destiny cringed, thinking that the neighbors would hear her as she tried to figure why was the woman screaming. Was it mental anguish? Embarrassment? Frustration? Was her white woman fragility getting the best of her? Destiny rationalized that it was all of the above and shook her head as a response.

She had seen girls unravel for her brothers when they were younger. But she couldn't imagine Jax's ex-wife, Chanel, letting anyone of Jax's mistresses see her lose control.

"Have some dignity," Destiny mumbled as she took a sip of her cocktail, still keeping her eyes on Victoria.

She looked at the knife still firmly in her hand. Suddenly she saw the dark red droplets all over her, like the morning she stabbed George Mason. She dropped the knife and started taking rapid deep breaths through her nose, trying control the unsettling feeling the memory awakened.

"I don't know what I was thinking when I came here… maybe I thought you would scurry off. You would cry and plead for my understanding. I even thought I might catch a glimpse of a growing belly," she poured more wine and quickly took a gulp like it was a shot of liquor. "I convinced myself that you just had to be pregnant for him to serve *me* divorce papers," she pointed at Destiny's midsection "But all I see *is a child*… a foolish child," she snarled.

Destiny wondered how long this would go on. She dialed Antonio again. She placed the phone on speaker as it rang and took a larger gulp of her cocktail. He didn't answer. She sent him an instant message to tell him that his wife was drunk in the living room.

Destiny caught an obscure glimpse of her own reflection in the shiny, white lacquered cabinets. She knew this wasn't the lifestyle she wanted to live. She didn't want to ruin anyone's happiness to gain her own. She didn't want to be confronted by women about her relationship with a man. Destiny knew she owed herself better, her mother's words engrained in her head. She accidently said them aloud while she watched Victoria take a gulp from her wine glass. "I am the prize."

"What was that? What did you say?!" Victoria shouted in an exaggerated fashion. She quickly grabbed the photo on the coffee table and threw it into the television. Destiny jumped back, even though she was far away from any flying shards of glass.

"You know what?" Victoria turned to Destiny. "You can have him."

Victoria voice was firm. But Destiny burst out in another fit of laugher — amused by Victoria's change in position.

"Oh! You think this is a joke? Don't you little girl?"

"Bitch, get out!" Destiny countered, her anger jumping out.

Victoria's eyes widened.

Destiny took another swig of her drink to avoid confessing that *she* didn't want *him*. That she was trying to comprise a plan to live out her truth with the man she had always loved. She wanted to be with the man that knew her and her flaws. A man that she could proudly take around her family. A man that could celebrate with her in any crowd. A man that whispered *I love you* into her ear at any given moment. Destiny knew Antonio wasn't that man. She dialed Antonio again. He still didn't answer.

"I've been with that man for as long as you've been alive, I helped him build his practice. He got his contacts from my family!"

"Victoria, I am not the root of the problems in your marriage!" Destiny yelled back. "Go home and remind him of what you mean to his life. To his career. To his entire being!"

"You think I haven't done that?!" Victoria screamed. "The man is full of himself. And now, I'm the laughingstock of Boston," she cried. With an exaggerated sigh, she poured the rest of the wine in the glass before launching the empty wine bottle at the television as well. This time, shards of wine tainted glass went flying all over the living room.

"That's enough!" Destiny yelled as she stared at the fractured screen of the television. "I'm going to call the police if you keep this up."

"This is my husband's—"

"Stop it! Your issues are with your husband. Not me!" Destiny shouted back. "HE made a vow to you, NOT ME!"

"And that's how I know he won't marry you," Victoria retorted, twisting her neck.

Destiny rolled her eyes and sipped her drink. She stared at her Blackberry, wondering why Antonio hadn't at least responded to her message, never mind the missed calls. There was a part of her that wanted to call Jasiah and ask him to turn around and pick her up. Her mind went to the farewell with her family huddled in a hospital room. Her eyes darted to her tote. She could hear her father's voice– *Don't hesitate.* With so many thoughts and emotions flowing, she could only clench her fist and take another sip. "I don't have time for this," Destiny declared, as she glared at the whimpering woman before her.

Destiny's patience had thinned out as she surveyed the mess Victoria created. The wine-stained carpet, the broken glass everywhere, the broken television sitting on the console and the broken picture frame on the floor.

"Why are you here?" Destiny questioned yet again, drumming her fist against the counter in a rapid motion as she spoke. "To vent? To see me for yourself? To humiliate the both of us?" Destiny slammed her palms against the countertop and leaned in. "If you were hoping to appeal to my empathic side, *this is not* the way you go about it."

"Fuck your empathy!" Victoria yelled. "You think I need anything from you, *little girl?*"

"Your presence *here* is evident that you do need something from this *woman*," Destiny spat back. "*And I'm telling you to go home and fight for your marriage there.*"

"You really don't love him," Victoria recognized. "This is all a game to you? Playing around with—"

"I said from the beginning that Antonio and I *do not* express sentiments of love and affection. He set those rules," Destiny admitted with a frustrated sigh. "I'm not the threat you think I am."

"Selfish bastard."

"I'm his play toy, a passing fantasy. A new accessory. I know my damn role. You need to go back home and claim yours," as the reality of her situation rolled off of Destiny's tongue, disappointment in herself settled over her.

There was a knock at the door. Destiny hoped it was Antonio. She figured his wife had somehow taken his key and that's why he was knocking. Destiny opened the door without asking who it was and was surprised to see the police standing there.

339

"How can I help you officers?" Destiny asked with mixed emotions. On one hand, she was glad to see them and put an end to Victoria's rant. On the other hand, she didn't know whose side they would take in the matter.

"We received a call about a disturbance, possible domestic violence."

"She's trespassing!" Victoria stood up, wine glass in hand, and stumbled toward the doorway where Destiny stood. "She doesn't belong here."

"I live here," Destiny countered in an even confident tone. If she acted as erratic as Victoria, she would end up in handcuffs. "Officers, she doesn't belong here. She is also destroying property."

"Destroying property?" Victoria looked at Destiny. "I'll show you, destroying property." With her warning, she launched the glass at a kitchen cabinet. Glass and red wine sprayed everywhere.

Destiny shielded her face with her forearms. Feeling a sharp pain, she screamed. Pulling her arm away Destiny's eyes widened when she saw a large shard of glass lodged into her arm.

Both of the officers grabbed Victoria while Destiny started to huff and puff as a way to release the mixture of pain and adrenaline flowing through her veins.

"We need a bus," an officer requested into his walkie talkie.

To be continued...

www.ingramcontent.com/pod-product-compliance
Lightning Source LLC
Chambersburg PA
CBHW061927170626
46813CB00006B/2320